# THE REVENGE OF HATATHOR

# THE REVENGE OF HATATHOR

*The Sphere Trilogy*
*Book Three*

Nassim Odin

2022

ISBN ebook: 978-1-954313-03-3
ISBN Paperback: 978-1-954313-08-8
ISBN Hardcover: 978-1-954313-13-2

Cover Design: your3dvision
Map: BMR Williams


Publisher: Odin Fantasy World

writer.odin@gmail.com
https://www.nassimodin.com

# Reviews

WINNER OF LITERARY TITAN GOLD AWARD

A dangerous conflict on an alien planet involves revenge plots and a wormhole-jumping orb in this final installment of an SF trilogy.
— The Kirkus Review

Odin creates a compelling and intriguing SF tale in this concluding installment in The Sphere of Destiny Trilogy, delving into the intricacies of life, love, revenge, and redemption.
— The Prairies Book Review

The book is full of action and there is absolutely no point where the action is dragging so it's a great book to read!
— Alice Branch

The Revenge of Hatathor is a fast-paced science fiction novel full of plot twists, double-crosses, and political drama. With dramatic action scenes, blood, and gore, this riveting trilogy will have readers on edge to see what the conclusion brings. — Literary Reviewer

**Dedication**

*To all the people interested in the pyramids*

**Al-Eard Soundtrack Musical Score**

Odin Fantasy World - You Tube Channel

***The Arrival on Al-Eard***
*Music Artist: Mecheri Kheireddine (khairsound)*

***The Misery of Space Traveler***
*Music Artist: Armen Voskanian*

***The Revenge of Hatathor***
*Music Artist: Arkady Akhidzhanov*

ⴰⵎ ⵓⴼⵍⵍⴰ ⵉⵅⴰⵜ ⵙⵉⵣⴷⴰⵔ

(As above so below)

# Prologue

In this third part of the trilogy, the book narrates the changes that the Kingdom of Akhom on an alien planet, Lyra, has gone through. This novel is written from an anthropological point of view, encompassing many changes that occurred in the kingdom's social, political, and religious spheres due to revolt.
The Kingdom is resourceful but has an uncertain future. Every character in the book has its apprehensions and fears towards the end. Al-Khidr's journey continues through all these alleyways, and he has to face the new challenges.

*Odin*
*2022*

# Contents

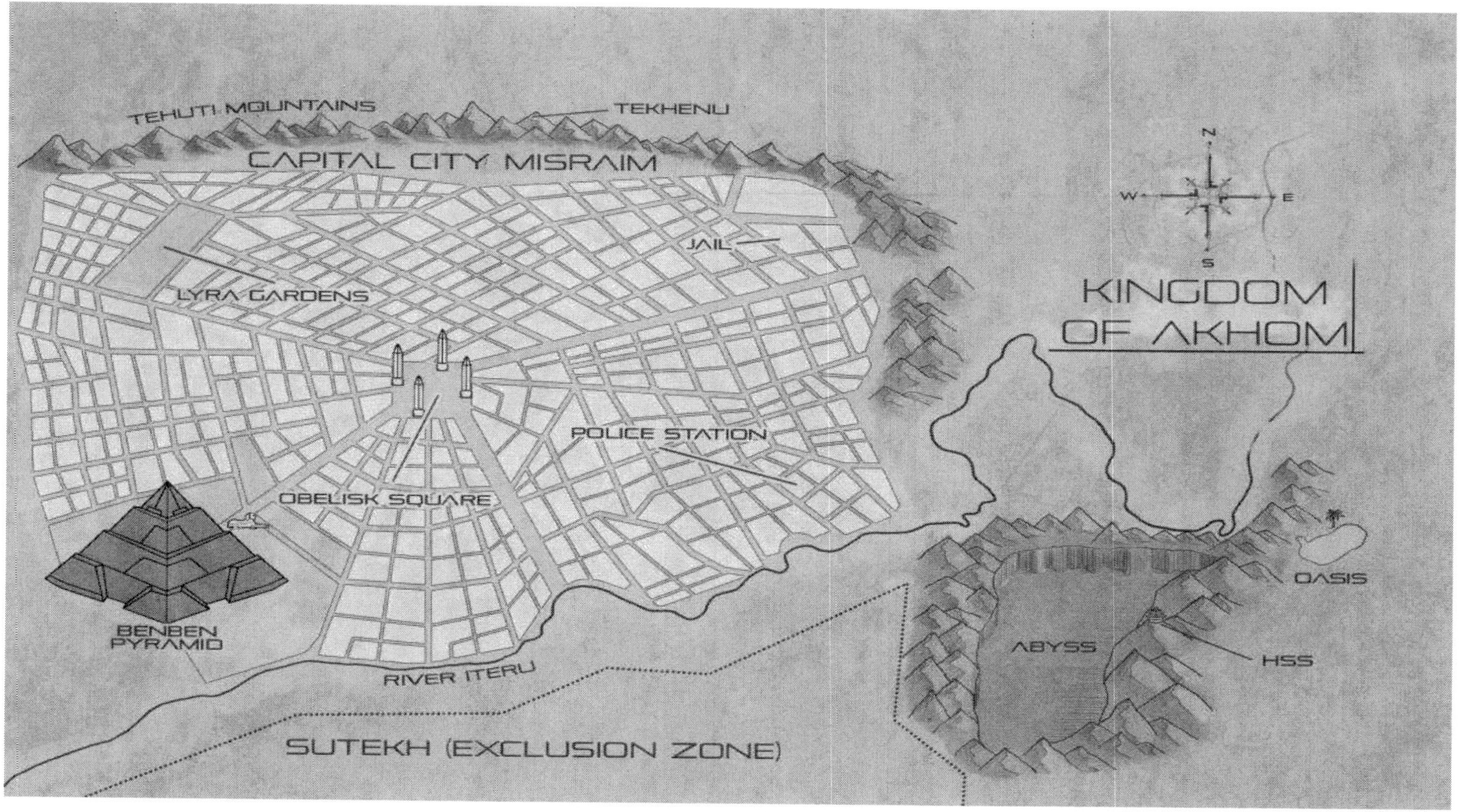
KINGDOM
OF AKHOM
N
W
E
S
TEHUTI MOUNTAINS
TEKHENU
CAPITAL CITY MISRAIM
JAIL
LYRA GARDENS
POLICE STATION
OBELISK SQUARE
BENBEN
PYRAMID
RIVER ITERU
SUTEKH (EXCLUSION ZONE)
ABYSS
HSS
OASIS

# Chapter 1

# The Qebhu

THE black matter was incessantly boiling inside the Maft-Shespt – the jump-sphere, and the cloud of bluish particles was forming over it. The particles were seeping through the pyramids' walls, creating a spherical cocoon of protective fields around the Egyptian pyramid. The sound of electricity arcing and crackling made strange music inside the pyramid. The sparks and electric discharges between the particles and the pyramid stones lightened the cosmic tunnel.

Al-Khidr was jumping from one plane of stars to another. He was supposedly going higher towards Vega.

The star that once was and may again be the north-pole of Earth. His body was shuddering as he was holding the jump-sphere in both hands, and the pyramid walls were constantly reverberating as a cocoon of energy zapped through the cosmic tunnel, creating music inside the pyramid.

The walls of pyramid were resounding, like persistently rattled sistrum. He was going back to the planet of Hathor. Inside the pyramid, Al-Khidr was lost between two worlds. Estelle was gone, and she will remain in his memories like a gentle breeze. She kept her promise by helping him identify the plants – the cure of Mutmut disease. She helped Al-Khidr to fulfill his promise, for which he came down from Lyra. "I lost all those who loved me. My mother, my father, my friends and now Estelle. Estelle, Ah, Estelle... You saved me, and you were a genuine friend and even more... I am sorry, Estelle. You were such a kind soul. I promise I will punish Hatathor if I ever see him again. Oh God, help me! Take revenge for the innocents who had died in saving me," he was weeping and beseeching.

The rattling and cracking outside the pyramid were communicating back to Al-Khidr like a constantly shaking sistrum. The sound had a calming and soothing effect on his nerves. The rattle's rhythm was in harmony with his breathing and heartbeats. It was like the cosmic tunnel was trying to make him recover from the loss. Due to the matching of the rhythms, he felt like he was floating – and indeed, he was floating between the stars. His mind slowly came out of the shock and realized the new reality.

The star tunnel was unfolding for him – the way to the distant world.

There were intense electromagnetic surges outside the pyramid – between the walls and the spherical energy field. Al-Khidr was oblivious to the reality that Hatathor was inside a crevice in one pyramid wall. He had created the crack using his sleeve-weapon Menkh-t Sekhem before the Egyptian pyramid took off from Earth.

Hathathor's hair was electrostatic from all the surrounding electromagnetism. It stood on end as the intermittent sparks jumped from the cosmic tunnel to the pyramid. Because of the electromagnetic surges, his sleeve weapon was no longer functional and had gone into the auto-save mode to protect itself. Thus, Hatathor was forced to remain inside the crevice; else he could be electrocuted and die instantly. He couldn't do anything apart from cursing. "Coward! You cannot hide longer. I will not let you destroy Lyra by bringing another plague from your cursed planet," Hatathor shouted. "I will save Lyra!"

The Egyptian pyramid was moving like a giant bullet through the Tepta Sehetch (tunnel between stars), spiraling upwards towards another Sehetu of stars (sky of stars at the higher level).

"How come humans are so lucky?" Hatathor uttered as he was astounded by the sudden turn of fate. *I miscalculated Al-Khidr. I had wiped out the pursuing*

*French army, and I had almost got hold of Al-Khidr. But God intervened, and it was He who turned the table.*

"O God, why do you help the weakest of your creations? Why did you choose humans over us? God, are Lyrians, not your creation?" He was uttering his confusion with sobbing eyes.

*Am I failing? Will Lyrians die again due to another Keb-based disease?* He was anguished even to think about it.

"O God, help. Save Lyra from the curse of Keb," Hatathor said.

I'll pull out the human from this pyramid and slaughter him as soon as we reach back. He decided.

Al-Khidr didn't know all these bitter feelings of Hatathor, as the rattling echo caused by stones has stopped him from hearing anything else. Indeed, it was making him feel drowsy. Inside the jump-sphere hidden compartment, he had the supposed cure of the alien contagion, Mutmut. "Ehsis and Nefertiti would be happy to see me, and I hope the leaves of the plant will give them the cure – the elixir." he was planning what would happen when he landed in Lyra.

***

In the sky of the kingdom of Akhom, obscure yet unparalleled bluish energy was building up. It kept intensifying until it became stable with a reverberating climax – ready to propel whatever it was hauling inside of it. The sky tore up above the city of Misraim, and a giant sphere emerged. The intense shockwave formed around the sphere, and the sphere became perpendicular to the planet Lyra and started descending straight down. Though the shockwave had slowed down the energy cocoon, it was still moving fast enough towards the capital city Misraim like a meteor.

The size of the sphere was enormous, and nothing inside of it being visible. Waves of white and translucent blue moved over its surface, their forms blending, diffusing, and reappearing. It was late at night when this sphere appeared over the Kingdom of Akhom. It appeared with no prior signature on the radars or weapons detection systems. But now it was over the capital and due to its huge size it cannot be ignored.

The kingdom forces were on high alert, and the sirens shook the entire capital. The space force was deployed, and the military spaceships were ordered to tackle the mysterious sphere. The defense forces had clear mission from high command to neutralize the threat to the kingdom. The shiny dark blue spaceships were basting off like a spindle piercing the sky – each one bears an insignia of vertical eye; the insignia represents the new kingdom. Meanwhile, the sphere took a sharp turn as it reached close to Misraim city, and now it was moving over river Iteru. The water of the river lurked towards the sphere but unable to reach it – a wall of water raised behind the sphere and fell back in the river as the sphere moved away.

# CHAPTER 1. THE QEBHU

***

Commander Kontar was in the central control room of the Space and Air Force headquarters.

"Commander, shall we fire on the sphere?" an officer inquired.

Commander Kontar was in a state of panic, and he ordered: "Yes, destroy it. We don't know who sent it. Fire from the ground!"

The laser cannons fired, but the sphere deflected the laser beams and continued moving unharmed.

"Nothing happened to the unidentified sphere," the officer informed the control room.

"Deploy the scanning mesh!" Kontar thundered.

"Approach the sphere with all sensors activated. Try to find what is inside it," another officer ordered on the communications network. The spaceships sped up and went ahead of the sphere. They opened the hatches, getting the devices ready. All pilots communicated with each other, and on the counter, they pressed buttons. A laser mesh was created in the pathway of the calculated trajectory of the sphere. The spaceships slowed down to let the sphere go through the laser mesh. The pilots started communicating with the tower. "The sphere is approaching the mesh. The gap is reducing; now 86.8 Supris, 73.4 Supris. . . 60.9 Supris. . . 49.9. . . Supri. . . Oh"

The pilots ejected their seats, and then explosions were heard through the communication line.

The officer announced in the control room, "Commander, we've encountered electronic system failure on all ships, and we have lost contact."

The pilots manually ejected themselves before the spaceships plummeted down and crashed into the desert.

"Commander, nothing happened to the sphere, but the mesh sends us some information. We have detected life-forms inside the sphere. Also, stones are present. No weapon system inside the sphere was detected," the officer announced. It was a relief for all, but the mystery remained.

*Who sent this sphere? And why?* None of them knew.

"The calculated trajectory shows it is moving away from the Misraim, and it is heading towards Qebhu!" the officer announced, and all looked at each other surprised. The sphere was indeed moving away from the capital as it was going towards Qebhu – the abyss.

"All spaceships, keep following the sphere. Maintain proximity with the distance of 150 Supris," Commander ordered.

***

*I wish I had my bident and I could pierce a hole through the pyramid to reach the human.* Hatathor thought to himself as the pyramid kept moving. Hatathor could see outside the sphere, and he got horrified seeing the spaceships fall into the desert. His yelling could not be heard. "Why does no one see me?" Hatathor was surprised.

Hatathor noticed the field of energy around him was moving out of the city. He knew he was away from the population, yet he was astounded. Through the sphere and the clouds, Hatathor could see the desert. The energy-sphere carrying pyramid was gradually making its way toward the mountains. He could see approaching Hept Sehetch Sheta (HSS) facility located just at the edge of an abyss.

"God! Don't let me fail," he whispered.

The sphere sped up towards one of the large, domed buildings of HSS. The entrance was too narrow to accommodate a giant pyramid. The energy-sphere collided against the metallic door between the two gigantic statues of standing Anubis. The gate had been carved in the mountain, facing the deep abyss. A loud boom echoed all over, and a massive cloud of dust erupted in the sky, covering the abyss. The sphere, carrying the pyramid, fell into the deep abyss. The statues were damaged, and parts of them also fell into the abyss, however the door remained intact. The energy-sphere took several turns during its fall. "Qebhu! (The Abyss!)" Hatathor was screaming in dread. He lost his consciousness as the inter-galactic jump and the trauma of imminent death had sapped his remaining energies. His body slid more into the crevice.

The sphere fell as the gravity of Lyra acted on it. While descending in abyss, it hit the mountainside and bounced like a ball and got deflected towards the middle of the abyss. However, it kept slowing down until it finally reached close to bottom of the pit. As soon as the sphere touched the frost, the sphere vanished, and the pyramid sank into the sand with its apex engraved.

Inside the pyramid, Al-Khidr was awake, but his brain moved violently inside the skull because of his fall. His motionless body was lying with eyes wide open, trying to regain a fixed point. At least I am not dead, he thought thankful.

***

"Commander, the sphere crashed with part of the HSS facility, and it fell into the abyss, and now we have no visuals," a military spaceship pilot reported. "The dust and sand are blocking the views," Kontar was sweating profusely and talking to someone on the communication network.

"We need a different type of craft to descend into the abyss to investigate further. It is a deep pit." the officer in headquarters said.

"General Desher called, and I need to update him. Do your job fast," commander Kontar roared.

All officers inside the control room looked at each other nervously.

***

It was conspicuously dark inside the pyramid when Al-Khidr realized he could move. He sat and held his head. He was feeling heavy and needed to get a hold of his train of thoughts. After a while, he rubbed his eyes and felt a thick liquid against his knuckles. "I wonder what that could be!" He brought his hand near to his lips and licked the liquid using the tip of his tongue. It was blood. He touched his forehead to see if the wound was deep, but to his luck, it was not. Suddenly, he realized that the jump-sphere was no longer in his hands. He was cramped into the apex, and because of the surrounding darkness, he couldn't see the sphere's whereabouts. But it was in vain. Al-Khidr peeped through the walls of the damaged pyramid and saw the white light growing frail. Is that the light of the orb? He thought to himself and rushed through the dislocated walls before the orb stopped glowing.

As he tried to lift himself out of the narrow apex space, he saw the glowing blue tint of the Maft-Shespt – the jump-sphere. He grabbed the sphere in his hands and used its light to navigate his way out of the pyramid. Al-Khidr looked around inside, and he saw an enormous crack in the wall; though not big enough to fit a human, he was down for a challenge.

He approached the crack and pushed himself inside it, though he was unsuccessful with the orb in his hand. Al-Khidr peeked through the gap and perceived nothing but a stream of white light pouring down on the sand. Al-Khidr pushed the sphere through the crack and dropped it onto the soft sand. Then he pushed himself through the gap and spouted half of his body out of it, grabbing onto the walls that were torn open from the middle.

Al-Khidr pushed himself harder, and with a jolt, a

large piece of the wall fell, opening up the gap for Al-Khidr to get out of the apex. He hopped and landed on his feet on the sand. There was a thin sheath of frozen moisture on the sand. He immediately grabbed the jump-sphere and glanced around to check where he was. There were mountains on his right and his left. Over his head were clouds and dust, stopping him from seeing the peaks of the mountains. It was a gloomy, shadowy world where the pyramid had landed.

Is this Lyra or some other planet? Are there hostile creatures around? all kinds of questions were circling in his mind, which added to his nervousness. Al-Khidr took a walk, and it appeared to him he was in some kind of abyss, with mountainous walls around him. What place is this? He thought to himself. He looked above him and saw the nebulous sky and a prominent plume of dust. Sometimes, the mellow moonlight pierced through the cloud and descended into the abyss. For a while, he sat on the sand and waited for the sky to clear up. He kept the orb in front of him and buried his fingers in the cold sand, scrutinizing the Egyptian pyramid. He saw how it landed on its apex and how badly damaged it was. The base of the pyramid was tilted and faced the sky. He sat hopeless in the sand. He did all to fulfill his promise, yet he landed in an abyss, God knows where.

He was hopeless and worries took over his mind for a while. Then suddenly, the ray of moonlight breached the cloud of dust and its light brought a ray of hope for him. He shrugged off all negative thoughts. He stood back, grabbed the orb, and thanked God for being alive.

He went to the pyramid, which was partly submerged in the sand. Intrigued, Al-Khidr picked a piece from the ground and said, "I cannot even imagine the intensity of the crash I am glad I was inside the pyramid."

He smiled at his words and let God guide him. He was facing the moons, Villio, and Umria. He closed his eyes and tossed the sphere. "If the sphere fell on its hole-side, I would go to my right-hand side, else to the left-hand side," he planned. He tossed the sphere and the sphere fell on its hole side into sand. He started walking in the right-hand direction, taking it as a lucky guess. While walking, he turned around and glanced at earthly pyramid one last time. The pyramid's apex was still buried in the sand between the mountains forming an abyss. The pyramid was casting shadows that were changing their shapes under the light that arrived at the base of the abyss through the clouds. Al-Khidr's was halfway between the pyramid and mountains when a gradually increasing roar rang in his ears. The roar was echoing in the abyss. "Oh, no!" Al-Khidr softly shouted.

The unremitting roaring was growing closer and louder. Al-Khidr knew that was the sound of a spaceship, so he ran fast towards the mountain and hid behind some big rocks and hid behind them to observe what was about to happen.

His conjecture was correct – it was a spaceship that

glowed in the abyss before Al-Khidr's eyes. It flew over the pyramid and circled inside the vast chasm. The spacecraft was roaring in the abyss, and it was probably assessing the scale of the disaster. A camera was attached on top of the spaceship – spinning at a moderate rate of speed, capturing everything as the spacecraft surveyed the crash site. Al-Khidr saw a green light flashing over the pyramid. What could they possibly be looking for? Al-Khidr wondered. The spaceship took flight with an abrupt surprise, and it approached the rocks. Al-Khidr immediately hid hoping he won't be noticed. His dark-colored dress helped his camouflage. His clothes remained intact on this travel.

I haven't seen these spaceships and insignia on Lyra before. Is it the Kingdom of Akhom or some other place on Lyra or even some other planet? A few moments later the spaceship turned and did vertical takeoff and flew out of the abyss, leaving a clear coast for Al-Khidr to begin his search. Al-Khidr waited for the roaring of the spaceship to go quiet. As he came back out in the open, he dusted his clothes, and started walking into rocks, searching for the way to go up to the top of the mountains.

The spaceship had confirmed one qualm that bothered Al-Khidr the most, and that was whether Hatathor was there with him.

# Chapter 2

# The Enigma

“WHAT now!” Al-Khidr exclaimed. He ran and sought shelter behind the rocks which were jutting out like giant needles. It was getting colder with every passing second, and Al-Khidr was frozen to the marrow. Although it was not snowing, the weather was hard enough, and the moisture froze over the sand grains. Al-Khidr clenched the alien orb close to his chest as if someone had descended to snatch it away from him. He watched four spaceships vertically landing in the abyss, beeping incessantly.

Being far away from the spaceships, Al-Khidr couldn't see much with his leaden eyes. His vision was hazy and ceaseless, with the chilly wind now carrying snow. Somehow in this inter galactic journey, he felt less tired as it had happened before.

*Maybe the stones of the pyramid saved me from the heat of the tunnel,* he thought.

He shivered, while profusely sweated with dread. These spaceships differed from what Al-Khidr was used to seeing on Lyra – they were different, with multiple searchlights reflecting against the crystal frost on the sand. The rime on the sand was illuminating the entire abyss. The four spaceships descended vertically near the Egyptian pyramid, flashing the searchlights on every aperture and ledge.

Al-Khidr had understood. The spaceship before had detected something, and this was reinforcement. He was intrigued to find more, so he stayed and watched. Soon, all four spaceships landed, and their doors slid open. An elongated carousel stretched before each entrance.

"Am I in Lyra or some other planet? What if it is not Lyra? They will kill me!" he said to himself, as he started to have doubts on what planet he landed. Al-Khidr, keep your head low. You know nothing about these aliens. I hope they are not monstrous. What if they smell my presence behind the rocks? I can run. Should I run or not? Where will I run? His mind was reiterating multiple pieces of advice.

Al-Khidr felt like a bird in a cage whose feathers

were clipped. He didn't know what to do. Al-Khidr looked at the ground to check whether any of his footprints were visible which could trace the aliens back to him. Luckily, the frost and sand with the encroaching cold had obscured his footsteps. He peeped over from the rocks to see if anyone had exited the spaceships.

The dark nebulous smoke released from the spaceships and started diffusing. Al-Khidr saw the silhouettes of a few aliens, but again, he was too far to make any concrete deductions. Nine to ten aliens emerged from four spaceships that descended in the abyss and formed a circle around the pyramid. They looked like humans or Lyrians, but they dressed strangely.

When the light from the ships reflected against their face, Al-Khidr noticed their faces were covered in tattoos of different colors, and they had long braided hairs. This is not Lyra, but some other planet.

"Man-at-arms, take your positions! We don't know what we are dealing with – put your masks on. Look for the sphere as well. Krono, are you sure there was no sphere here?" one of the braided aliens asked.

"Yes, master Asubia? I scanned every corner" one of the other braided aliens stepped forward. He seemed to be the leader's favorite and pilot who arrived earlier. "Check the body lying on the side of the pyramid. Tell me if he's conscious or dead," said Asubia, their leader.

"Be right back!" Krono bowed his head and went towards the body lying on the side of the pyramid.

There was a slight beep sound emerging below the

body.

Krono flipped the body and saw a man in a blue frock coat. The uniform was tearing apart. The beep sound intensified, and it was issued from the sleeve device. "Is he alive?" the leader squinted.

"Master, he is wearing some device. He is alive but unconscious," Krono shouted in surprise.

"Probably the sphere fell into the abyss, and the pyramid was inside it?"

"Oh!" said the leader and ran towards the body.

"He could be a spy of Ehsis. We will not be sure until we perform facial retinal recognitions and execute the biometric modalities."

"Do the Kostiva Maneuver. Perhaps he will regain consciousness, and then we interrogate him."

"Very well, Asubia," Krono replied.

Because of the distance and sound of the spaceship engines, Al-Khidr couldn't hear them very well. He was silently observing the aliens. He couldn't comprehend what was happening on the other side of the flipped pyramid and realized his mistake that he hadn't surveyed the area much.

*What is there?* he thought to himself.

One possibility that came into his mind was infuriating. Was that Hatathor? The blood flooded his eyes. He wanted to take his revenge immediately, but couldn't handle all these aliens alone.

"It will be suicide!" he stopped himself and started thinking logically.

Hatathor was far away and hadn't entered the pyramid with me.

Al-Khidr continued observing.

Krono flipped the body and sat on its back with both hands around the neck. He then pulled it towards him. The guttural sounds came out of Hatathor's body, but he was still unconscious. Al-Khidr, sweating profusely and hiding between rocks, was unsure about what was going on, as he could not hear clearly. Krono released Hatathor, turning toward the leader, and declared, "I am afraid that he might be in a state of coma." He flipped the body back into a face-up position. Meanwhile, another alien studying the pyramid approached the leader and said, "It does not look like it was made using the rocks of Lyra." "What do you mean?" the leader demanded an explanation.

"Come and see yourself," the alien replied. He walked with the leader and Krono to the pyramid and asked them to put their hands on the walls of the Egyptian pyramid. "This is not from Lyra, we don't have such rocks on our planet."

"That is unusual," Asubia remarked.

"Sambi, climb up through this opening over here and search."

"But the heat sensor detects nothing," replied Sambi.

"I understand your concern, Sambi. But we can never be too sure, can we?" replied the leader. "Just jump up there and see if you can find anything." "Very well," replied Sambi. He jumped, as if canceling the gravity, and landed on the ledge of the pyramid. Using the sensory flashlight, he walked inside and explored the pyramid's apex that was buried in the sand. The sensory flashlight helped him look through the walls, but the heat detector didn't detect any signs of life once again. Sambi came out of the pyramid and declared there was no one inside.

"Hm, strange. The sphere vanished, and a pyramid appeared," replied the Asubia.

He turned back to Krono, who examined the unconscious body.

"What are you doing with the specimen, Krono?"

"His clothes, Asubia – look, they are tearing apart," replied Krono.

"Looked like the poor guy went through a lot of stress."

"I see," replied the leader. "Remove his torn clothing and take him to the Tekhenu."

Krono gestured to two other aliens, who went inside one of their spaceships and came out, pushing a stretcher. They moved the stretcher around the pyramid where Hatathor lay inert. They stripped Hatathor off and put him on the stretcher. Hatathor's body had scratches and scars here and there.

"Did you get photographs and collect samples?" he asked.

The female alien nodded her head in response. "Yes, Asubia."

"Good," their leader remarked. "Let's move now."

As Asubia's word resounded in the midst, everyone immediately packed into the spaceship, ready to fly. Soon they took off, leaving Al-Khidr to explore the cold abyss. When the spaceship could no longer be sighted in the sky, Al-Khidr came out. He was cold and scared. Above all, he didn't know what to do or where to go. Since Al-Khidr didn't know yet, what planet was this?

He continued searching for a way up.

*If this is Lyra, then why couldn't I recognize the people. Perhaps another planet speaking the Lyrian language or part of Lyra that I am not familiar with?* he thought to himself.

# Chapter 3

# The Seka Awaken

HATATHOR opened his eyes, and he moved his arms hysterically towards his face. In his last memory, he was falling into the abyss. His eyes were bloodshot red, and his breaths were intensifying with every passing second. “Where am I?” he uttered.

He sat quickly and looked around. It was a round room with a single metallic wall that surrounded it. A big rectangular light was hanging above him. And he was surrounded by several people.

“Who are you, and what is this place?” Hatathor asked.

Hatathor was making sense of his surroundings. He was feeling heavy-headed.

The four men in front of him raised their hands over their heads, while nodded their heads. The men put the palms of the right hands on top of the dorsal side of the left hands. It was a sign of deep respect at the Lyra to do such a posture. "Seka qau! (The warrior awakens!)," they shouted in excitement.

One moved forward to kiss the dorsal side of Hatathor's left hand. Another one called back to others in the lobby. The slogans shook the building.

Seka!, Seka!, Seka!....

Hatathor started recalling the trauma. He was inside the crevice, holding onto the wall of the Egyptian pyramid, and then it fell into the abyss. The bloody Kebian (human) was inside the pyramid. His memories were flashing in his mind.

Hatathor sat on the stretcher and realized that he was naked.

"Where are my clothes? Who are you, people?"

"We are brethren, my lord."

"Brethren of whom? I have no siblings." His head was still heavy, and he was a bit confused. By this time, Hatathor started to get furious. He looked at his hand and found that his sleeve weapon was not there. He quickly jumped from the stretcher and stood in front of them. He was ready to make them suffer and took a man by the neck and pulled him towards him.

"Where is my sleeve?" Hatathor asked threateningly for his weapon.

"Where are my clothes?" Hatathor shouted.

One of them quickly approached and offered him a military uniform composed of a pair of pants, a shirt, and a cape for Hatathor to wear.

"The clothes you were wearing were worn out, master. We found you unconscious lying near the pyramid," the man said.

He handed the new clothes to him and said: "Here is a new Takhr (military tunic) for you".

Hatathor took the clothes and put on the blue shirt and trousers. He put on the cape as well, which was red.

"We also detected high levels of radiation, though they were not that dangerous for Lyrian breeds." The man said further.

Asubia looked at Krono, and he ordered him with a brief nod. Krono went inside, and after a few minutes, he appeared again with Hatathor's sleeve weapon, who was now fully dressed.

"We will give this to you, but first, you meet Tor (The King). He is waiting to see you." Asubia requested.

"Tor? Who is your king?" Hatathor inquired.

"Follow me!" Asubia went out of the room, and Hatathor valiantly followed.

He saw many men and women in the corridor when he entered. They were all saluting him in a specific Lyrian way of honoring by raising hands and making an arch at forehead level.

Hatathor felt privileged, but he hadn't seen these

people before in his life, as far as his memory went.

Hatathor walked through some long capsule-shaped corridors. He was familiar with the technology he was witnessing before his eyes, so he knew this was not Earth, and these people weren't humans but must be Lyrians. He had the dj vu feeling that he had been in this place before.

The corridors were white, with pipes of all shapes and sizes stretched across them. After a long walk, they stood outside a large door. "You may go inside now. Push the door, and step inside, please," stated one of them in a thick accent. It appeared to Hatathor they were using some kind of device to translate, but he let that thought waver. At first, Hatathor hesitated because he didn't know what to expect on the other side of the door, but then he thought there was no other way out of here, so he pushed open the door, ready to face whatever stood behind it.

It was a large hall and it looked like a throne room. It looked familiar to Hatathor as he entered.

As he advanced he saw a man in the room. There was a throne in front of him, but no one was sitting on it. The room was large and had a transparent wall overlooking the mountain range. Hatathor could only see the back of a man. The man's face was towards the window, but his pierced ear was visible. He was wearing a helmet. The man turned to face Hatathor. He was smiling and moving his hand over his black beard.

"You!" Hatathor exclaimed.

The man with an image of a closed eye in the vertical position on his forehead laughed and said, "Yes, me! Come, my friend. Ankhamon, son of Heka, welcomes you again on Tekhenu."

"Ankhamon...," before Hatathor could complete his sentence, Ankhamon corrected him. "It is King Ankhamon."

Hatathor was lost. He couldn't comprehend what Ankhamon had just said.

"What do you mean, king Ankhamon?" Hatathor demanded an explanation. "I think you haven't heard. We destroyed the Ehsis support army with the help of rebellion when you were sucked into the Tepta Ankh (The star tunnel). With the help of revolutionary generals, brethren took Ehsis's support army by surprise. We entered the capital and got control of the Benben pyramid. Ehsis and her staff escaped to some other planet," Ankhamon paused, "We are still searching for that devious woman."

"What happened to generals – Eli, Oseria, Dodvan, Popious and others?" Hatathor asked.

"They are now the war heroes, and I made monuments in their memory," Ankhamon said with a smirk.

"What? They are all dead?" Hatathor asked, demanding an answer.

Ankhamon kept silent.

"You could have stopped the war," Hatathor said.

"You are saying this – you, Hatathor? It was you who created a sinkhole in the kingdom – the power vacuum – someone had to fill it," Ankhamon said.

"You were not here, but I was here. How do you expect me to stop the war and brewing mutiny among the generals? The generals wanted to keep me like a puppet, but I decided not to become one. We are the brethren of awakening consciousness, and we see what most of the other Lyrians failed to see, especially those who were living in the fool's paradise," Ankhamon said.

"Who is the commander-in-chief now?" asked Hatathor.

"General Desher," Ankhamon said.

Hatathor laughed. "I feel like I am dreaming. The Kingdom of Akhom changed so much in a few days," Hatathor said.

"A few days–Nay, a few years, Hatathor!" Ankhamon said.

"Looks like the farther in-universe you go, the jumpsphere stretches the time and space like a vortex, and everything is distorted," Ankhamon said. "I see," replied Hatathor. He was speechless.

"Is that all you wanted to say?" asked Ankhamon.

"You are the Seka – the warrior, Hatathor. Remember, in exchange for a favor, it was I who informed you about your father, Seth, and you still have to return that favor to me," Ankhamon asserted his expectations.

Before Hatathor's arrival, Ankhamon was portraying him as a savior. He reminded Hatathor of his promise to accept him as his king if the government is toppled. "I will discuss this later with you," said Hatathor.

"Your allegiance to me is part of your promise. For the brethren, you are a true warrior, Hatathor. You endangered yourself to protect the Lyra. You solely jumped into the wormhole. We are proud of your bravery and courage. I am sure that you must have neutralized the threat to Lyra. You must have killed the human," Ankhamon said.

Hatathor said: "No, Ankhamon, I failed to stop the human. He was far more cunning than I had thought, or maybe it was all destined by God." "What do you mean? Did you fail, Hatathor?" Ankhamon shouted.

"I did everything I could to stop him . . . ,"

"Lyrians have a deep regard for you. If they came to know about your failure, they would be heartbroken," Ankhamon said.

"First, I must search for humans. He must have brought back something from Keb with him."

"Do you know where he must be?" asked Ankhamon.

"Perhaps the question I should ask you!" replied Hatathor. "You found me, but you couldn't find the human? He was inside the pyramid, and I was out in the crevice."

"According to my men, there wasn't anybody else except you there!" Ankhamon argued.

"I thought that today, I'll met a warrior who had stopped the human from coming back to our planet, but I am wrong!" Ankhamon said sarcastically. "Stop being sarcastic," Hatathor shouted. "As your king; I am also your friend. Therefore, I shall allow you to go look for him if you promise to bring me the sphere."

Although Hatathor didn't show it, he was unhappy with Ankhamon being the king. He wanted to object to himself, but he also wanted to get out there, so he played along. "Before I get you the orb, it is important we destroy the plants' leaves which the human has because if we don't, there won't be a kingdom to rule, Ankhamon." Reluctantly, Ankhamon agreed. "Fine, you win!" In his mind, he knew Hatathor was the only person who could get him the sphere that he badly wanted, so he allowed Hatathor to begin the search for the human.

"You may look for the human," Ankhamon said with a mischievous smile on his face.

Hatathor didn't reply. He had an earnest look on his face. "But before you leave, there is something I must ask you for."

Hatathor, almost out of the room, turned around, looked Ankhamon in the eye, and asked, "What is it?"

"My men have been talking to Lukmas, but he won't talk. We believe he knows where Ehsis is hiding." Without responding to Ankhamon, Hatathor was about to walk out of the room when a young man in full military General attire entered the throne room. He moved forward, and he bowed to the king with military precision.

"General Desher! It's wonderful to see you here. Come and meet major general Hatathor!" Ankhamon said excitedly.

General Desher stood upright and saluted the Tor Ankhamon, then he turned and faced Hatathor. He was a stern-looking man with no beard, wearing a dark blue uniform and a red cape with many medals on his chest. General Desher smiled and looked sternly at Hatathor. Hatathor grudgingly saluted General Desher. Desher looked at Hatathor from head to toe and said to Ankhamon:

"Luckily, we found the major general beside the pyramid; otherwise, he could be trapped in the abyss."

"No mountain can stop Hatathor," Hatathor said.

Desher looked back and smiled and said: "I can reinstate you on the rank of major general,"

"Reinstate?" Hatathor said in a surprised tone.

"I was on duty when I had left Lyra," Hatathor said.

"Desher..." Hatathor wanted to say more, but before he could say anything, Desher stopped him by raising his hand.

"General Desher – not Desher, I suppose you haven't forgotten your training," Desher reminded Hatathor of the military decorums.

Hatathor kept quiet.

Desher started walking around Hatathor. "A lot changed here, major general. Our values, our culture, and also our leadership," saying this, Desher looked at Ankhamon and moved towards him.

"We support our King, Tor Ankhamon, son of Heka and Holy mother Ahmose, who has set new values for the society," Desher said. "By the way, who is the

Holy Mother, Ahmose?" Hatathor asked.

"Mother Ahmose – she is the now the mother. Lyrians need a mother, and Ahmose fills up the psychological lacuna in people's minds. She used to be my disciple, a trustworthy and stalwart supporter of the brethren's cause. I am sure she will be pleased to meet you," said Ankhamon.

Hatathor looked at Desher, who was smiling. He couldn't believe what he was hearing.

*How much psychologically, politically, and emotionally the Lyrians had changed,* Hatathor thought. *I'll meet you soon, mother.*

"Do Lyrians need so many changes?" Hatathor asked.

"Yes. We cherish our values and our new way of thinking," Desher said.

"General Desher, we will talk about it again, but now I have to search for the human," Hatathor said and looked at Desher and Ankhamon.

"Yes, major, you may go now," Desher said as if telling him he is the new boss now.

Hatathor walked out of the room; he walked past another Lyrian walking towards the throne room. Kontar was a sleek man with a vivid bony structure on his face and long hair. He smiled and respectfully saluted Hatathor.

"You summoned me, Master?" Kotar asked Ankhamon.

"Yes, Kontar," said Ankhamon. "I need you to do something for me."

"It will be an honor, Tor Ankhamon," replied Kontar. "What can I do?"

"Being Lord of Security, I want you to accompany Hatathor and keep a close eye on him. Report everything to general Desher or me," Ankhamon ordered. "You mean we spy on Seka Hatathor?" Kontar said in a baffled tone and looked at General Desher, still in the room. "Yes, Kontar- you may call it spying or whatever you like. But Hatathor has just arrived back on Lyra, and it will take him time till he readjust to the new lifestyle," Ankhamon said.

***

Hatathor came out, and a man gave his sleeve weapon back to him. Hatathor took it, but his mind was overly active and overflowing with possible conflicts with Desher. He clenched his fist in rage.

Should I like Desher or I hate him? he asked himself.

Maybe Ankhamon got what he wanted, but he does not understand the danger looming over Lyra. The human is back, and he has the sphere or perhaps the plants; I should keep my focus on my aims, he reminded himself.

Hatathor walked and reached some guards, and he asked a guard where the jail was. The guard told him that Ankhamon made a dungeon in the mountains. He walked towards the dungeon, where Lukmas was held as a prisoner.

*I must dig out of him where Ehsis is hiding*, Hatathor thought to himself.

He walked through the corridors of the catacombs, navigating his way to the newly created dungeons. The guards stood up when they saw Hatathor walking towards them. His face was red, and he was in no mood for an argument. In his mind, he had already decided to fight the guards if they tried to stop him, and he knew he was going to win with all the fighting abilities he possessed. "Open the door. I am here to see a prisoner."

"I am sorry, but can I see an approval?" one of the guards asked.

Hatathor was triggered. His eyes were now bloodshot red. However, before he did something, the other guard said, "Let him in." "What do you mean?" the first guard argued.

"He is Hatathor – the man I told you about," said the other guard. "I apologize on his behalf. You may go in."

The guard entered a passcode outside the dungeon on a keypad, which opened a door, leading a narrow way inside a dark room. When Hatathor walked inside the room, the lights flicked and turned on. The floor sounded metallic under Hatathor's steps, and on each side, there was a long capsule-shaped tube filled with a liquid substance, big enough to fit a human. Hatathor took a stroll, looking at tubes closely, trying to recognize Lukmas. "May I know who you are looking for? I may be able to help," said the guard from before, standing behind Hatathor.

Hatathor looked at the number of tubes that were in front of him. He knew it would take him a long time to find Lukmas that way, so he turned around. "Lukmas," said Hatathor. "I would like to see him in the interrogation room."

The guard ran towards one tube and pressed some buttons on his tablet. The viscous translucent fluid started draining from a capsule-looking shell. Once it was drained, the being inside the capsule was visible. The guard pressed a few more buttons, and a nebulous smoke came out of the capsule as it was opened. The man dropped to the floor. He was going through convulsions and coughing. The room was also partially filled up by the smoke. Hatathor saw Lukmas at his feet. He was incessantly coughing and begging Hatathor to let him go. The guard picked Lukmas up and forced him to walk inside the interrogation room built inside the dungeon while Hatathor followed.

"Leave us alone now," said Hatathor.

The guard left and closed the door on his way out. Now, it was just Lukmas and Hatathor. "Would you like something to drink?" asked Hatathor. Lukmas, trying to catch his breath, nodded.

"Then cooperate," replied Hatathor. "Tell me, where is Ehsis?"

"I don't know. I have told everyone a hundred times, I don't know," replied Lukmas.

Hatathor slammed the table before him and shouted, "Liar!" He looked Lukmas in the eye and continued,

"I will ask you again, where is Ehsis?" "I don't know. Please, let me go. I don't know anything," cried Lukmas.

"I didn't want to do this, but you left me no choice," said Hatathor.

"Unlike everyone you have talked to before, I tend to use violence. How about we start with your fingers?" Hatathor grabbed Lukmas's hand and slammed it on the table.

Lukmas did not see that coming. He was telling the truth, and he didn't know how to convince Hatathor to put aside his wrath. . "I swear–I swear, I don't know where he is. I may be his general, but I was not with him when he escaped. There can be thousands of places where he can be right now. Trust me, keep me prisoner, if you must, but believe me."

Hatathor released his hand and said, "I am done here." He walked out of the room, and following that, the guard walked inside the room and took Lukmas away.

***

Hatathor walked out of the facility and looked around. Everything made sense to him now. He knew where he was and where to go, though he was a bit agitated about the whole Ehsis and Ankhamon thing; after all , considering he wanted to be the king.

While he was there a lady guard came forward and bowed to him and said: "Greetings, Seka Hatathor.

We are so delighted that you have returned safely."

"Mother Ahmose already foretold a savior from the sky," she said further.

"Prophetess Ahmose, who is she?" Hatathor asked.

"She is the Reverend Mother – the Great Seer. She is a clairvoyant. We used to call her the mother while we were in Tehuti mountain, but now the epithet is officially given to her by Tor Ankhamon." The lady guard informed Hatathor.

"Ah, I see," Hatathor uttered in a surprised tone.

"Her lodge is on the mountain nearby. No spaceships can fly over her lodge, so one can only meet her after climbing mount Tass.

*I need to meet the Prophetess to know who she is*, he thought.

Hatathor thanked the girl, and another gaurd approached and said: "Seka Hatathor, we have made a ship ready for you".

Hatathor was surprised as new model of spaceship landed near him with new kingdom insignia. He went inside and was impressed with the new technology the Lyrians were using. Hatathor tested his sleeve weapon to see if he could still produce a protective hemispherical energy shield around him and generate a shock wave to repel enemies. The sleeve weapon was functioning flawlessly thanks to Vega radiation levels.

*I am all set for the mission, but something is still missing!* He thought.

"Ah, the bident," he said to himself.

Hatathor tracked the weapon storage room, and he

went to get more arsenal, but two guards blocked his way, which was strange.

"Let me in," Hatathor demanded access, but the guards refused to move from their place. They stood in front of a double door armored with a metal that Hatathor didn't recognize.

"Nobody gets it without a written notice from Ankhamon," one of the guards replied. The guard had a firm look on his face.

"Ankhamon sent me," Hatathor argued.

"And you don't have a written approval," the guard replied.

"I do not follow orders." Hatathor pressed the buttons swiftly on his sleeve weapon, and a protective shield formed.

While the men were baffled, their head-officer entered and ordered: "Give Seka whatever he wants."

Hatathor entered the arsenal room and picked a bident.

Hatathor walked out of the facility, making his way to the dock, where Ankhamon had readied a spaceship for him.

"There you are!" Kontar welcomed him. "Your spaceship is ready for flight," he declared.

With an attitude, Hatathor hopped into his spaceship. While getting familiar with the controls, he turned around and saw that three more spaceships were being loaded for flight behind him. Hatathor hopped out of the vessel and confronted Kontar. "What is this? I thought I was going alone!"

Kontar knew he couldn't tell Hatathor that Ankhamon had asked him to spy on him, so he lied.

"The human has the orb with him–and its energy is unpredictable. Our men don't know what he is capable of." "Don't be afraid. Orb is not a bomb", Hatathor said.

"Let us all go," Kontar insisted.

"Alright then," Hatathor said.

"You will lead the mission," Kontar added. "So, which way do we head?"

"Where are you human," Hatathor said, and he started looking at the display of his sleeve weapon. The device had a small screen on it. Hatathor pressed some buttons, and the device beeped, and a holographic map appeared, giving Al-Khidr's location. He showed the location to Kontar, and he immediately recognized the place. "Abyss, how he had reached the pit?" said Kontar. He looked at Hatathor and hopped into his spaceship with his fellowmen.

Hatathor didn't respond and went into the spaceship to begin the mission.

# Chapter 4

# The Culture

"THINK, Al-Khidr, think!" Al-Khidr chanted, strategizing a way out of the chasm. He glanced around to find another way, but his prospects were not looking good. The mere way out of the abyss was to ascend the mountains, which Al-Khidr couldn't do, given the fact that there was frost on the rocks. He simply couldn't take the risk of damaging the orb - his only way out of Lyra. He walked along the mountain, looking for a lower step to begin his way up the cliff.

The track was arduous, and with every fleeting minute, it was getting cold. The breeze carried frost on its wings that limited Al-Khidr pace. He walked on over-slippery rocks and that was overwhelming and stressing. Al-Khidr prayed for the frost to melt, but his prayers went unanswered. After all, God wouldn't have changed the entire climatic make-up of an alien planet just to ease out the struggle of an ordinary human being. The odds were against him, and he had to live his fate. The breeze started to get colder and more powerful and Al-Khidr knew he had to find a shelter; otherwise, he would freeze to death. He looked around himself again, and saw the same cliffs, stretched where until where an eye could perceive. Al-Khidr felt chilled to the bone.

*How will I overcome these mountains?*

As he was walking, supporting himself onto the wall, all of a sudden his hand got into a hole. surprised, Al-Khidr looked closely and saw there was a crevice in the mountain. *It was hidden from sight, but what a blessing it was!* he thought.

He found a cave that brimmed with hope in his heart and mind.

Upon entry, the warmth that lurked in the cave overflowed Al-Khidr with happiness. It was not hot, but at least it was warmer than outside.

As he went deeper into the cave, he noticed that the cave had some lights reflecting inside. His footsteps sounded as if the brittle shards were splintering under his Egyptian cowhide sandals. Where this light is coming from?

He was looking at the floor for a wood or a twig

that could warm him up, but he couldn't see anything flammable. Suddenly he noticed that sphere is also issuing some light though not very luminous.

"Ah, the sphere!" He exclaimed.

The sphere's light was not sufficient, but by bringing it closer to the floor and nearby rocks, he could perceive them. He realized that the cave had sharp ridges. A noise stopped him in his exploration. There were a few ships outside. *Is someone still looking into the pyramid? I had hoped they wouldn't return! Do they know I am here? I hope I wasn't seen!* The thought made Al-Khidr uncomfortable.

The spaceships were hovering at a slow speed, in their research mission. However, the cave's opening was too narrow, and from above, it looked like a simple crack in the mountain that couldn't lead to an ampler which could have been perfect for someone seeking shelter.

"You said the signal came from here, Hatathor," the pilot of one spaceship, known as Kenem, complained.

Hatathor was looking anxiously at the tracking unit. The tracking system showed that the prisoner was somewhere close. However, the signal was distorted.

"I know what I said, but something is wrong, I guess," replied Hatathor. "The trackers seem to be malfunctioning." "Let me check with other units," Kenem said.

Kenem contacted the other pilots in the search party, and all responded negatively. "These ships are not designed to capture the signature of primitive and weak life forms. No signature on our ships," Kenem announced.

"Share the visual of your military tracking unit's screen with us. I am sending you the sharing protocol," Kenem proposed to Hatathor.

Hatathor reluctantly pressed buttons on his tracking unit and shared his screen with the spaceship's onboard tracking unit.

"This is what I was talking about–a new signal every second. The tracker probably has battery issues at the moment or might have been broken."

"The tracker isn't broken or low in battery, Hatathor," Kenem replied. "These mountains have Amris inside them, and you know Amris emit radiation which could disrupt our tracking electromagnetic signals."

"Oh, yes, Amirs is causing this distortion in signal!" Hatathor agreed.

"I guess we'd have to rely on our eyes now since this is where you got the signal for because most of our technology is useless here!" Kenem said.

"I see," said Hatathor.

"I think it is better if we come back later. The blizzard seems to be worsening. Besides, the prisoner is a human. He couldn't possibly survive this cold. We should deploy a search party to find his corpse after the storm." Hatathor said further about Al-Khidr.

"Sound like a plan, Hatathor," replied Kenem and commanded the others to turn. "Turn around. The mission has been aborted for now."

Five spaceships out of six turned around and flew back to the base, except the one spaceship that Hatathor was flying. He was confident that the prisoner was alive and hiding somewhere. Hatathor took matters in his hand and lowered his spaceship into the abyss. The lower he descended, the beeping was gradually increasing. But again, Hatathor found nothing but snow. He landed near the pyramid and went inside the pyramid to look for the orb, but all he found were only the French military uniform shards, which were of no use now. "Curse you, Al-Khidr," yelled Hatathor. His scream echoed and echoes of his voice came back to him. Al-Khidr, lying on the cave floor, opened his eyes but he decided not to go close to the crevice.

"I am being tracked. Oh God, save me from these ruthless aliens," Al-Khidr prayed.

"Curse you, prisoner, and curse this tracker!" Hatathor yelled again and flew out of the abyss.

Al-Khidr picked up the orb and continued to explore the cave. As deeper he found the cave was like a catacomb, an intricate maze. Many tunnels were interconnecting, which made the exploration challenging. However, Al-Khidr went with his instincts and continued walking in the cave.

***

Al-Khidr was feeling thirsty. The inter-galactic jump has sapped his energy already. He needed to figure out how he would survive on this planet, which didn't look like Lyra to him. He sat on the floor of the cave and started praying Allah. The exhaustion threw him into slumber. When he woke up, his head was on the cave's floor, and his ear was touching the ground. There were no hauling echoes of the blizzard. Light was coming inside the cave through multiple crevices in the cave walls. It was morning already, and he could see the interior around. The cave was dazzling in the multitude of reflections. The rocks looked like mud smeared over the glass, as if the giant glass shards were protruding from the cave's ceiling.

Multiple beams of light converged to the center of the cave - like a halo.

He took a shard from the ground and immediately recognized it. It was the piece of the same flowing glass – the Amris.

He shouted: "I reached! I reached back." He cried and thanked God for bringing him back to the Lyra.

*Nefertiti said that Amris is only present on Lyra.* The thought energized him now that he was sure he was in the right location. He took a few pieces of Amris and put them in his pocket, thinking that he might need them later.

Then he walked further inside the cave and suddenly he felt coldness at his feet. He looked at the ground. There was a puddle of water like fluid which was not overflowing. The water below was clear, crystal-clear. Al-Khidr could see his reflection in the pool of pristine water. The sparkling water under the reflective rocks of Amris created an ambiance and it was a mind refreshing experience.

He tore a piece of his clothing and threw it in water. Nothing happened. He went closer, and no fumes were coming out of the liquid. He dipped the tip of his finger, and nothing happened. As an alchemist and maker of acids, he was sure drinking water.

"In the name of Allah," he said and took a scoop of water into his palms and washed his hands.

He quickly quenched his thirst and continued his climb. The Amris inside the cave reflected the light multiple times, and the entire interior was dazzling. He noticed that the floor was elevating, and he realized that he was moving up. He continued his climb through the cave for hours. He even took short naps to regain his strength. Luckily, there were the water ponds along his path and he was able to at least quench his thirst, fooling the hunger he had started feeling. Finally, the cave's inside was changing, and it seemed that was getting closer and closer to the top. He could feel and fresh air. He gathered all his energy and continued climbing, and finally, he could see an opening. He ran and was now he was standing on the flat floor.

He was so astonished by the sight that he thought he was hallucinating. He rubbed his eyes and blinked a few times to figure out what he is looking at. He could see from afar a dwelling.

He continued to walk until he finally reached the dwelling. The architecture was ancient, as per Lyrian standards. With a rumbling stomach, he continued strolling. He found many dilapidated houses and abandoned buildings, but he couldn't locate a single life form. He wondered what it was like to live here. He noticed warning posts on every corner of the block, and he could read the signboards in the lyrian language.

The warnings read: "You are in the forbidden zone. Beware, no one may trespass, Sutekh... Life imprisonment will be given. Leave the Sutekh...."

This is a forbidden zone–probably the place that Nefertiti had mentioned. The place struck by the Mut-mut disease.

What caught his attention was a clothing shop. Al-Khidr knew he had to keep a low profile, and for that, he had to blend in. He walked into the shop and picked a dusty outfit, which was much better than the French frock coat he was wearing. He dusted it off and put it on. It fitted quite nicely.

***

Hatathor was still in his spaceship. Suddenly, his display panel beeped, and a voice said: "Update, major general?" asked General Desher. "The look on your face tells me you failed."

"I am working on it, General."

"King Ankhamon wants the human to be displayed for public viewing," said General Desher.

Hatathor didn't respond to that.

"Give me some time, General, and I will catch him. I am not doing this for some show. You know that any pathogens from any alien planet can put us in a very compromising situation. We need to get our hands on him as soon as possible!" Hatathor said.

"Yes, I knew it already, so do it as soon as possible," Desher said in a stern tone.

Hatathor's brown skin turned red. "Just give me a week, and I will get you the human!"

"Alright then, you have 10 days," said General Desher. "But if you fail, I'll do this my way."

The communication was closed abruptly. In frustration, Hatathor took the sleeve weapon off his arm and tossed it in the corner of the spaceship.

# Chapter 5

# The Insurgents

THE drone was approaching the ruins of the ancient city, destroyed ages ago in battle by the rival planet Sovidos, even before King Ptah. It looked like a huge crater with porous rocks frozen in time as if the lava splashed and froze from outside. The hue of the rocks was black, and within the chambers of its pores, a queer silver glowed.

The crater, now called Kneph by a Lyrian geologist, was made by destroying the second major city of the Kingdom of Akhom in the east. The war between Lyra and Sovidos was not going to stop until

King Ptah threatened to evaporate Sovidos using the hall of death weapon system of Akhom. Fortunately, the threat stopped the battle. King Ptah later made underneath the Kneph an underground bunker-like facility with access to the communication systems and security cameras of the capital Misraim. After the military mutiny, Ehsis fled into hiding with her small supporting military troops, police, and some scientists. When the uprising had broken out, she had came to this secret place. The Kneph was an underground place especially made for unexpected situations, military coups, etc. The site was secret and only known to Ehsis, and a few very well-trusted military staff.

The Kneph was equipped with sizable laser weapons and three spaceships to escape the planet.

"I never imagined I'd need to use this place," said Ehsis.

"But what do you suggest we do now?" asked Nefertiti, standing before Ehsis and looking into the drone data.

The drone was part of surveillance protocols that needed to be done every day.

"For the first time, I don't know Nefertiti," said Ehsis. "I don't know if we should plot an attack on Ankhamon or live our remaining lives here in Kneph until they are captured or killed."

"If you don't mind, may I suggest something?" asked Nefertiti.

"Your suggestions are always welcome, Nefertiti," said Ehsis.

"I think we should plot an attack because if we stay here despite whatever the resources we have, we will die anyway. So, why not die fighting for what's rightfully ours?" suggested Nefertiti.

"Oh Nefertiti, I understand your enthusiasm. However, we don't have enough men to march against Ankhamon," Ehsis expressed her concern.

"Guardian Ehsis, I will take care of that problem. As your attack commander, I'd like to ask you to let me organize this counter rebellion force. Most of my friends are from the police force, and I know they will help us out during these trying times," replied Nefertiti.

"You have all my trust," said Ehsis, "but we have to act slowly for the time being. We need external help. Maybe some other planet will help Lyra."

***

"What the heck!" exclaimed Rostau.

"Now what happened?" asked Semed.

Rostau was a tall, slender, energetic man of 26 years old who had completed his Lyrian Academy of Space Explorers training just before the rebellion. He had straight hair with a sky-blue color and transparent eyes. His face was long and angular, like a hawk, but his arms, chest and legs were thin and strong like a gymnast's. Semed was a clean-shaven, chubby guy with a prominent forehead and curly hair, also trained at the kingdom of Akhom's military University of Space Engineering and proved to be the best cadet they've ever had. His piercing, emerald green eyes were evidence of his intelligence and capability.

Rostau and Semed were well-versed in the art and technology of spacecraft, orbital tracking, drones, and guided weapons. However, Guardian Ehsis had given them the stupendous task of starting an ancient device.

Commander Rostau was working on the ignition system of Mavira (Meteor in the Lyrian Language). He had already spent 17 hours trying to fix the ancient ship manufactured in the times of King Ptah. At the end of the wedge-like spaceship, the nozzles were roaring, though there was an intermittent power gap, and the whole craft was shaking.

"Try to run the analytics on the on-board controls," said Semed. "Looks like there is a disconnection between the panel power and the ignition system," Semed added. "Yeah, I'm checking it out," Rostau replied. Rostau was always irked by advisors, especially those from his friends.

"Take it easy, man," Semed assured him.

"Guardian Ehsis wanted to see the results soon, but damn this machine is not smooth," replied Rostau.

As Rostau spoke, the main control board was short-circuited, and the power went off with sparks. "Ah, not again," Rostau shouted. "I told you there is a power issue here between the panel and the ignition," said Semed, pointing it out for Rostau.

Suddenly, their conversation was stopped by a constant beeping which circled the room. If it were regular days for them, it would have been a safety alarm. However, the sound was deliberately lowered since they were hiding and couldn't jeopardize their location. Soon after everyone had sought shelter at Kneph, Rostau and Semed programmed the beeping to sound lower and installed them in every chamber of the underground cave which looked like a beehive. There were many openings in every enclosure where people worked on different things. These chambers, just like a beehive, were octagonal and weary walls of porous rocks. Inside the room, the spaceship Rostau and Semed were working on with their team, was sitting obsolete. There were two metallic tables were standing with papers and blueprints on them. Because of that, paper balls were scattered around the dustbin in the corner, which was already full.

"Let's eat. I hope they cooked something good today," said Semed.

"I think we should be thankful for what we are getting considering the situation," replied Rostau sarcastically.

"Well, it is not a bad thing to be hopeful," Semed countered. "Come on, let's go now. We will work on this piece of junk later."

The five men slithered themselves out of different slots of the spacecraft. The slots in the spaceship were too narrow to accommodate a person, and no one could have imagined going that deep inside the spaceship. However, their dedication towards a better future and Ehsis's orders coerced them to try to make the ancient technology rerun.

"I think I am stuck. Pull me out," shouted Semed.

The rest of the men chuckled.

"Come on, guys. This is not funny," remarked Semed.

"Rostau?" called Semed again.

Rostau slithered back into the slot and stretched his hand for Seemed to reach it, controlling his laugh. "Come on now," said Rostau.

Semed grabbed his hand, and Rostau pulled him outside.

"Thank you," said Semed, dusting his clothes. He paused and looked at the guys laughing at him. "Come on now, and the slots are too narrow."

"Perhaps you're too out of shape, Semed," said Rostau.

"Seriously? Look around you. How can one stay fit amid such circumstances?" countered Semed.

Rostau laughed. "Then aren't you supposed to be losing weight instead of putting it on?"

The guys laughed with Rostau.

"You know what? Forget it!" shrieked Semed. "Let's go eat now."

As they walked out of their chamber, they met other refugees and workers, making their way up to the dining hall. They all went inside a descending tunnel in a drill, which led them to a cavern. The cavern was dimly lit. However, the porosity of rocks helped them to get fresh air. They walked in the dark passage of the cave, which was a narrow passage of

70 m in length. After making their way through the shuttle, they entered a large dining hall crowded with men and women. "I hope we get something good to eat today," Semed iterated.

Rostau looked at Semed with an annoyed look on his face in response.

"What? Remember what I said about being hopeful?"

"You are unbelievable," remarked Rostau.

Everyone queued up for the food, and there were already 30 men and women ahead of them. "Damn it, we should have hurried, but somebody got stuck," said Rostau, and they laughed again. The people in the hall had unkempt hair and shabby clothes. Most of them were former police officers, and some belonged to the military before the unfortunate mutiny happened. Rostau and Semed got into the line along with their team and patiently waited and followed the queue, waiting for their turn to get served.

A bulky lady was serving the food to everyone in the queue. "I wonder if they even wash the things they cook," said Rostau. "I mean, who washes so many dishes?" Rostau looked at Semed and replied, "Well, when was the last time you were assigned this duty?"

"Hey, let's not make this personal," said Semed.

Rostau chuckled at that and asked, "Can you read the menu for me?"

Semed squinted and tried to read the screen installed above the serving counter. "It says delicious wobbling insects poured over some hot gravy. Wait, isn't that what we had two days ago?" Rostau shrugged in response.

After waiting patiently and following the queue, their turn to get served came. Rostau and Semed walked ahead with their trays, and the lunch lady served them their food. "It looks better than yesterday's stuff, though," said Semed.

"Man, this looks delicious!" Rostau responded. He looked at the serving lady with appreciative eyes and added, "Good work!" The dining hall accommodated about 12 metallic tables placed side by side. Even the walls in the dining area were especially manufactured to survive nuclear fallout. However, everyone was seated at the tables having their lunch. The refraction of the daylight was making its way through the big bulletproof windows into the room, which gave life to the dusty murals on the walls. The sound of the spoons against the metallic plates was reverberating in the hall, and the people were discussing their several projects.

A buzzer was heard as they talked, and that diverted everyone's attention. Everyone looked at the doorway and saw Nefertiti standing. As usual, she was dressed in a police uniform. "The Guardian Ehsis is entering the hall," she said and stepped aside, allowing Ehsis to enter the room. Through the dark shadows, Ehsis entered the dining hall wearing a white gown. She looked older than her age and her platinum blonde hair was falling freely down her shoulders. Her skin was wrinkled, but even without makeup, she looked flawless. She looked around with a smile on her face and gave a short speech while the men and women listened attentively.

"I know things are difficult now, but I want you all to know that Kneph is old, but no sounds can go out of these walls. It was the master security plan of King Ptah, for he knew we would need such a place. Although I know you guys are working hard to make the technology function best and as good as what the brethren had stolen from us, we cannot beat them unless we reach their level. I am pleased that we got your loyalty and help. We will soon take the kingdom as we are the true owner of the planet. We will obliterate the deceived cult, along with the treacherous generals who had supported them." The dining hall roared as the words of Ehsis had etched hope on their hearts sunk in despair. One of them stood up and shouted, "Liberate general Lukmas from their prison." Another followed, "Long live Guardian Ehsis."

Guardian Ehsis was the State Secretary in queen Hathor's time. But when the mishap occurred, she fled along with some royal military force to Kneph. The crowd chanted, "Long live, Guardian Ehsis!"

"As much as I appreciate their enthusiasm, I will not allow the food to get cold," said Semed, slurping the gravy and the wobbly insect. "This is tasty." However, Rostau was still listening to all the roaring that bombarded against the walls of the halls. He was smiling, looking at Ehsis. Rostau always adored Ehsis for her bravery, and he believed in her. This was the reason he even agreed to work on Mavira. "I guess they used fresh pieces today instead of using the preservatives like they normally do," replied Rostau, looking at Ehsis until she went to her chair, which was slightly different than the regular chairs.

"As long as they do not stink, it is okay for me," said a girl sitting in front of Rostau and Semed. The men laughed at her remark.

"Stop making fun of the food. Just eat it. Gulp it down," said Osahar as she was always annoyed when someone commented on food. Osahar was a former clerk in the central police station where Al-Khidr was imprisoned.

However, the guys were unwitting towards him. "I wish I could go out and grow some vegetables," Semed continued.

"No way! You're not allowed to go out. Pokiah was warned, and he only went 2 km away from here," replied Osahar. "Ehsis and Ofiah had given the current grade instructions to all personnel that we cannot go beyond the 5 km zone and only within this 5 km premise we can hunt birds or insects. Luckily, there is a hidden excavation channel that is leading us to the Amris. If it were not close enough, we never would have enough fuel to power up Kneph."

"True," Rostau agreed.

"Sometimes, they get fish from the river underneath Kneph. But due to security reasons, Ehsis only allowed it once every two months." "Damn you guys need to chill. I am just making a joke," countered

Semed.

"I heard that Ankhamon's men were sighted near HSS," said Osahar.

"We are lucky in several ways. Ankhamon and his men don't know we have access to the CCTVs of the Misraim," Semed said.

"I hope they don't know that until we take them over. The only thing is that we are short on men here. Otherwise, this would have happened earlier," Kopher added to the conversation.

"Not until we fix the ships," Rostau shrieked. "They were made in the period of King Ptah. Since then, we have had a lot of technological advancements. Unfortunately, they are in control of Ankhamon, though he doesn't know how to run all of it."

"Ankhamon only won because of the treachery of major general Hatathor," said the Kopher. "He killed the mother Hathor in vengeance."

After Kopher's statement, a sullen silence took over. They all stopped talking and ate their lunch with curves stretched across their faces. The frowns on their forehead implied they were sad. Semed, however, while eating, looked up and glanced across the room. He saw everyone was suffering. He saw how Ehsis didn't look like she used to, how everyone was coping with the situation. Semed was sorry. He knew he couldn't do anything, so to himself, he vowed to work as hard as he could to get the spacecraft started. He smiled to himself and ate his lunch. Rostau raised his sight and witnessed the smile on Semed's face. Although Rostau didn't say it, he knew Semed had realized something. He nodded to himself and ate his lunch.

***

Shiphrah was in her room in Tekhenu, and she was looking through the window towards the vast Tehuti mountain range. She was carrying both jewelry and weapons on her gorgeous Kalasiris. All four fingers were charmed with rings, and the golden chains attached to her golden armband were adorned with precious stones. She was wearing a robe that looked like an ancient Egyptian dress of some goddess. It was azure, with a pattern of spangles and pearls. Shiphrah, daughter of Ankhamon, was a seductive beautiful young woman.

A servant arrived and informed her that her father was looking for her. She turned as if she was a warrior who had vowed to protect the kingdom and walked none other than any military general. "Tell him I will be there shortly," she told the servant.

It had been a long time since her father had summoned her like this, and unlike last time, she had no clue why. The last time Ankhamon called her, he had planned a party for her, although this time, her birthday was nowhere near, so she was clueless. She quickly put on a silk gown representing royalty and got rid of all the weapons around her waist.

Walking like a lady, she entered the king's chambers while guards stood straight. "Father, did you call me?" she said, flipping her smooth brown hair.

Shiphrah's long hair was a cascade of glimmering red, and the waves contrasted against her smooth skin.

"Yes," Ankhamon said. "Hatathor is back!" he announced to his daughter.

Her heart jolted into her chest. She giggled with a half-open smile as if some private joke of her own secretly amused her. "Oh, what wonderful news," Shiphrah said. Every breath from Shiphrah was like a night's worth of perfume, the kind that arouses whispers and dreams. It was a scent of musk and water, a mingling of forest and river.

"We'll talk later!" Ankhamon said to the four brethren men who were already inside his chamber. They smiled at Shiphrah while leaving the room. Shiphrah, however, ignored them all, and she had already given her heart to someone she hadn't met.

Shiphrah had mentally given her heart to Hatathor. She liked strong men those who could fight and kill for the honors of the race. Ever since Hatathor went to Keb (Earth), she started seeing him in her dreams. She even had a picture of Hatathor in her room. She hadn't met him, but she was sure that she would be the only girl in his life.

"Seka Hatathor has arrived, and he wanted to see you," an officer entered and announced.

Hatathor entered the room, saluted the king, and saw the lovely Shiphrah.

Shiphrah was blushed; finally, she saw Hatathor in person for the first time. Her heart was right he was the man she wanted. Her face lit up when he approached and forwarded his hand and said, "I am Hatathor, and you are Miss,"

"She is my daughter, Princess," Ankhamon said.

"Shiphrah, I am Shiphrah!" she exclaimed with nervousness.

Hatathor had broad shoulders with a firm jaw. Shiphrah thought it made him look stronger. Hatathor liked the young woman, and her attitude and the way she carried herself were what he wanted.

Ankhamon noticed Hatathor was looking at his daughter again and again. He smiled and said, "Why don't you guys go out and have some drinks on the top floor of Tekhenu? Previously, it was a dump yard, but now it has been made to view the entire capital city. Plus, the food is good." Hatathor didn't mind going to the top floor with Shiphrah for some drinks. After all, this was all he needed after having a long day contemplating a strategy to get to Al-Khidr, a wonderful time with a beautiful girl. Shiphrah couldn't stop blushing, and she was enjoying this. "After you," said Hatathor, gesturing for Shiphrah to walk.

Shiphrah bowed, depicting her royal ethics, and walked towards the door, while Hatathor nodded at Ankhamon and followed her. He held the big door open for her as Shiphrah walked outside. Hatathor closed the door behind him and joined Shiphrah in the corridor, which led them to the stairs. Although they were walking together, they were both too flustered to start a conversation, both blushing.

"Would you like to take the elevator?" asked Hatathor.

Shiphrah turned around and saw how busy the elevator was. Although the others would have let her through because she was the king's daughter, Shiphrah didn't want to build that image of her in front of Hatathor. Therefore, she refused. "We can take the stairs," she smiled. "Sure," said Hatathor.

"So, what do you do, princess?" asked Hatathor. Shiphrah blushed. "You can call me Shiphrah," she said, thinking of an appropriate response to give to Hatathor. Although she trained like other brethren, she wanted to appear more lady-like to Hatathor.

"I read, write, bedazzle, and try to be the perfect daughter."

Hatathor was surprised by Shiphrah's response, as he didn't expect that answer. "What do you mean, try to be the perfect daughter?" asked Hatathor. "When you are a princess, people think your life is easy. Little do they know, it is a strenuous life since you have to be perfect in everything," replied Shiphrah. "I understand," replied Hatathor, thinking how to keep the conversation going.

"Sometimes, I wish I could flee these walls and experience the world," Shiphrah added.

Hatathor had found his cue, and now he knew how to carry the conversation further. "Well, that won't be a problem," he smiled. "Maybe Princess can give me more time, and I can introduce her to the world."

Shiphrah smiled. "I would like that."

While walking up the stairs, Shiphrah tried to get a hold of the handrails, compelled by Hatathor's charm.

She missed it and tripped on her high heels. Hatathor used quick reflexes and stretched his hand to catch Shiphrah by the waist, all the while looking into her eyes. The time seemed to stop for both of them, and everything turned slowly as they kept looking each other in the eye. "Are you okay, Shiphrah?"

"Yes." Shiphrah's lips quivered with her hands around Hatathor's neck. "Thank you."

Slowly, Hatathor helped her back to her feet and confirmed again. "Are you sure you're okay?"

Shiphrah nodded in response. Her cheeks blushing.

After a while, talking about their lives, they finally made it to the top floor. It was close to dusk, and the gleam of the day was soon to set at the horizon. They could see the beautiful setting Vega from the top floor balcony.

The Tekhenu's top floor was turned into a dining hall, as Ankhamon mentioned. The dining hall walls were covered with fine art and aesthetic murals. There were multiple accent walls painted in a lush combination of black and white. At the entrance, a man dressed in black and white greeted them. It was a fancy place. There were four upholstered armchairs around each table. "Wow, this place is nice," said Hatathor.

Princess Shiphrah and Major Hatathor, we have been expecting you," the man dressed in black and white said. "The royal staff has called and made a reservation for you both already," he added.

"Its an honor for me to spent few hours with you

Princess," Hatathor said.

"Shiphrah just call me Shiphrah," she insisted trying to become more informal.

"I have heard so much about you. Your chivalry and courage to face the old regime is exemplary," she added.

"I did what I thought was best for our kingdom and people," Hatathor said.

Hatathor was not the dating sort, but he tried and did it with confidence. Meanwhile, Shiphrah appreciated his gut and didn't seem to mind it at all since she had secretly given her heart to him.

Hatathor and Shiphrah were escorted to their table and were handed a menu. They both went through the menu and ordered the finest drink for themselves, with some exotic worms from a neighboring planet. While they waited for the food, Hatathor told Shiphrah about his adventures on Earth, and after having the delicious meal and drinks, they stood on the balcony that overlooked the entire kingdom.

The slightly cold wind set the scene for the couple as they enjoyed the beauty of the Tehuti mountains in the Vega twilight which was making them beautiful. The raising moons looked more prominent while they both stood there with their hands tied together, enjoying the tranquility of each other's presence.

***

Shiphrah was lying in her bed inside her master bedroom. She was experiencing a spontaneous feeling of frivolousness today. The ecstatic mixture of happiness and mischief was taking over her completely. She was daydreaming about Hatathor and fantasizing about him. She was hoping that soon she would get married to Hatathor, the magnificent warrior that Lyra had. And she imagined the day he would kiss her on the wedding floor in front of the massive crowd of Lyrians who would bless them. She got goosebumps at the thought of that divine moment, and she rolled over her bed, her dreamy eyes taking her to heaven. She began caressing her neck at the thought of Hatathor touching her and pulling her into his firm and sexy arms.

Oh, I would melt like butter in his muscular arms, she fantasized, trying hard to experience that feeling with her eyes closed and moaning softly. "How would I look when I'd be his bride," she was imagining, with an unusually flustering glow on her cheeks, eyes sparkling like neon lights, and butterflies filling her stomach and making her shriek inside her head with a feeling of mad ecstasy.

"Hatathor hasn't told me what he likes," she told herself loudly, with a broad smile spreading across her exotic face. Instantaneously, she jumped out of her bed, opened the door of her wardrobe, and began pulling out her innumerable dresses excitedly as though her wedding was due to take place in an hour. She began putting on new dresses to see which one would look sensually attractive to entice Hatathor.

And thinking no further, she acted impulsively and

called Hatathor.

"Hello man, where are you?" she muttered with mild franticness.

Hatathor was not answering the call, which made Shiphrah frustrated, and she threw the phone violently on her bed.

"Damn! This guy is just so overwhelmed with duties and burdening responsibilities he doesn't have time for anything else," she grumbled, folding her arms and sitting on the bed with the innocently disappointed face of a little girl. Shiphrah had always been a spoilt brat, who had been granted everything she desired before she even asked for it to her father, Ankhamon.

"Oh, my dear Hatathor where are you? Your lover lay breathless here for you," she began singing slowly, falling back on her bed with her gorgeous arms spread widely.

"Come into my arms, and we shall be taken to heaven, come into my arms, and we shall ride the vehicle of love. You seem so far, yet so close to my heart. I find you so cute. Let's break all walls that keep us apart; let's tear the distance that keeps us adrift. For my heart and life belong to you, and you shall see how we rule the whole wide world as the greatest king and queen."

***

Ankhamon took his time and walked to his daughter's room, trying to find the right words to tell her why he had actually summoned her. After about 10 minutes, he walked up to her room. Shiphrah was surprised to see her father at this hour of the night.

He looked at her while he sat on the royal chair in his only daughter's spacious room.

"Father, why do you come here? I could have come to you," Shiphrah said.

"I was thinking of your late mother. Had she been alive, she could have guided you better. I kept quiet but then I decided to share my worry with you," Ankhamon said. Shiphrah looked at him with a puzzled face. "Sweetie, I would like to advise you," he continued.

"What?" she asked in a surprised tone.

Ankhamon saw the picture of Hatathor on the side of Shiphrah's bed. He frowned and looked at his daughter and said: "Darling, things differ from what is portrayed in public. Do not take some news too seriously."

"What, father?" Shiphrah asked.

"I want you to spy on Hatathor for me," said Ankhamon.

Suddenly, the smile disappeared from Shiphrah's face. "What?" she exclaimed.

"Spy? Why? I thought he was one of your most trusted allies?"

"Things are not always what they seem. I am afraid, but I believe he is too adventurous sometimes, which may put us in an odd position," replied Ankhamon. "I can see that you like him, but he is not a man you can trust as a longtime friend, Shiphrah. And besides, there are other men. You may date him but not as a friend you know what I mean."

Shiphrah was puzzled. She didn't know what to say or how to react.

"Besides that, I think General Desher is much younger and more suitable for you." Ankhamon continued.

"I don't know Desher well yet," exclaimed Shiphrah.

"Exactly. That is why I am saying this. You don't know Hatathor either, and keep my advice that the best suitor for you is General Desher, not a low-level military major General," Ankhamon said, and he walked out of the room.

# Chapter 6

# The Mount Tass

HATATHOR was walking on the Lyrian-made stairs, going up on the mount Tass towards a grand lodge. Along with him were many devotees of the Mother, including men, women, children of all ages. There were many people, and it looked like that the Holy Mother had many followers and disciples. The devotees were chanting the mantras prescribed by the reverend Mother for soul uplifting and mind focusing.

The terrains were rocky and thorny plants were growing all around. Hatathor was wearing a somber white attire as requested by holy Mother that all visitors to the lodge had to wear a white garment and climb the mountain with bare feet. The garments were similar to the toga the Keb people wore.

After the climb which lasted roughly forty-five minutes, upon reaching the summit, Hatathor saw that the top of the mountain was flat. There was a long queue of people entering the rocky structures and then going out. People were climbing the stairs, and Hatathor didn't understand where they were going, so he asked a passerby. The passerby told Hatathor that they were going into the holy pit. In the middle of the rocks there was a pit, but from where he stood Hatathor didn't have a clear view and couldn't figure out what was happening there. He waited in queue, waiting for his turn to see the mother.

Slowly, the line advanced and Hatathor got the chance to get closer to the pit. He first climbed the stairs and reached a platform. The platform was huge and had another set of stairs leading to the inner core of the pit. Hatathor moved further, and there he saw people in the queue going to a woman sitting in a cross-legged position. She was wearing a cloth covering her head, and she was facing the opposite direction, so Hatathor could not see her figure. After some time as line advanced further, Hatathor got the chance to look at her. The Mother was a white-skinned woman with long white hair. Her eyes were closed, but she raised her hand each time a devotee came closer for the blessings.

A pregnant woman came forward and said: "Mother, is my child dead inside me?"

The Mother took something in her hand which was lying near her. Hatathor was surprised to see that it was a hand of the dead Lyrian. Mother Ahmose placed the hand on the lady's belly, and the pregnant lady cried with happiness. "It moved!" she shouted in joy with tearful eyes.

Then a disabled older man came, and Mother took a crucible full of water, and she poured the water on the head of the disabled man. She uttered a mantra while her eyes were still closed.

With pure, clear water of Iteru,
With the bright, shining water of Iteru,
Seven times and again seven times,
Sprinkle, purify, cleanse!
May the evil Rabisyu depart!
May it step to one side!

The man left the scene with grateful eyes after receiving the blessings.

*I don't think Ahmose is even Lyrian; this is not the way we cure the people*, Hatathor thought for a moment.

As Hatathor approached her, Mother Ahmose opened her eyes and she pulled the cloth over her head away, and turned her face towards the sky. Her hair got electrostatically charged and got lifted in the air. She stared, saying in an electric voice:

"The Savior arrived back as the spirits informed me."
People were engulfed in awe as they watched the voices coming out of the Mother Ahmose.

Hatathor was watching the entire scene with confusion and bafflement. Mother Ahmose uttered in her trance:

"Spirits told me; One is coming from the sky from Keb. He will destroy us. Spirits are saying. Another one came from the sky. he will save Lyra from the curse of Keb."

People listened with a sense of awe and wonder. They were looking at Hatathor and Mother Ambrose. Suddenly Mother shouted in an electric voice: "Ah, I see death. Death everywhere. Fire and blood Lyra will be reborn again from fire."

"An alien has arrived on Lyra he will doom us all Stop him, Kill him, Seka, kill him, savior."

Mother Ahmose now looked straight into Hatathor's eyes. Hatathor shivered to see that the Mother had a deeply wrinkled face and completely white eyes. She said: "One Lyrian here has to kill the alien from planet Keb, or else he will die by the curse of planet Keb."

After uttering this, she collapsed on the rock. Some devoted woman quickly came forward and covered the Mother's face with the cloth she was wearing. Hatathor and others were asked to leave the mount Tass as Mother Ahmose had entered in her seance and no longer met people.

As Hatathor was descending, he asked around and

discovered that most of the people were living in the Tehuti mountains and were going to Mother for healings. The Mother had lost her husband when the Mutmut appeared, and she left the Misraim and moved to the Tehuti mountains together with her son. She had been a supporter of Ankhamon for a very long time and had foretold the appearance of a savior who would kill Queen Hathor the great harlot who impregnated herself after her husband's death.

Hearing this, Hatathor had a fishy feeling about Mother and her plan. He decided to dig out the truth later, when the time would have been right, as the woman was extremely influential; approaching her too fast might bring nothing good. But one thing was certain to him, she was the prophetess of doom and she was enticing him to sacrifice his life for Lyra.

*I'll do whatever I can to save Lyra but not to fulfill some cultist agenda!* He thought.

"In case you didn't know, she is also the mother of General Desher," one lady informed Hatathor.

*This mystery is getting deeper. She and her son are up to something, but first, I should get the sphere from the human and find Ehsis*, Hatathor thought.

***

It was night in the kingdom of Akhom, and General Desher was with his Mother Ahmose at the dining table. Their servants were not allowed to be present on mount Tass. Only their security guards were allowed to approach the mountain at this hour. But they, too, were not allowed to go to the top of the Tass. The winds were howling on the mountain, while Desher and Ahmose were discussing in private.

"Today, Hatathor arrived here. I recognized him. I guess he was impressed."

"Yes, Mother. You know how to surprise people," Desher said laughingly.

"I hope Shiphrah marries you, and it will make us even stronger than the king," Ahmose added.

"I am constantly receiving messages from Mosaka," she continued," the king wanted our plan to be done as meticulously as possible".

"I understand, Mother. You should not worry. I'll do whatever I can to help our people," Desher said, and both smiled.

## Chapter 7

## The Unfamiliar World

AL-KHIDR looked up; the sky was clear. The circumstellar debris disk surrounding Vega's star was visible. "Seems like Lyra to me," he told himself as he continued to walk. Since he had changed his outfit, he almost blended in with the locals, or at least that is what he thought. Al-Khidr was unwitting of his surroundings until he started paying a bit more attention. Before that, he knew he had nothing to worry about because he had been to Lyra before. He knew how to communicate with people, eat with them, and blend in. Although the language was the same, Al-Khidr didn't know that Lyrians had access to advanced technology, enabling them to understand every language spoken.

Al-Khidr was walking through the bustling streets of Misraim. He had been on Lyra before, but now it was changed. The people had strange symbols on their faces. They ranged from spiderweb-like patterns to flame-like images. They seemed to be carved into their skin or tattooed into their flesh. Although Al-Khidr was unsure about what had happened, it fascinated him.

With that, people had a wide variety of elaborate and intricate hairstyles, and their clothing differed from what he was accustomed to. Most of them had strands of hair woven in tight patterns down to their knees. The air was filled with the smell of burning incense and was mixed with the scent of herbs. Whatever it was, it was a new kingdom – a kingdom as if arisen after desolation, but with ashes still on its body and face. People walking in the street were looking at him as he walked around. This was making him nervous because, although he thought he blended in, the reality was that he actually didn't.

He realized this the moment he started paying more attention to everything around him.

*What's wrong with me? Is it my dress, or do they recognize me?* He thought to himself.

Then he realized that the clothes he was wearing, although they were Lyrian, they were still much different from others. His clothes were old-fashioned as per current Lyrian standards. Also, he didn't have a tattoo on his face.

Before Al-Khidr left Lyra, there were flying vehicles present. But now they were no more, and people walked. So, he asked a passer-by, "It's weird not to see any flying vehicles around."

The passer gave him a strange glance and retorted, "Hermes is dead!"

Al-Khidr was shocked to learn that. He continued walking and reached the obelisk square. There were no posters of either Ehsis or Hathor around. However, there were speakers attached to the obelisks, and a song was being played on repeat:

Our hope, Ankhamon,
Brethren hero, Ankhamon,
Man of wonder, Ankhamon,
Pride of the kingdom, Ankhamon.
Our hope, Ankhamon,
Brethren hero, Ankhamon,
Man of curiosity, Ankhamon,
Pride of the kingdom, Ankhamon.
Only one can be victorious,
Only one can prevail,
Ankhamon! Master Ankhamon!

The eulogy was an amalgamation of phrases written in praise for a leader called Ankhamon. Al-Khidr felt like he had heard this name before. But when and where? He couldn't recall at the moment.

The balcony he saw in the previous visit, where Queen Hathor addressed the nation, was still there, but it was broken.

"What happened to normal and sane people?" He wondered. Al-Khidr continued exploring with a puzzled face. After strolling for some time, he reached the Benben pyramid. The statue of Anubis was damaged, and its head had been re-carved and changed into a Lyrian looking person. The access to the Benben pyramid was prohibited by law. A warning was flashing at the check post. The door was sealed with welded metallic bars. The Benben square had no guards around. He walked around the Benben pyramid to explore more. On one side of the black pyramid, facing the garden, a banner was fluttering. It had a giant image of a bearded person with black eyes, pierced ears, and a tattoo in the middle of his forehead. The tattoo was placed on the forehead with a partially opened eye in a vertical orientation as if the third eye was about to open. The man in the banner was shown with long hair, and he was wearing a beastly hide on his shoulder and holding a helmet near the right side of his chest with a laser weapon. He found the same banner exhibited across the road. Master Ankhamon was standing in every corner in all his dignity. Al-Khidr also saw the banner with an image of a woman. It was written on it: "Mother Ahmose will guide us all!".

*Who was she?* Al-Khidr had no idea!

He also saw the posters of Ehsis and many others – Military personnel, law enforcement officers, and civilians. There were red crosses over Ehsis's face. He went closer to the posters to learn more. Hefty rewards were announced to capture her alive. He was shocked. Al-Khidr was lost. He was trying to comprehend the new reality of the kingdom. Ehsis was no longer a guardian. Instead, she was a pariah.

A plaque was installed in front of the pyramid, and the golden-colored words engraved on the stone plaque read:

> "Wars - unite the nation."
> – Master Ankhamon.

The name sounded familiar again as if Al-Khidr had heard this before. It was a war memorial, and hundreds of names were written on it with the message: In memory of martyrs who died to establish the purity of the kingdom. Through their blood, the nation regained consciousness. They will be remembered forever with prayers and thanksgiving.

This was shocking. Now things were getting clearer. Al-Khidr recalled Nefertiti's words from before a cult living in the mountains called the Brethren of awakening consciousness. *Are these guys on the roads are the same cultists?* Al-Khidr thought. *Have they taken over Lyra while I went to Earth? The attack on HSS, was that the beginning of the rebellion?*

A lot of questions were bothering him. He couldn't ask anyone what had happened in Misraim. He was afraid, as he was not aware of people's loyalties. Luckily, he was not wearing the French military uniform.

He now needed to put some marks on his face to belong to the cult.

***

He started moving in city, eavesdropping on conversations of the sellers, passer-by people, and school-going teenagers. After a while, he found that the population is divided. More than half was afraid of the Brethren cult. *There are supporters of the new regime present,* he thought.

*Where did Ehsis ran away? Had she left Lyra? She could be dead.*

He was horrified to think about these possibilities. Then he worried more. "What if the cult gets a hold of me and confiscates the jump-sphere or destroys it? These crazy people can also lynch me. After all, they know I am a human." He wanted to hide the jump-sphere before he was caught with it. But he did not know where.

*Would Nefertiti still be in the police station?* he wondered. *I need to change my appearance.*

He had some Amris shards in his pocket. He learned from Nefertiti before that Amris is a fuel. He took a piece of cloth from his muffler and put it in front of him. He started a fire using friction. He knew that starting a fire in public places was illegal, but he had no option left to do it elsewhere.

He noticed many security cameras in the square near the Benben pyramid. He couldn't do his arsonist act there, and he needed to go somewhere else, and he knew his journey wouldn't be easy.

Standing, he turned around and glanced at the city–the city he no longer could recognize. Al-Khidr had understood that while he was gone, the war had raged, and what he was looking at was the result of that ugly affair. The once-lucky city was no longer happy but deluded and scared to retaliate against Ankhamon. Al-Khidr had to hide the orb first, for he knew it was just a matter of time before he got arrested. Although everything came to him as a surprise, he hadn't forgotten that whoever was behind this may want the orb. The orb that Al-Khidr had with him.

# Chapter 8

# The Signature

*A Few days ago*

NEFERTITI was in a hurry as she was moving down the spiraling staircase. It was still dark and dawn was yet to come. She needed to move fast, as she was summoned by the Guardian – Khnemes Nasut Sabut (The Guardian of Ancient Wisdom) as called in Lyrian. It must have been important as her name was announced thrice on the central communication network, and she was requested to come urgently. There must be some reason for the call at this hour of the day.

She was moving down in Kneph, a vast cave with openings like a beehive. In the middle of the cave, there was an ample open space. The cave was near the ruins of a destroyed ancient city of bones. In the war of Embecah in Lyrian year 345,6900 Sovidos destroyed the Nusaar city, and the cave was formed because of a Sovidian bomb explosion on mount Kass. Within minutes, Kass was turned into a porous structure with caves. Sovidos were finally retreated after a significant loss. King Ptah later transformed the cave into a secret hideout in the eventuality of another attack.

Nefertiti reached the central command room, which they called Cove. It was located deep under the hive and was like an enormous hollow metal ball. Guardian Ehsis looked worried, as she was looking at the many screens. She had been looking anxious for many months. She hadn't noticed Nefertiti as she was busy giving instructions to her officers.

The central station was encapsulated in a metallic sphere protected by layers of lead claddings to prevent radiation penetration – in case they would have been attacked. There were some more secrets attached to it, which only Ehsis knew about. The display panels inside the Cove were all lined up circularly on the walls and in the center. On an elevated platform, the central seat was installed. When Ehsis finally sat on her commanding chair, Nefertiti approached her and knelt while looking at the ancient Guardian. Ehsis noticed Nefertiti and said to her: "Come, Nefertiti, there is something significant I want to show you. A sphere has been reported to have breached into our atmosphere. It fell from the sky and went into Qebhu (abyss)."

Nefertiti was surprised to hear the news. "Could it be Al-Khidr?"

"I don't think so. I suppose Maft-Shespt are not supposed to create such huge cocoons."

"Wait, we have visuals. I show you," Ehsis said.

Ehsis ordered some of her officers to play the video on one of the screens. It showed a sphere surrounded by a shockwave entering the sky of Lyra. The colors of the sphere were changing, and it was not visible what was inside it.

"It entered the abyss two days ago. We learned from our spies that some spaceships also descended into the abyss shortly after that. "I want you to go into the abyss and find out what is there. But beware. Ankhamon's cultist could spot you and you know that he has been relentlessly looking for us." "Guardian, I will not disappoint you," Nefertiti said determined.

"You cannot go there on a spaceship as you might be spotted by the air patrols. But we have prepared a transporter for you – a hovering vehicle with an indistinct signature on the tracking devices. If anyone actually noticed it, they would think that a bird was flying. Rostau and Semed will accompany you. They are not only excellent combatants but also are talented engineers. I already passed on to them the instructions, and they should be here soon." Ehsis added. Nefertiti nodded in affirmation. She knew very well Rostau and Semed. They were two friendly but naughty guys. As she was thinking about the trip, the two guys entered Cove. They knelt to Ehsis, and she said to them:

"Hello Commanders, Officer Nefertiti is ready to go with you. Your mission is to provide her assistance to descend into the abyss to undertake the necessary research."

***

Nefertiti quickly prepared a rucksack and caught up with Rostau and Semed, who had already reached the surface. The hive and Cove were located deep inside the mountain, under their feet.

There were mountains all around and the landscape where they were standing looked like a vast, porous crater. The sponge-looking rocks were protruding from the surface in a chaotic formation. The hovercraft was a piece of old technology but still functional. The color of the crater camouflaged it very well. Rostau was checking on the hovercraft's engine, and Semed had already gathered the items which, according to him, could be required on this trip. Nefertiti saw some new laser guns, pairs of torches, very long ropes, an infrared camera, jetpacks, water, food and Amris fuel. Semed threw a gun towards Nefertiti which she caught midair.

"This we refined. Try it out," he said to her.

Nefertiti looked at the gun in her hands and asked: "Would it generate a loud boom?"

"No. We have upgraded it; try it out!"

Nefertiti took the laser gun in her hands and aimed at the distant rock.

As she pressed the trigger, short-pulsed beams hit the rock which melted, creating a more grotesque landscape.

"Nice gun!"

"You keep that one," Semed said.

Rostau moved towards her and said: "Meet the Bird."

"Bird?"

"We call this hover –Bird."

She laughed. She patted the hover as if it were a pet.

They got into the hovercraft. Nefertiti sat in front alongside Rostau, while Semed was in the back seat. The engine was relatively silent, and the speed was slow. They started moving East towards the abyss.

"Hold on, officer," Rostau warned as he maneuvered the Bird over the barren landscape.

"Hold on to what? This thing is barely moving," Nefertiti retorted, and Semed let out a giggle.

"The insects we eat crawl faster than your beloved bird, Rostau." Semed countered, and Rostau harrumphed.

"You speak as if you weren't sleeping in the workshop when I slaved away to revive a dead technology," Rostou jabbed.

"Sleeping? Preposterous!" Semed bristled in his chair.

"We need to maintain our cover," Nefertiti intervened. "I hope you aren't taking us to the slaughterhouse, Rostau. Ehsis would hate to lose such capable minds." "I wouldn't dare, trust me! Hold on," Rostau warned again, and while Nefertiti caught herself just in time, Semed was pushing hard against his chair.

"Wait-" Semed began, but Rostau only cackled in reply. The sudden shift in the terrain roughed up Semed a little too violently despite the safety belt around his waist. "I told you not to use those thrusters," Semed shouted, but Rostau only laughed in reply.

"I don't take orders from you, my friend," Rostau snickered, much to Semed's indignation. Nefertiti was looking at the cerulean expanse of the shimmering sky. Back in Kneph, they could not venture far, and this restriction had taken a toll on everyone who relished the open ambiance and winding landscape. Semed and Rostau were still going back and forth, and Nefertiti was glad to find distraction in their quarrel.

"Look, a real bird!" Semed shouted as he pressed his nose against the glass window. "We must hunt it and take it back," Semed pleaded, and Nefertiti sighed. "We are on a mission far more important than satiating your cravings, Semed," Rostou replied. Still, Nefertiti knew he was already looking for a way to expand the objectives of said mission.

"Men and their appetite," she tutted while the two engineers went back and forth with the things they miss eating. By the time Semed was done arguing his point about the nutritious disparities their people were bound to suffer in the beehive walls of Kneph, Rostau had advised his friend to take up dieting hundred times over. By the time they reached near abyss, Vega was about to set. To avoid being seen, they hadn't switched on the lights and were content with lurking in the shadows. According to the forecast, the weather was getting cold, and they had to finish the job before Vega rose again. The signals from Cove could not reach them as they were already out of range. They needed to rely on a primitive compass to understand where to go.

They had been flying for eight hours when Rostau said: "Let's stretch a bit," and stopped the hover. The ground was no longer sandy but a mixture of mountainous rocks and sand.

They came out of the vehicle and started eating their sandwiches. The land before them was quiet and shrouded in darkness, creating an environment of foreboding. "Guys, is it a good idea to eat outside?" Nefertiti asked as she craned her neck to examine the stretch of the land in front of her. "No worries. I guess you are a police officer," Rostau commented, but when Nefertiti arched her eyebrow in question, he continued while laughing, "that explains the nerves and suspicion."

"That is why the army is better than police," Semed teasingly added.

"Haha–so funny!" Nefertiti said annoyed.

"Did you bring something to eat?" Semed asked Nefertiti when he saw her searching through her bag.

The witty engineer was drawn to food like an ant drawn to a sugar cube.

"Looks like I forgot to put it in the bag," Nefertiti said dismissively, and Semed nodded in understanding. Rostau gave his friend a skeptical look, but Semed only muttered, "I am not offering her my sandwich, if that's what you are hoping."

"I am alright," Nefertiti assured Rostau, who was now shooting daggers at his friend for his lack of manners. "I took a big breakfast before coming, so I am not hungry yet." Rostau smiled weakly while Semed continued to munch down his sandwich. Nefertiti took out her camera and started looking towards the abyss. The abyss held its name and offered nothing but darkness to prying eyes. Semed and Rostau looked into the distance blindly, their mouth in sync with each bite they took off their sandwiches. Suddenly, Nefertiti saw high radiations emitting from the ground and creating a strange moving landscape. "Hey, what's that?" she asked while pointing at the odd phenomenon.

*Are these dunes moving?* Nefertiti wondered in astonishment before peering into the camera and yelling in worry, "Why is there a radiation build-up?" Rostau pushed the last bit of his sandwich into his mouth and got up from his perch beside the Bird. He then came forward to look into the camera to see with his own eyes what Nefertiti said.

What Rostau saw through the camera lens made his body shudder involuntarily, and before Nefertiti could inquire the change in his demeanor, he started backing away. “Guys, quickly! Into the Bird,” Rostau yelled a warning as he picked up their meager belongings scattered about on the ground. Semed whipped out his camera to look into the distance to determine the source of his friend’s discomfort.

“These are Tenems – the underground-creatures,” Semed shouted as he hurried past the clueless Nefertiti. Just when the two combatants reached the hulk of the Bird, they realized that Nefertiti hadn’t moved from her place. Semed ran back, grabbed her by her wrist, then pushed her towards the yawning entrance of the Bird. The three scavengers were thoroughly rattled, considering this new and horrifying development. Rostau kept cursing under his breath as he tried to start the hover. Just as they got inside the hovercraft, they noticed the ground started to shake.

Tenems were grotesque looking creatures which were approaching them fast from the south. Rostau’s hands shook nervously as he tried to start the engine again, but it appeared to have gotten jammed.

“Damn it. I need to go out to check the engine.” Rostau grumbled as Semed screamed about the approaching creatures. The interior of the Bird was now thrust into chaos as warning lights, and signs flashed on the control panel.

“Just shut it down!” Nefertiti shouted as the hovercraft shuddered in the wake of an impact against its hulk. “They are probably coming towards us because of the heat generated by the hovercraft.” Semed said. But before Rostau could act on Semed’s advice, something hit the Bird hard, making its three passengers shriek in fear. The hover rolled over on its side; it took 6-7 turns before the flipping came to a halt. Semed, Rostau and Nefertiti took the worst of the flip, for they were not strapped in their chairs. Nefertiti's head had hit something round and blunt, making her temple swell in protest. Semed was rolled on his side, trying to keep the contents of his stomach in his body. Only Rostau was still holding his ground despite the chaos that had erupted around him.

Short, black, feathery creatures appeared out of the sand and surrounded the hover in odd synchronization. These hideous and unfriendly creatures had all the charisma of a dead, bloated body as they covered the hover with their bodies. As Rostau struggled with the control panels' switches, Semed, and Nefertiti took positions beside the glass windows, their weapons aiming the approaching targets. Then, they cracked open the windows and fired laser shots. "Smoke them out!" Rostau shouted, and his companions wasted no time opening fire on their hideous targets. Shots rang out in the wilderness. Tenems had been exoskeleton beasts with feathers and hard shells over them that appeared like muscular turtle shells. But as laser shots penetrated the shells, they buckled and cracked, popping like bottles filled with liquids. The fluid from their insides puked out and spread all over the sand. With a faint smell of blood, the rotten aroma filled the air.

***

"Now, how do we hide the bird?" Nefertiti asked.

Rostau took out a black bag from the Bird. He spread it out and it looked like a thin black rubber sheet. Semed and Rostau stretched the sheet and spread it all over the hover. Then Rostau pressed a button on a small panel at the edge of the sheet and the whole sheet transformed into a sandy texture, so much so that it was no longer looking like black rubber, hiding it completely from sight. Semed smiled and nodded his head.

"That's incredible!" Nefertiti said.

"I never thought that we have such things," she added.

Semed and Rostau laughed.

"Guys, we have to go down now!" Nefertiti said while she was looking down from the edge of the abyss.

"Yeah, guys, it's time to descend into the pit," Rostau said languidly. The fight with the odd creatures had dimmed his charismatic flare, but he was still excited about the next phase of their mission.

"We especially designed these jet packs so their radar signature is very low. The brethren will not be able to detect them," he added. "I never tried it; I am a bit nervous," Nefertiti announced worriedly.

"Sometimes the descent can be dizzying and vertiginous, but we heard the police are trained for every kind of mission. Legends says you guys can do anything," Rostau said teasingly.

Nefertiti, Semed and Rostau started their descent using the jet packs, and while they were descending, they used an internal communication system to talk to each other. But because of the presence of Amris in the nearby caves, that was interfering with the communication frequency, their voices sometimes sounded broken as they talked. The sound was floating through the air, like a bubble that popped every time it contacted something.

"Wow, I never tried this before, but it's so wonderful," Nefertiti shouted.

"Hello guys, slow down! I have acrophobia!" Semed shouted.

Semed saw Rostau moving away from them, so he cried out slightly concerned, "Hey, where are you going?"

"Don't act like a real bird! Be careful and don't hit the rocks," Nefertiti shouted.

It was an unexplored world of sharp ridges, jutting out of the mountains at odd angles. They all appeared to be pointed at the sky like needles, stopping people from climbing.

"This place is so damn good!" Rostau said while flying.

The lights from the moons of Lyra were following them as they were spiraling down into the abyss. The ground was still not visible. The only thing they could see was the structure of the mountains, which made it seem as if they were descending into some magical place.

After the descent of several time-cycles, thanks to the gravity of the Lyra, they finally reached the bottom of the canyon. There was a thin layer of frost on the ground, and over their heads, clouds were blocking out the moons light from touching down.

"My God, I was not expecting that – it doesn't feel like I am on Lyra," Semed said. "Lyra is a mysterious planet." He continued, while Nefertiti and Semed looked around in awe and wonder.

"This place is surreal!" Nefertiti said.

"Why is there a mist suspended over there?" Semed looked over his head.

It was a magical place with a frosty, sandy floor, covered entirely in mist and clouds.

They could now see in the distance the inverted pyramid with its apex sunk into the sand. The pyramid's base looked as if it had been jolted out of the ground by some high-temperature laser cutting which had melted the stone.

They started going around the pyramid, inspecting it from every angle.

"These stones are not from Lyra. I'll take a sample," Semed said.

Suddenly Nefertiti felt like she had stepped on something – something unlike sand was under her feet.

When she lifted her foot, there was a sharp and acrid smell that she recognized as the smell of blood and smoke.

Her eyes scanned the ground, intense and wary as if she was trying to convince herself that she saw it.

She saw a pair of boots and clothes. The shoes seemed to have belonged to someone in an ancient army – something similar to what you would find in a museum. She took a sniff: the clothes had a scent – mostly of sweat and blood – that lingered on the fabric.

"Guys, check this out," Nefertiti exclaimed as she inspected the ripped clothing.

"Maybe we can bring it to Kneph and do a scan," Semed said to Nefertiti, who was looking at the pieces of clothes.

"It doesn't look like a Lyrian garment," Nefertiti noticed. Rostau climbed the pyramid and went inside. He took out a small torch from his pocket and inspected the interior. Though still intact, the pyramid shape was a cracked structure that had gone through many structural stresses during the interstellar flight.

"Hey guys, there is nothing inside except dislocated stones."

"Collect the clothes and boots and let's go back before anyone else comes," Nefertiti ordered, and Rostau started packing the clothes and boots immediately. They were all set to go when they noticed Semed went to the base of the mountain. He was pretty busy exploring something that was on the ground. Rostau and Nefertiti went to him and said: "We are about to leave. What are you looking at?"

Semed said nothing as he looked up towards the top of the mountain, which he couldn't even see. The clouds had covered the mountain top. He turned towards Nefertiti and Rostau and said: "Hey guys, you see this Anubis head? It fell from the top".

"What's up there?" Semed said and then they all exclaimed: "Hept Sehetch Sheta!"

***

The moment they were back in Kneph, they went straight to Ehsis' office. Nefertiti took out the torn uniform pieces and the worn boots from her bag and placed them on the Ehsis's desk.

Ehsis stood up, wringing her hands in front of her to soothe the storm raging in her head.

"What is this?" Ehsis said surprised.

"This is what we have found in the abyss. Near that, there was an inverted pyramid which had its apex sunk into the ground," Nefertiti said. "A pyramid in the abyss!" Ehsis repeated and sank into her chair as if she was brooding over something. Semed called for a scientist to run tests on the things they had collected on their mission.

Dr. Zokiva arrived, and he took the samples and started scanning them using a handheld gadget. "These clothes are not made from any synthetic material. They are made-up of some biological grade fabric. Some primitive planets still use such type of clothing, like. . . ."

"The Keb!" Ehsis said before the scientist finished his sentence.

"Yes, Madam. Keb should also have such type of fabric," Dr. Zokiva confirmed.

Nefertiti looked at Ehsis and said: "Do you think he returned?"

The room went silent as the Guardian weighed down all the possibilities. At last, she replied, "Seems likely."

# Chapter 9

# The Lyra Gardens

Al-Khidr entered the Lyra Gardens and he was fascinated as it was nothing like of any other garden he saw back on Earth. The trees were tall, and they were moving as if dancing together. There were a multitude of flowers growing over the multicolored rocks and glittering stones, as if the stones were made by jinn. It was a beautiful place to relax and a great place to put the tattoo on the face, if you were a human in need of a camouflage on an alien planet. There were ponds with water so clear he was able to see himself in the still surface.

There were some people jogging and children playing, so he had wait until the Vega set in the west.

He reevaluated his plan and instead of burning the piece of clothing, he thought of burning some dried twigs instead. He collected them from underneath the trees and carefully went to a secluded corner near a water pond.

*In case Amris is too flammable, I will push it in the water*, he decided.

He took a shard of Amris and started rubbing it over the ground. It took him a bit of time to ignite it and then he quickly put the twigs over the fire. The twigs started blasting like firecrackers. He was horrified, as he expected that twigs would burn like they would have burned on Earth and convert to ashes. Instead, they were blasting.

He quickly pushed the burning twigs into the pond. On a closer look he discovered that the whole place was artificial. There were no real trees or flowers! He dug into the grass and found that it was not real either.

Then he decided to do what he wanted initially, so he took out the piece of cloth from his bag and set it on fire.

He gathered the ashes and using a twig made a tattoo on his face. He now looked like one of the brethren.

***

Nefertiti and Al-Khidr were lying beside each other looking at the night sky back in Lyra. Al-Khidr was shirtless and Nefertiti was wearing a loose nightgown.

She turned her body towards Al-Khidr and placed her arm on his chest.

"Al-Khidr," she whispered, caressing his bare chest tenderly and with immense passion.

"Yes, Nefertiti," he replied softly, continuing to stare at the sparkling stars in the night sky.

"You are so warm, my love," she whispered in his ear, and planted a soft peck on his bearded cheek. Then, she pressed her head against his chest and he placed his rough palm on her head and casually played with her silky hair. "Your body is the warmest thing that I have ever experienced on this planet of Lyra, where is hardly any warmth, be it physical or emotional," she expressed, rubbing his chest with utmost sensuality and affection for him started building up inside her. "And your hair smells ravishing, my love," he complimented her, continuing his play. Then he looked in her eyes.

"I feel like I'll be lost in your eyes and may never be found by any mortal being of this universe. Your face glows brighter than the moon of Earth." Nefertiti's heart melted with every word spoken by Al-Khidr and she gazed at his handsomely charming face and asked him the question that had been tormenting her for quite a while. A question that wouldn't allow her to fall asleep peacefully at night since the day their love had blossomed.

"Do you think we can be together forever, Al-Khidr?"

He didn't respond but continued to play with her hair and gazed deeply at the night sky. Nefertiti called his name twice but he pretended as though he hadn't heard her. Then suddenly, he pointed at the night sky with his left finger.

"Do you see the stars in the sky, Nefertiti?" he said, and she nodded slowly.

"There are innumerable stars in the sky right, even if we try to count them, we simply cannot. I promise you my love, that till my last breath, I will fight to try and stay with you the same number of years, as the number of stars present in the night sky right now," he affirmed, and placed his finger down.

Al-Khidr's words had an inexpressibly profound effect on Nefertiti such that a gush of tears erupted from the corners of her eyelids. She wiped them away quickly with her sleeves and moved up towards her lover's face. To her his face seemed to shine brighter than the stars in the sky. Placing her soft palm on his rough bearded cheek, she got her face close to the side of his nose and pressed her nose against it. Her heart was racing at that point and she wished to stay in that position for eternity; she wished to obtain miraculous powers which she could use to prevent Vega from emerging out from the night sky and take away that precious night from them. Al-Khidr lifted her somber face with his hands and bringing it close to his lips, he kissed her tenderly. As their lips met, sweet and relaxing music began playing inside Nefertiti's head, providing her body with an inexplicably soothing sensation. Her soul seemed to dance to that music, and all the stars present in the night sky seemed to have fallen onto her soft lips, while they were being grazed and cherished by the smooth ones of the love of her life. They kissed passionately for nearly an hour, which felt like mere a few seconds for Nefertiti. Finally, their lips parted, and Nefertiti began gazing deeply into the intense eyes of her love with immense passion. She caressed his cheek tenderly, her soft fingers finding grace and tremendous pleasure in the simple, yet powerful act of affection.

"I have tasted the stars on your lips," she said, moving her fingers from his rough cheek to his firm lips and pressed them softly. "I have never felt something like this before, Al-Khidr. What sorcery was played by your lips on mine? That despite kissing you for a prolonged period, I still feel like a thirsty animal, who is gasping to drink the elixir out of your lips".

"If it was in my hands, I would have kissed you the entire night, Nefertiti. Your lips are the divine goblet that the almighty Lord has assigned for me to drink from and relish in its entirety." he claimed, placing his fingers on her lips and grazing them softly. The act made Nefertiti's heart beat faster than lightning, and channeled electric current across every nerve within her body. She closed her eyes to relish the luxurious sensation thoroughly and her fingers lay motionless on Al-Khidr's lips.

Nefertiti woke up from her dream. She found herself alone in bed. She was dreaming about him Al-Khidr.

"Oh Lord, what shall I do?" she said to herself.

"Ehsis set the protocols. Why Vega is not coming out faster!" She was anxious and felt the urge to go to Misraim again and search for Al-Khidr.

"I cannot wait much longer!"

She made up her mind and started putting things in her bag.

She took necessary things and the most important was the Ar-t-Heru tracking unit removal. The tracking was still functional and brethren's management didn't know that rebels supporting Ehsis had hacked their security system. The transmission frequencies and encodings were most important in this game. Nefertiti was using the tracking unit, one of the police gadgets, which she still had.

Lyrian police had been dismantled by the rebels. The headquarter where she used to work was sealed along with other government buildings and were declared as no entry zones. Ankhamon wanted the full control. He was the king, the judge and the executioner.

***

The hover flew a few supris above the ground, swirling the air at high speed, causing the wind to brush Nefertiti's face fiercely. Nefertiti was lost in desperate thoughts, and a swarm of fear bubbled inside her. *Am I doing the right thing? Is it betrayal? Will I get killed by my own people?* These thoughts wandered inside her mind continuously slowly ripping away her decisiveness. She thought of Ehsis, and what she would think of her breaking the protocol and doing something like that. For a second, she even considered turning the hover around and going back. However, the thought of her beloved Al-Khidr, whom she loved more than the whole world kept her from going back and diminished her anxiety and fear from her heart and restored her determination and strength.

The atmosphere felt rather chilly and uncomfortable, as the hover flew at top speed, delivering a rather chilly sensation across Nefertiti's body. Luckily, she was wearing a jacket. The sky displayed the light of dawn, emitting tranquility across the entire horizon and creating an atmosphere of pure romance and sensuality. Nefertiti's heartbeat slowed down as she experienced the aura of the blissful atmosphere around her. And instantaneously, the thought of Al-Khidr entered her mind which drove away all the coldness from her skin. The romantic atmosphere around turned her nostalgic and she recalled the brief, yet, priceless moments that she had spent with Al-Khidr.

Her thoughts vanished as she saw a shooting star and her nostalgia had ended, and her mind came back to the present time.

Half an hour passed, and Vega began emerging gradually, pulling aside the blanket of the night and bringing with it the rays of a new day with the promise of new hope. She opened her eyes, and basked in the rays of Vega which lifted up her mood and made her hopeful that she would surely be reunited with her love, Al-Khidr. Nefertiti slowed down the hover, and looked down below, and for the first time she realized that she was miles away from Kneph. The thought of Ehsis still worried her a bit. She still felt a little guilty for breaking the protocols and moving outside without informing her. She wasn't afraid of being punished or facing her wrath, rather she feared that her trust might shake and she would be removed from her good books.

For a brief moment, Nefertiti, imagined a time wherein she hadn't met Al-Khidr.

*What if we hadn't met? What if life back here on Lyra would have never become so rebellious for me?*

Her mind was filled with mixed feelings.

*Is Al-Khidr back? Is yes, has he brought the supposed cure of Mutmut? How did he survive so far?*

She was horrified of the thought that he could be captured by Ankhamon's secret police.

But then she put her worries aside as she was not so sure who had actually arrived in the pyramid. These thoughts wavered across her mind and she imagined every possibility that involved Al-Khidr's absence. *NO!* She screamed loudly inside her head, brushing aside the thoughts that spoke against Al-Khidr. *How can I even think of a life without my love? She rebuked herself, shaking her head. A life without Al-Khidr would be meaningless and purposeless. I could never even think of a life without him. He is the man of his words and he will surely come back!*

As these thoughts ran through her mind, she fell back into nostalgia again and recalled another precious time spent with Al-Khidr.

Instead of going towards the abyss, now she was heading towards the Sutekh. The deserted spot no Lyrian would have dared to enter. She had to take the risk as this was the only safe way to enter Misraim. She just needed to cross over the river Iteru.

She stopped the hover in Sutekh and parked it in front of some deserted shops. The bushes and weeds were growing everywhere. They were coming out of roads and pavements. The place had been deserted for years.

"It's better for you to stay here!" she said to the hover as if it's a living thing.

She wrapped her hair like Ankhamon supporters and made some quick removable tattoo on her face. She wanted to look like the people in the city to avoid suspicion. She put on a mask before coming out of the vehicle. Only her eyes were visible. The mask prevented the spores of Mutmut to enter her system, even if even if she would have been exposed to them for a long time.

She climbed down the hover and started walking towards Iteru.

The dawn of Vega was about to happen. The birds started gathering over Iteru to hunt for fish.

She remembered the day she sat with Al-Khidr on the bank of the river.

"*Would he recognize me? Do I still look beautiful?*"

After all, she hasn't seen herself in the mirror for many days.

## CHAPTER 9. THE LYRA GARDENS

The war had changed everything. The aesthetic sense was lost as if it was sucked out of them by brethren. "Why am I feeling so nervous," she said to herself.

The tracker started blinking, as she previously switched off the beep sound from it. She noticed the prisoner's position near the Lyra Gardens or Benben pyramid (disrupting signal). She had reached the outskirts of the city using the hovercraft and left it outside. Then took the city's underground hyperloop network to get close to Lyra Gardens. She started going towards Lyra gardens. As she had no vehicle she had to walk as fast as she could. She looked into her jacket and checked the status of her gun. All was set as it should have been. It was morning now, and the tracking was constantly showing the prisoner 1001001 location inside the Lyra Gardens. She reached the place. The garden was only 300 Supris away. She took a deep breath. "*The game has begun!*" she said.

***

"It looked wonderful," Hatathor said to the ambassador of planet Honkira.

"I accept your gifts," he said further.

"It is an honor Tor Hatathor. We are your slaves," the ambassador said further.

Hahaha, Hatathor laughed.

"You Ankhamon! You will be the gardener in my palace."

"Thank you, Master Hatathor," Ankhamon said.

"All kneel to the king!" Ankhamon said to his brethren: "All kneel to King Hatathor!"

As all were kneeling, Al-Khidr entered the hall and threw the jump-sphere right at him. The jump sphere moved in the air like a ball. All brethren, including Ankhamon, were still kneeling. No one stood up to capture Al-Khidr.

Hatathor saw the jump-sphere approaching, and he lifted his hand to save himself from the hit. But lo-and-behold he looked at his hand, which looked like a dried twig. He threw the sphere in shock and started jerking his hand violently.

Hatathor woke up. He felt a gush of pain in his hand. He was looking his both hands and flipping them in confusion. He was panting and sweating profusely. "It was a dream. A bad dream! I would not let this happen to me. I need to find the bloody human," he said to himself. He looked around the room. The sleeve was on the side table. He quickly took it and activated the tracking unit in it to see where the human was. A distorted and disrupting signature was generated. It was a broken signal, an intermittent one.

"Why bad things always happen to me? I need a new sleeve. New arms. Stupid Ankhamon is wasting money just on his palace and protocols." He pressed the buttons again. This time signal was clear.

"What!" he uttered. "I am a coming, human!"

***

Al-Khidr was sleeping in the Lyra Gardens when a gush of pain erupted in his wrist. He woke up and pressed his left-hand wrist. "*I am being tracked, or is it something else?*"

He had hid his sack in the tree trunk underneath which he was sleeping. The sack containing the Amris and the Sphere was well camouflaged into the tree because it had the same color. Also, he wanted to hide it while he was sleeping. This was the safest thing to do because he did not want to be caught by brethren police with the jump-sphere. He got up and shrugged off the thoughts. He straightened his back and took the sack out from the hide-out. He looked into it and he started shaking the bag. A flying bug came out and flew off.

The chirping birds were signing the morning prayers in chorus. It was a pleasant morning with a fresh breeze. He thanked God that so far no one had captured him. Al-Khidr noticed some fruit trees in the garden. The fruits looked like the apples on Earth. He remembered his last experience with fruit, Shaqarqabi, but these fruits were not real. The entire garden was a Lyrian-made piece of art. Lyra was a sandy place, and did not have so many varieties and species of the trees. He started strolling in the Lyra Gardens. Today his plan was to visit the area of the police station. "Maybe I meet Nefertiti today. Hope for the best."

He was quite positive that he would meet her.

Being an alchemist, Al-Khidr was curious about

the materials and he wanted to inspect the fruits. So he climbed up the tree and plucked a fruit. He smelled it first. It passed the test. There was no bitter smell. He tried to cut open it, but the fruit was just bouncing back to him. He put the artificial fruit into his sack and he was about to climb down, loud sirens could be heard all over the area. "Maybe the police are passing by. Or are they coming for me? Nay... They don't know yet that I am back," he convinced himself, and continued moving up the tree. Suddenly, he noticed few drones moving in the garden.

He got nervous. "*Oh, God help!*"

The drones were scanning, and they hadn't reached yet the place where he was.

"I cannot go out! The police is outside," he reevaluated the entire plan.

He quickly pulled the branches towards him. By the time police surrounded and entered the gardens, he was completely hidden inside the tree. Police was now inside the gardens. The police had cordoned off the gardens, and that was the reason why no one could enter the premises.

"I was tracked!" he realized, but it was already too late.

"Search the garden. Check every nook and corner. Anything unusual. The human is here! Seka informed, he'll be here soon," their chief ordered.

*Who is Seka? Do they mean warrior?* Al-Khidr thought to himself.

The police spread into the gardens and started

their search. Al-Khidr was sitting in the tree, watching every move of the brethren's secret-police. He saw a few of them gathered near the pond where he had burned the twigs the previous day. They were talking and taking photographs.

As he was in the tree, he first saw how the drones went down, then the officers dropped, one after another. There were no fire-shots heard.

The remaining policemen panicked and took shelter, while trying to find out what was going on through their communication network. Suddenly gun shots were heard. "A Mis N Tkahbacht," he whispered to himself in his mother-tongue. "*Someone attacking the brethren? What's going on?*"

Within minutes, the policemen were wiped out by a very skilled masked man.

Al-Khidr was horrified to see that the masked person was coming towards the tree towards him. As the masked man reached the tree, he said: "Come down quickly. As fast as you can. We need to run."

Al-Khidr realized God had sent the help. But who did he send?

He came down and the masked person removed his mask. It was Nefertiti.

Al-Khidr quickly moved down the tree and then jumped. He was right in front of her – his love. He moved forward and kissed her. Nefertiti said: "Welcome back to Lyra!"

"I am back to complete the Aladdin story," he laughed, and hugged her.

"I missed you so much," he said with sobbing eyes and kissed her.

"Me too," she said. She gave him a mask to cover himself, and they both ran out of the gardens.

"We are short of time. They knew already that you are here."

"How is Ehsis?" Al-Khidr asked.

"I will tell you everything but you need to speed up, mister." Nefertiti was better than him at running.

Nefertiti ran to a parked vehicle and broke the window. Al-Khidr followed, and they climbed in the vehicle. She took a gadget out of her bag and somehow connected it on the handle. She threw a gun at Al-Khidr and said: "This is for your safety. Just fire, don't think twice!"

She overrode the vehicle security and it started moving on the road.

Nefertiti was driving slowly, as she wanted to avoid suspicion.

Al-Khidr took the jump-sphere out of his bag and showed it to Nefertiti.

"It has the leaves!"

Nefertiti glanced at him graciously.

She was a totally different person and didn't look like a Lyrian police officer, but more like a bold Arab lady. She now had long braided hair and no make-up. Al-Khidr smiled.

"You look more beautiful!" Al-Khidr said to her and kissed her again on the cheek.

"We got a disrupted signal, most likely because of

Amris. We were so worried about you. The day you went to earth. That was the day–the war started. Hatathor has joined hands with Ankhamon. They took our loyal military by surprise and we had to flee the city. I will take you to Ehsis. She will be glad to see you back." "But who is after you? How come they can chase you? As far as we know the brethren had no tracking for prisoners like you have," Nefertiti asked. "Is it Hatathor?," she asked. "He went after you, right?"

"Yes. He followed me and killed my friend and he wanted to kill me as well, but I had escaped and I returned here; hopefully he remained back on Earth."

"Were you the one who arrived in pyramid, wearing the military uniform?" Nefertiti asked.

"No!" Al-Khidr said and then he realized:"Wait, someone was outside the pyramid. Some people came and they were looking around. Now I understand they found Hatathor there."

Before Al-Khidr could say anything, the loud sirens were heard again, and they were getting louder and louder.

"We are being chased!" Nefertiti announced.

"I remember you used to have flying vehicles," Al-Khidr mentioned to Nefertiti.

"Have we had the Hermes, we could have gone out of the city by now. Coward Ankhamon barred people from using it. He feared people might attack on his Tekhenu." She replied then she took a look in the rear-view mirror and shouted: "Heads down. I saw

Hatathor. He is chasing us... God, what can I do?" she exclaimed.

***

It was nighttime, and the mount Tass was brightened up with torches of all kinds, giving it a surreal appearance. Mother Ahmose was waiting for one of her devotee girls. The girl entered and bowed to her. Ahmose smiled and said: "Minkava, do you know why I called you?" "Only mother knows." "You put this into Hatathors spaceship. But beware, its only for your eyes and hands." Mother brought out her hand under her peplum, holding a small pyramidon with a strange marking on it and blinking red. Minkava bowed and took the pyramidon into her hands. It was a device that looked like a small pyramid and had holes that were blinking. "Your command will be fulfilled, Mother!" she bowed and went out with complete determination. Ahmose was smiling with a smirk on her face.

# Chapter 10

# The Hope

"OH, where are you girl?" Ehsis said with lips that were dry and cracked.

She was walking anxiously in the Kneph. She was worried and her heart was sinking. Many officers around her were trying to console her.

"I will give her a punishment for breaking the protocol," she said, then she said to herself: "What shall I do. I cannot even punish her."

"Call Rostau and Semed! They are to see me immediately," she shouted at the staff.

Within minutes, Rostau and Semed knew that something serious was going on. As soon as Ehsis saw them, she stood up and said: “Nefertiti has gone to Misraim. She sneaked out and went on her own on your hover. She is probably looking for Al-Khidr. I need you to find her. Let’s hope they don’t get to her before you.”

Semed and Rostau were not expecting that Nefertiti would do this. They had to look for her. They have no other choice.

***

The blood rushed into Al-Khidr eyes, and he said: “I’ll kill him. He killed so many innocent lives on Earth. Including my friend Estelle. But... but how come he came back?” Al-Khidr was baffled.

“We found a uniform near pyramid in the abyss, so it must have been him,” Nefertiti said. “Maybe he climbed on the pyramid as a last resort, as he might have had no other option left,” she suggested.

Al-Khidr recalled that the jump-sphere was activated, and before he could think further, the energy cocoon had formed around the pyramid, and maybe Hatathor just climbed on it at that time. “Stop the vehicle and let us kill him!” he said to Nefertiti as he was boiling in rage.

“Calm down. We cannot kill him now. He is not alone. The whole Ankhamon cult is supporting him. We will deal with him when the time comes. Now we escape!” she convinced Al-Khidr to hold his reins.

Nefertiti was driving fast, with a speek of close to 300 km/h, in Earth's terms. Hatathor and the brethren were following them. They placed barricades on the streets, and Nefertiti had taken many turns to avoid them.

Nefertiti received the notifications that someone was trying to contact her. While driving, she commanded the vehicle: "connect me to the contacting vehicle." "Pull it over, or you will die," Hatathor said in a growling tone.

"Go to hell!" Nefertiti shouted and sped up.

Suddenly some drones moved over their heads. The drones started positioning themselves and getting close to the vehicle that Nefertiti was driving. Al-Khidr looked through the window and shouted at her: "These things are getting closer!"

The drones were equipped with powerful magnets, and they all stuck to the vehicle rooftop. The engines were running, but the tires lost contact with the ground. Within minutes, their vehicle was lifted several hundred feet above the ground.

Hatathor and the brethren stopped the vehicles, and they all started looking triumphantly at the drones. The man who was controlling the drones also came out of his car. Nefertiti aimed at Hatathor and fired. She missed, and some brethren also responded by firing back at her.

"Stop it. I want them alive!" Hatathor tried to stop them from firing, while taking shelter.

A shot had hit one of the drones, and it started

burning. This tilted the vehicle titled, as the drone drifted towards the river. "They will take us to Tekhenu and interrogate us," she said.

"What shall we do now," Al-Khidr said, "and what is Tekhenu?"

"I'll explain everything," Nefertiti said.

They both started looking out through the window. The drones were taking a turn over the river Iteru.

"Jump into the river before it's late."

She pressed a button, and the doors opened. Without a second thought, they both jumped into the rushing waters of the river Iteru.

They swam out of the water, and while panting, they saw that drones had landed and abandoned the vehicle on the Sutekh side of the river.

Nefertiti took out a communication device from a secured water and fireproof pocket and sent a message to someone. "They should be here soon!"

***

"Seka, they jumped into the river! . . . I am dropping the vehicle down and following them with the drones," Kontar said as he was the man controlling the drones. "Damn!" Hatathor shouted.

"I am sending a team to look over the river."

Hatathor tried to track Al-Khidr, but there was no sign of him.

"What the hell? This technology sucks!"

He started cursing the engineers who designed such a faulty gadget.

In his rage, he threw the tracking device away.

"Give me an update as soon as possible," Hatathor shouted.

***

Hatathor became so furious at Al-Khidr and Nefertiti's escape that he couldn't control his anger. He banged his fist against the vehicle's bonnet, creating a significant dent on it. His fury knew no bounds, and his eyes blazed with the fire of hatred and frustration. His blood began bubbling like boiling water placed on a lighted stove. His mind was racing with the images of Al-Khidr and Nefertiti jumping out of the vehicle and into the lake.

Hatathor made a tight fist out of his palm and flexed his muscular arms out of intense rage, displaying the veins in his heavily built body.

"Ahhhhhh!" he shouted, punching the air like a wild beast. Kontar looked at him with terror in his eyes, as though he expected him to transform into an absolute beast and attack everyone. *How the hell in Lyra can that darned human escape again from my clutches? How can fortune favor that human scum again?* Hatathor's mind kept blasting with these thoughts as he breathed heavily with immense outrage. "Damn!" Hatathor shouted.

"I am sending a helicopter to look over the river." Hatathor tried to track Al-Khidr again, but there was still no sign of him. "What the hell? This technology is the worst shit I have ever seen!" He was cursing the engineers who designed the gadget. "Kontar!" he yelled, glaring at him like a fierce lion about to pounce on its prey. "Your technology is a worthless pile of bat droppings! Couldn't your people create some helpful piece of tech that would function correctly?!" Kontar looked at him with an something between rage and fear. He felt if there were someone else in place of Hatathor, he would have ordered the drones to shoot him for his bold tone.

"Hatathor, our technology is the most advanced on Lyra at the date, and nobody, absolutely nobody, has access to such advanced tech," he asserted calmly. "Bullshit! It can't even track a pathetic human scum like Al-Khidr, and you call it the most advanced."' Hatathor spat on the ground with disgust. The moment he got the device from Hatathor, he attempted to track Al-Khidr. However, he failed too and after a few more struggling attempts to get any sign of the human, but it was in vain. Sweating profusely, he called one of his men to try it. The tall, slim man held the tracking device and made several attempts, but, unfortunately, lady luck didn't seem to smile at Hatathor yet again, and the man failed miserably.

"Useless! Everyone's piece of flesh on this planet is utterly useless. And that includes Ankhamon's army!" he lamented, continuing to punch the air in bitter frustration. "Incompetent piece of donkey dung, all of you!"

Kontar gawked at him with a mixture of fear and sympathy. He was feeling thoroughly disappointed at the human and Nefertiti's narrow escape. He started experiencing the frustration and hatred felt by Hatathor while feeling bad for him, such that he didn't even care about the curses he threw at Ankhamon and his army. Abruptly, in a fit of immense fury, Hatathor snatched the tracking device from the man's hand and threw it away. "Give me an update as soon as possible," he shouted, marching off to his vehicle.

***

Semed and Rostau were in the Sutekh –the no-man's-land. It was part of Misraim city but now a shanty spot. They were wearing masks to avoid contraction of Mutmut disease.

The weeds and bushes have grown from the walls of the buildings were now invading the streets. The hover was striking as it moved over the empty streets. It was quiet, and there was deserted desolation feeling about the town.

They reached the place where, according to their tracker, the Bird was parked. They came off their hover and started searching the area. They called her name several times, but there was no sign of Nefertiti.

They located the Bird.

They got close to inspect it to make sure that it was the vehicle they were looking for.

"She's here, but for what purpose?" Semed said. "Isn't she looking for Al-Khidr?" He said further.

"I guess this is a part of her strategy. After all, she used to work as a police officer," Rostau said.

"But we have no other way to find out," Semed replied.

"Yeah, that's the problem," Rostau agreed.

"Well, I guess we have no other choice but to wait for her. We don't know where she could be." Semed said.

Rostau was confused about what to do. Suddenly Rostau received a message.

"We are being chased. I need help. Come quickly..."

With another beep sound, the location came through.

Rostau looked at Semed, "She just beeped me and sent the location. It's.... It's close, and she is right across the block." "You handle the Bird, and I am taking the hover," he said and threw the keys at Semed, "Follow me!"

***

Nefertiti and Al-Khidr were still at the river bank. Behind them was Sutekh. She had lost her mask in the run, and it was not safe to enter that area without a mask. The river flow took them downstream. "Some things are coming!" she looked through the camera and said.

"These are the same drones. They dropped the vehicle, and now they are coming here... Jump into the river again. They cannot track you as long as you are in the water. We don't need to go deep into the river, just submerge our heads until these drones are gone."

They jumped again into the river. Several quadrotor drones were surveying the river, looking for their signs. The white drones comprised two pairs of counter-rotating rotors and propellers at the vertex of a square frame. An array of tiny cameras was attached to their bottoms, which possessed many sensors to scan and locate the target efficiently. The drones sounded like the buzzing of a swarm of bees that moved faster than the speed of a standard earthly airplane towards their kill. The array of cameras and sensors was constantly adjusting and swerving here and there. They were looking for the target – Al-Khidr. Nefertiti made some hand signs inside water, gesturing to Al-Khidr to hold his breath until the drones were gone. They remained inside the water for some time until the drones moved to scan other area.

They came out of the water and started running away from the drones and towards Sutekh. But before they could reach Sutekh, a group of six Lyrian men jumped in front of them. They all had tattoos on their faces and were nearly seven feet tall and towered above Nefertiti and Al-Khidr. Ankhamon's men were equipped with laser guns and began circling the lovers like a ravenous pack of wolves who hadn't eaten for weeks.

"Nefertiti and Al-Khidr," called one of the Lyrian men. He was bald and had intense grey eyes. "We are not here to kill neither of you but simply to take you to King Ankhamon. However, if you attempt to make any smart move, we shall fry you with our laser guns," he threatened, aiming his gun at them, and the other five Lyrian pointed their weapons at them, too. "So it's wise that you love birds co-operate, and place your hands behind your neck, come with us quietly, or put an end to your love story here. The choice is yours." He finished talking, still pointing the weapon at them. Al-Khidr and Nefertiti looked at each other intensely, as though trying to read each other's minds and think of a plan. They let out a sigh of defeat and placed their hands behind their necks, and the group took them. Nefertiti and Al-Khidr walked beside each other while the bald man was following behind them with his gun pointed at their backs while the rest of the alien men followed him.

They walked for a few minutes, and suddenly, Nefertiti tripped and fell to the ground. She grabbed her leg and began moaning in pain. "Ah! My ankle got twisted. Please help!"

"Nefertiti!" exclaimed Al-Khidr, and bent down to tend to her. The bald Lyrian got closer to them, pointing his gun away for a moment. Before he could bend down and touch anyone of them, "Now," whispered Nefertiti, and in a flash of a second, Al-Khidr jumped up violently and smashed the back of his head against the bald man's chin. The man's chin began bleeding, and his gun slipped away from his hand. Al-Khidr then delivered a tremendous punch to his stomach and knocked the wind out of him. The other men began firing at Al-Khidr. However, he grabbed the bald man's neck and placed him as a shield between him and the many laser shots fired at him. The laser shots hit the man's back, and he let out a gruesome agonizing scream. The men kept firing till their guns ran out. Instantaneously, Al-Khidr threw the fried alien aside and bent down on the ground. Within a second, Nefertiti came running from behind him and placing her foot on his shoulder; she leaped into the air and landed a terrific kick on one Lyrian who tumbled backward and collided with the others who collapsed on the ground like bowling pins.

The alien men got to their feet and surrounded Nefertiti, who raised her fists and got ready to battle. They attacked her simultaneously and landed various kicks and heavy punches at her. However, being a proficiently trained police officer, she defended their blows with her elbows and punted one man squarely on the chest, making him fall backward on the ground. Al-Khidr joined his iron lady by running in the middle of the fight and punched one of them on the back of his shoulder as the alien howled in agonizing pain, then grabbed his dislocated left arm Al-Khidr lifted him in the air and tossed the heavy muscular man on the ground. The rest of the aliens unitedly surrounded them, making the lovers stand back to face them. Suddenly, they dashed towards the two, but the muscular men stood no chance against the duo, as Al-Khidr bent his torso, thus, allowing Nefertiti to stylishly roll over his back and deliver a powerful strike on the alien's face with her foot, which began bleeding profusely as he fell on the ground. The last two aliens got into a fistfight with Al-Khidr, who applied his mightily raw strength and lightning-fast punches on their faces and chests to knock them out instantly.

The fight ended, but the defeated men of Ankhamon tried to rise again. Before they could get back on their feet, Nefertiti rolled over the ground and, seizing the bald alien's laser gun, she blasted all of them like insects on the floor. Al-Khidr and Nefertiti had just moved their eyes off each other when two drones appeared out of nowhere and began blinking at the sight of them. The lovers held their hands and made a run for it. They approached the riverside again, and there they saw two masked men running towards them. Nefertiti clenched the hand of Al-Khidr tightly and said: "We need to jump into the river again!"

The men waved their hands and shouted: "Hey, it's us!"

"What took you so long?" she said, recognizing the voice.

Rostau and Semed fired at the drones, rendering them dysfunctional.

"We have to run out of this place as fast as we can. It's not safe to remain here," Semed said.

"Already got the bird," Rostau said to Nefertiti. They all ran and reached the vehicles. But before they could set in, Rostau received the call from Ehsis.

"Have you found Nefertiti?"

"Yes, Guardian," Rostau said, "and I have good news for you. Nefertiti had found Al-Khidr," "He's back! Thanks, God. What a wonderful news! Now, you come back as soon as possible, but you have to listen to me carefully. There is Ar-t Heru seal installed in the wrist of Al-Khidr. Do not forget to remove it before you leave Misraim."

"Understood, Guardian, we will do as you commanded," Rostau said.

He disconnected the call and informed others what Ehsis had instructed.

Nefertiti looked at Al-Khidr and said: "I should have done this long before."

"We do not have any first-aid kit here. Be strong. It will hurt you, but we have to do it for the safety of yours as well as that of the Guardian." Rostau went to the Bird and started looking into its compartments.

"Who is Guardian?" Al-Khidr asked, in a curious tone with a completely confused look on his face. "Ehsis. She is the Guardian," Nefertiti said.

"What? How come? Why are you referring to Ehsis as the rebel, Nefertiti?"

Nefertiti looked at Al-Khidr with a somber expression on her face. And with a brief pause, she began narrating the painful events that had occurred. "Before you departed from Lyra for Earth, Hatathor had joined hands with Ankhamon and waged war against the rest of us. Ankhamon could have never defeated us if not for the betrayal of that bloody Hatathor. They slaughtered many of our people and we, Ehsis, along with the rest of us: few military men, police officers, and a handful of scientists had to go underground when the rebellion broke out," she paused, and her expression turned even more severe and disturbed than ever. “What happened then? Where did you people go?” he asked softly, gazing into Nefertiti's eyes with extreme tenderness.

Nefertiti caught her breath and continued slowly. “There is a secret hideout located towards the east of the kingdom of Akhom called the Kneph. The ancient city lay in ruins since it was demolished a long time ago during a brutal battle by a rival planet Sovidos, in an era before King Ptah. But, the Kneph is an underground area built and developed by King Ptah particularly for adverse situations. The place was, and is, a top-secret facility known only to Ehsis,”

Al-Khidr kept gazing into her eyes with extreme tenderness. It had been so long since they had had a meaningful conversation together, and he recollected the moments of love and romance they used to share before he had left for Earth when Nefertiti used to lie on his chest. They used to talk while they stared at the sparkling stars in the night sky. Al-Khidr moved his hand forward, intending to grab Nefertiti's, but before he could do so, Rostau came back with a small device. “This is a laser cutter. We use it to put the metals. The good thing is that I can control the beam's intensity, and I have set it to the minimum level. It will still be painful, but I'm sorry I have no other option left,” he said and gave the cutter to Nefertiti.

“But after the removal of the seal, how do we close the wound?” she asked. All looked at each other.

“I have a tape. Hopefully, by the time we reach

back to Kneph, it should be fine," Semed said.

"I know you're a powerful man," she said while looking into Al-Khidr eyes.

"For the safety of all, I'm ready for it," he said and closed his eyes.

Nefertiti asked Rostau and Semed to hold AL-Khid's hands. Al-Khidr clenched his fists.

She placed the cutter a small distance away from the skin and started the laser. She could almost see his skin melting away, and the smell was overwhelming. Al-Khidr shouted in pain. The tears started coming out of his eyes, but he didn't move his hand. Nefertiti made a straight slit over the Ar-t hero seal. The blood started dripping from Al-Khidr's hand as she moved the flesh on the sides. The chip was now visible: it was clamped into Al-Khidr hand like a spider sitting inside his wrists.

The three sensors that had been underneath were now visible. They were right under the three holes: one on the top, one on the right, and the third on the left, altogether making an upward triangle.

The sensors had to be burnt carefully using the thin laser beam in order to remove the chip safely and make it dysfunctional. After the sensors stopped functioning, the spider looked device had to be pulled out carefully with the help of pliers. The sensors were green and were blinking over the veins. Rostau was pumping the blood dripping out of Al-Khidr's hand using a small dripper he usually used for hover parts lubrication. It was a crude surgery but an essential one to execute. Al-Khidr was lethargic with pain, and his body began sweating profusely.

Nefertiti looked further. The sensors were connected by a switch and some wires where nanoscale prints were seen to be blinking. "This can be very dangerous, as they can generate an electric shock, which can make all of us unconscious," Nefertiti said to the others. "The first thing I have to do is to make these three sensors delicately dysfunctional one after another." I learned all this as a police officer, as it was part of my training. The device was designed like that to prevent the removal. The escaped prisoners find it complex to remove." She said while burning the three sensors, which were actually underneath the three holes. The holes were made in the skin the first time the seal was installed.

The thin laser beam had burned the sensors to a crisp. The sensors smelled like burned electronics, and the skin smelled of burning rubber. "Fetch me a plier Semed," demanded Nefertiti, examining the chip so closely as though she could see through it. Semed retrieved a plier from a drawer on the dashboard near the driver's seat and threw it at Nefertiti, who caught it flawlessly with her free hand. The plier was quite heavy and possessed a silvery luster. Nefertiti held the tool in her free hand, and without breaking a sweat, she clamped the spider-looking device using the plier's fangs.

"Finish it," Al-Khidr shouted in agony.

Al-Khidr's hand was shaking in the last few moments, and the whole chip was out, along with the burned sensor. "It was a small piece but a very troublesome thing."

Then, they climbed into the Bird and the hover.

Al-Khidr was holding his hand and was in pain. Rostau started the hover, and they started way back to Kneph. A feeling of immense relief broke across Nefertiti's face at the hover's flight, and she sat comfortably on the seat beside Al-Khidr, whose hand was ablaze with excruciating pain. Al-Khidr succumbed to the unbearable pain in his hand that looked gruesome after the chip's removal. He tried to keep a straight face but couldn't as his wrist burnt intensely. His lady love took his hand and stroked it as tenderly as she could.

"Just a little longer, my love, and we shall reach the Kneph, and your wrist will be treated as a matter of urgency," she assured him, placing her tender lips on his rough hand and planted a sweet kiss on it. Nefertiti's kiss seemed to diminish the pain a bit for Al-Khidr as he stared into her gorgeous eyes. The hover traveled east, and the lovers busied themselves in looking at the scenario that transformed gradually from the bustling city to the tranquility of the desert. Despite the air-conditioners operating at their highest, the scorching heat of the desert rose the temperature inside the vehicle, and they began sweating. They traveled for a few miles before bidding farewell to the heat as the landscape altered from the sandy environment to the lush greenery of the mountains.

The air turned colder as the hover soared higher and higher across the breath-taking scenery of the mountains. “Beautiful, isn’t it?” breathed Nefertiti in Al-Khidr’s ears, as she gawked at the marvelous view outside, which seemed to make her pupils larger and her eyelashes sparkled.

“Not more than you, my love,” he responded as he moved his face towards her and gave a soft peck on her lips. Instantaneously, the scenario changed to a deserted city, where no soul, could be seen. Then a gigantic crater emerged, consisting of innumerable porous rocks that seemed to have laid there for centuries. And finally, the Bird entered a substantially dark cave that led them deep into the ground, and they all reached the Kneph safely. The brethren failed to get the signature in time, before they got to safety.

***

Al-Khidr was surprised to see the Kneph. It was a porous rock structure, and he descended into a cave in spirals until he reached a place that looked like a giant beehive. He found himself in the middle of an open field, and all around him were small caves. The top of the cave was also closed, and there was no chance for Vega lights to reach this place.

Nefertiti then took him into another spiral pathway, and he reached a place which the Lyrians called the Cove. It was a large metallic sphere, which was stuck in the rocks. The sound of gushing water was reaching his ears. It was a strange echo there and reminding him of the sistrum sound–the one he heard while coming from Earth to Lyra in the tunnel between the stars.

He entered the Cove, and there were openings all around the walls, as if they are in a bee hive. He saw Ehsis, and she jumped from her elevated seat at his sight. She stepped down from her command station and came to Al-Khidr.

"Welcome back, human!" "Blessings on you, Guardian," he replied. "What is this place?"

"We will tell you everything, but first, we need to check your wound."

A lady came forward and gave him a glass of some kind of sherbet. He drank it all. "It's a nutritious drink–vitamin water, which it will help you in recovery."

Nefertiti took Al-Khidr to the emergency medical facility, and the doctors cleaned the wound. Then they moved a device over it, and the flesh came closer, and the wound was healed within a few minutes. Al-Khidr felt the excruciating pain in his wrist evaporate like smoke. As the device healed the wound miraculously and painlessly, he felt nothing at all while the device worked its magic-like operation onto his burnt flesh. Meanwhile, Nefertiti brought a torch, and she threw a blue light on the seal. The seal was still visible, but it carried a scar over it. She switched off the torch. The seal had again become invisible to his eyes. "Now, everything shall be alright. Hatathor cannot track you anymore," she assured him, with a captivating smile that felt as soothing as a hot waterfall and as glorious as spring for Al-Khidr.

"Thank you for this," he said, returning her a tender smile.

"We now execute the de-radiation sequence!"

The doctors announced, and Al-Khidr was placed in a pod.

It reminded him of the procedure that he had gone through before he had left Lyra. However, his heart felt significantly light this time, and his mind was clear, with no anxious thoughts buzzing around. It took some time, bur Al-Khidr was finally out of the pod.

"It was a vital procedure to perform, Mr. Al-Khidr," the doctor informed him, and he nodded at him in approval. The moment Al-Khidr got out of the pod, the doors slid aside automatically, and a towering man, wearing a silver metallic suit and a metallic helmet possessing a transparent glass that showed his face, emerged. He carried a metallic suitcase, which seemed relatively light, as he held it effortlessly in his right palm. He walked towards Al-Khidr and handed him the suitcase. And at Nefertiti's nod, he took it. The man then instructed him to place it perpendicularly on the ground and hold its handle. He followed the instructions, and the moment he did so, the suitcase miraculously transformed like clay and took the shape of grey metallic armor similar to the one the man was wearing. The armor was hollow from the back and perfectly suited to fit Al-Khidr's physique, and he knew exactly what he had to do.

"Remove your clothes before moving in, my love," instructed Nefertiti, and everyone, including her, left the room. Al-Khidr removed his rugged old clothes and threw them aside on the ground. Then, slowly, he placed his body inside the hollow armor, and the moment he did so, the armor bound itself around his body perfectly. Al-Khidr felt an unusual ticklish sensation inside the armor, which was neither too tight nor too loose, but simply perfect for him. And despite it being metallic, he felt no sweat leave his body as the armor somehow seemed to control the internal temperature. And neither did he feel suffocated inside the metallic case, which astonishingly seemed to feel more comfortable than any regular attire.

"Everyone can come back. I am clothed," Al-Khidr shouted somewhat nervously, as Nefertiti came rushing inside as the doors opened. She looked at him with her eyebrows raised and lips pursed out of sheer admiration. Al-Khidr moved towards her, and his walk felt as light and subtle as it usually did and didn't make him think he was placed inside a case made of metal.

"You look fabulous, and to be honest, slightly more handsome than usual," she complimented, winking. And before Al-Khidr could utter another word, she said. "Let's eat now; I am starving like hell," she announced, and grabbing his metallic arm, she took him to the cafeteria.

***

"It's better. I also search myself," Hatathor said to himself.

"Kontar, make your team more active and alert. You have selected a bunch of lazy guys." "I am sorry, Seka!" "I need a small spaceship. I don't like helicopters. Send it fast!" Hatathor shouted in a rage. Within a few minutes, the spaceship arrived, and Hatathor along with Kontar went towards the other side of the river.

# Chapter 11

# The Escape

THE food in the cafeteria was not very appetizing. It consisted mainly of an insect soup that looked muddy brown and tasted substantially rancid with a tinge of bitterness. It felt a little disgusting to Al-Khidr, who wasn't accustomed to eating insects. Besides that, crusty bread was slightly moist and hard to chew. And a mixed vegetable stew was on display, which looked as though it had been made of vegetables that had rotted for a month. Al-Khidr's heart sank as he noticed the food on display and attempted to control his grumbling tummy, which had been empty for the last few days. The food seemed even worse than what he used to eat in the police station cell. Although he was not very enthusiastic about it, he couldn't afford to make any excuse not to fill his stomach as he had to eat since he was damn hungry. Nefertiti noticed the unavoidably intense look of disappointment on Al-Khidr's face and instantly knew that he didn't like the food as well. She said: "Ever since the rebellion happened, we are here. Perhaps you remember we were all in the Hall of Stars, and there was an attack ongoing. I was unconscious when you and Hatathor went into the wormhole. Later, Ehsis woke me up and took me, along with the scientists, to this secret cave-like facility. And we descended into the caves underneath the HSS facility and rode the starship to escape from the city. It was a huge surprise, as none of us had seen this facility before. General Lukmas had made the spaceships ready for our escape. However, he faced the rebels, and during the bloody battle with them, he was captured alive," she paused, holding the spoonful of insect soup in mid-air as she stared in space and recalled that painful memory with a somber expression on her face.

"After that, Ehsis left and reached Kneph using a highly advanced technology called Cloaking' that completely concealed her spaceship from radars. That became a secret known only to her and her guards. The military rebels, along with Ankhamon, searched for her far and wide but in vain. This place is thoroughly equipped with cloning technology and radar jamming equipment."

She paused again, sipping her soup slowly, and continued.

"Ah, poor General Lukmas. We learned he is still inside prison somewhere in the dungeons of Ankhamon."

"Who is Ankhmaon? Sorry, I forgot. I have a vague idea that you told me about him," Al-Khidr asked.

Nefertiti explained the Ankhamon and his brethren of Awaken Consciousness cult. "They called Hatathor a savior figure," she informed.

"How come Ankhamon became so strong?" Al-Khidr asked.

"The military general couped. They wanted to install their puppet and control him. But Ankhamon was shrewder. He was a journalist and knew well what to do in such a situation. He promoted the junior-ranked generals and removed the old ones. Then he exercised his powers and gave positions to his brethren in bureaucracy. Also, he continued with his cultist mentality and took over almost all power structures."

"Ankhmaon destroyed the Hermes system. He said that it's like flies moving over the dung. But in reality, he was afraid that anyone could reach Tekhenu in the Tehuti Mountains. Now only the ground vehicle is allowed. I guess he is taking all of us back into Stone Age to make his kingdom strong," she said further. "It's deplorable that happened. But what shall be our next move now?" he asked.

"For Ehsis, the foremost step is to get the cure for Mutmut and make a vaccine for it. Attack on Misraim will be suicide, as we are too few, and this place is a hide-out made to escape some other planet. But Ehsis said that she will strike back."

"I see," Al-Khidr said. "I guess you have finished eating. Let's go back to Ehsis and give her the sphere."

"Wait, a minute!" Nefertiti exclaimed. "Before we do that, we have to do one important task."

"What is it?" demanded Al-Khidr, gazing at her stupidly, utterly confused.

***

"It's a little heavy," Al-Khidr commented as he held the laser gun and scrutinized it thoroughly inside the Kneph's training arena. "Do we have to do it now? "Yes, genius. If we are going to save Lyra from the rebels and overthrow Hatathor and Ankhamon, we need to teach and train you to use one of these laser guns." Al-Khidr looked at her for a few seconds and then nodded silently in approval.

"Alright then, watch and learn," she instructed, grabbing one gun from a shelf. She held the long gun, which closely resembled an earthly sniper, above the shoulder level with both hands and aimed it at a faceless mannequin with a target board in its chest that stood nearly a hundred supris away. Al-Khidr followed her actions accurately. She sought the dummy through the gun's eyepiece, then pressed a button at the weapon's center, and Al-Khidr did the same. Nefertiti's shot hit the bull's eye flawlessly and burned a hole through it. Al-Khidr's shot hit the wall, right above the dummy's head.

"I am hopeless," lamented Al-Khidr, keeping the gun aside.

"Relax, my love. You are a rookie, and someone even hitting the wall at your level is quite an achievement," Nefertiti claimed with an encouraging smile. "Let's give it a few more shots."

She handed him the laser gun, and they resumed the practice session. This time Nefertiti guided Al-Khidr by standing beside him and placing her hands on his as he held the gun. She made him aim at the bull's eye, and he pressed the button. The laser shot sailed through the air right across the bull's eyehole made by Nefertiti. "Now try it yourself," she said, moving aside. Al-Khidr was thoroughly determined to master the laser gun, and, with complete concentration, he fired four shots at the dummy. The first went right above its shoulder, and the second hit its groin area; the third hit its shoulder. However, the last one struck on the right side of the target board.

"Bravo Al-Khidr!" she cheered, clapping her hands with a broad smile on her face. "You have learned it in just five shots. Brilliant!" "Well, I had an excellent teacher," he said, throwing her a flirtatious smile.

"Come on, Ehsis must be glad to have it," she said with a half-giggle, while Al-Khidr gave a nod of approval. The lovers held hands, moved out of the training arena, and walked towards the Cove.

***

Al-Khidr looked into his sack and said.

"To God, we all shall return! We have to go back!" Al-Khidr said anxiously. "But why?"

He was frantically searching for his sack and moving his hand in it. "I lost the sphere!" "What? Are you serious?" They all shouted back.

"Yes... yes. It's not here!"

"When did the last time you had it?" "I had it with me all the time. It was in the sack when I left Lyra Gardens, and it was even there in the vehicle. Oh God, I hope I didn't lose in the river," He took out the gun and gave it to Nefertiti.

"This is the gun you threw to me when you entered the vehicle. When I was jumping into the river, I dropped it into the sack and then jumped into the river. I didn't realize that sphere had gone out."

"Oh!" all exclaimed.

Ehsis looked at Nefertiti and Semed.

"Where is Rostau?"

"He is sleeping!" "I guess it's a hard day today," she said.

"Maft-Shespt cannot be left like this, and anyone in the brethren cult might misuse it. I ask you guys again that you look for it," Ehsis ordered.

"Al-Khidr, you also come. I have a hunch that sphere likes you," Nefertiti laughingly said to tone down the tense situation.

***

They got close to the vehicle. Its glasses were broken, and its metal frame was dented. Bolts and hinges were bent. The drones have dropped it on the ground. The tires were burst out. Semed searched inside, but found nothing.

"I should have awakened Rostau. He sometimes finds things which I cannot find!" Semed said regretfully. Al-Khidr was still searching, and then he found the sphere was stuck between the seats. He took it out and showed that to others.

"Wow. I told you. This sphere and you are staunch friends," Nefertiti said, and all laughed.

"Some entourage is coming. It doesn't look good," Semed said, while looking through the camera at a swarm rushing towards them. "Semed you go back. As per protocol, we should all not leave together but separately. We have only one vehicle, and I suggest you take the vehicle. Al-Khidr and I will go to the city and hide there," Nefertiti said.

"What about the sphere?" "I keep it," Al-Khidr said.

"Ah, I cannot think much," Semed said.

"Hurry. They will be here soon." Nefertiti said while running towards the buildings.

***

Hatathor vehicle was flying over the buildings, then dunes, and finally, he reached the river. He noticed the abandoned pile of metal. It was the vehicle that Nefertiti was driving, which the drones dropped.

He landed and went towards the abandoned vehicle and scoured it, but there was nothing inside which could grasp his attention. Suddenly, Hatathor gaze stuck at the sand.

"Kontar, look here. Before we arrived here, there were people here," he said.

He was scrutinizing the sand. Kontar also knelt and also looked.

"There were three of them. Look at the footprints," Hatathor said.

"At least two of them went towards the city," Kontar concluded. "I'll look around. You go search into the city. Inform all security and intelligence." "The human was inside the vehicle, and a girl protected him."

"Very well, Seka!" Kontar said and went towards the city.

Hatathor stood up, and he looked at Sutekh. He did not want to enter, because he had feared that he could contract Mutmut. Since the childhood, his mind had been hit by psychological trauma and the fear of contracting a disease!

It was a phobia that had made a fearless lion like Hatathor into a terrified cat. His face was sunken in, his skin turned pallid, as though he hadn't slept in ages. His eyes widened, and the upper lids rose as they strayed to the horizon in an inexplicable fear. His lips became so dry, as though they hadn't tasted a single drop of liquid in weeks, and they were pursed in intense pain. His nose turned reddish. He became rooted to the spot as though someone had nailed his legs to the ground, and his body went completely numb as the blood in his veins froze. The beating of his heart slowed down drastically, and his chest became so heavy and began banging so wildly, as though a wrecking ball had been tied against it. Intense fear had paralyzed him from head to toe, and profuse sweat had enveloped his entire muscular body as though a bucket of cold water had been poured onto him.

The newscaster's voice was resounding in his head, a voice that had been trapped in his mind since his childhood. "The disease ... The Mutmut ... the contagion."

He recalled the news report: "Sutekh is a big graveyard!" a man shouted at the police.

He sat on the sand and held his head in his hands. The horror of the dream was haunting him again. The sounds of flowing rivers were turning into screams rising from Sutekh. He started feeling like his head was shaking, and he fell to the ground, and he started smelling the rotten flesh.

He started feeling like he was living in another world. He kept looking for a way out, but nothing but sand surrounded him. He closed his eyes and wanted to return to reality.

He was drifting into sleep, into an unknown world. He was whispering: "Stop, human, he will unleash a disease on us!"

# CHAPTER 11. THE ESCAPE

***

Al-Khidr and Nefertiti were back in the city. Every passing second was increasing their nervousness. They were wearing hooded jackets and were walking separately, but close to each other. Al-Khidr did not want to lose the sphere again. They felt like every passer-by was looking back at them. “Intelligence is all around! Just be careful,” Nefertiti said to Al-Khidr.

They were briskly walking, but they did not know where. They walked, and suddenly they entered a square with two statues. They were installed in the middle of a pound and were facing opposite directions with their backs close to each other. “This is the statue of Usir, and this is the statue of Seth. King Ptah ordered to erect these statues.” Trees surrounded the pond. The leaves on the trees were turning brown, bright orange, shiny, and dotted with red. The air around the trees smelled fresh, and the leaves were falling over.

It was all surreal, reminding the viewer that the Lyra was now a dying planet!

Al-Khidr was awestruck for a moment. He felt like history passed in front of his eyes. Seth killed Usir and Ptah told a lie to his people. A lie, concocted for a good reason, shattered the lives of all those who lived in the kingdom of Akhom. The mutiny defaced the beauty of the Akhom–turned it into a gloomy world ruled by a dystopian king.

“What a fall for a civilization!” he said to himself.

Nefertiti shooks him, and he quickly came back to his senses.

"Let's go. What are you thinking?" she said.

"Wait, where are we going?" he shrugged off her hand and said. "I am fed-up of this running and this unending game of hiding. I am tired!" Al-Khidr said as a gush of tears formed on the side of his eyes as he started sobbing . He was rooted to the spot and refused to move. He was sweating profusely and rubbing his eyes with one hand, as tears were trickling down his reddish cheeks.

"How long are you going to run for, Nefertiti? Everything will perish one day!" he said to her.

Nefertiti was flabbergasted and kept staring at him with her eyes widened. She was not expecting such a turn of emotions. "Al-Khidr, we will prevail. The truth will prevail, we will take back our city victoriously and defeat the treacherous Hatathor and the rebels!" she shouted back, unable to believe her ears. She felt as though a rock had struck her head. The scenario of the mentally and emotionally strong man whom she loved breaking down so briskly and so unexpectedly was something she had never expected in her wildest dreams. For Nefertiti, a surprise attack by the rebels would have been less outrageous in this scenario than this sort of behavior by Al-Khidr.

"Yeah, right!" he exclaimed with a tone of despaired sarcasm in his breaking voice. "And how many lives shall be sacrificed while we hopelessly struggle to do so? What if Ankhamon takes the sphere and destroys it, or Hatathor kills me? What will you do after that? What if they eventually find the Kneph and slaughter Ehsis and the rest of her soldiers? Look around Nefertiti and see for yourself. This is not the Lyra where you were a police officer, and it has changed so drastically that it is unrecognizable! Come out of your fool's paradise and see the bloody goddamn truth!" He shook Nefertiti's shoulders harshly and clenched his teeth out of sheer frustration and an unexpected feeling of helplessness.

Nefertiti yelled back: "Yes, I know! But let's not give up so quickly and so easily, Al-Khidr!" She paused for a few seconds, trying to regain control of her emotions. Being a tough police officer, she had never previously allowed her feelings to go out of control, no matter how horrible or ridiculous the situation was. She shook her head, regaining complete control of her emotional balance, and said calmly: "But you are right. We must hide the sphere somewhere. But where . . . ?" she turned motionless for a few moments and began pondering about all the places, placing her mind under immense pressure, and suddenly, a brilliant idea flashed inside her head. She removed Al-Khidr's hands from her shoulders, looked around, and ran towards the ponds where the fountains were sprinkling. She looked over the water towards Al-Khidr, and statues blocked her view.

She came back to Al-Khidr and said: "Give me the sphere!"

Al-Khidr took the sphere out and asked: "What

are you going to do with it?" She took the sphere from him and jumped into the pond. The water was knee deep. She walked towards the statue that was carved from bronze. Usir bag was cut deep with a hollow space. She took the leaves out and placed the sphere inside the bag, and covered it with leaves. She quickly came out and looked around to ensure no one noticed her. She said:

"It's safe now. Let's hide somewhere before anyone's eyes fall on us. We will get it later!"

***

Al-Khidr and Nefertiti were still in the park, and they felt like they were being watched by trees and the buildings overlooking the enormous garden. They all looked like giant monsters with thousands of eyes looking at them.

Al-Khidr and Nefertiti continued their brisk walking, and they could see neon lights of the advertisements. The entire landscape transformed from nature's lush and breath-taking greenery to the city's sparkling and glamorous ultramodern side. The quiet side of the creation of God was changing into the hustling and bustling artificial area of the city with its awe-inspiring and towering skyscrapers. The change of scenario diverted their attention for a few moments from their desperation and instilled immense curiosity and awe in their eyes. They walked nearly two hundred supris, and a vibrant bazaar was about to come. "I have never seen this place before," Al-Khidr expressed loudly, inquisitively ogling the glamorously urban side of the city, his pupils widening with every step they took and mouth hanging.

"Me either," Nefertiti said softly, unable to get her own eyes off the unexpected glamour surrounding them. The neon lights were dazzling like a disco ball and enveloping themselves in the slim bodies of Al-Khidr and Nefertiti. Thus, creating an aura of sensuality and stupor. "Queen Hathor did not like such places. However, Ankhamon had created a new type of business, and he wanted to make people forget the past and accept the new reality," Nefertiti said.

Al-Khidr looked at the neon lights in awe and wonder, which had lights of different colors reflecting all over the place. The bazaar appeared extraordinarily crowded and noisy that Nefertiti and Al-Khidr could barely hear each other's voices. "It's bright and beautiful," he exclaimed, getting completely lost in the oblivious nature of the radiant lights dancing in the city. "Don't get too carried away by this glamor and craze Al-Khidr," warned Nefertiti irritatingly as she noticed the awe in his eyes. "It's deceptive and merely an oblivion for misleading the people of our city."

Various genres of music were being played in the bazaar.

"There are hotels, shopping malls, cinemas, restaurants, nightclubs," Nefertiti mentioned casually, as Al-Khidr was looking around like an overwhelmed tourist. The music was played by electric instruments, which were loud and beaming with life. "Hey, I need to go to the restroom," Nefertiti said.

"You just stay here. I'll be right back," she instructed and went towards a shopping mall. "Oh damn! I feel the pressure too. I need to find a restroom too!" Al-Khidr said, and they both went inside the shopping center. He was amazed by the things sold in the bazaar.

Al-Khidr came out of the restroom earlier than Nefertiti. He was amazed by the things sold, and gradually, without even realizing it, he lost his way. Some beautiful girls were sitting in the corner of a shop and were enticing him to come over. One came forward and introduced herself. "Hello, I am Alora. Do you have viboors?" she said, and kissed Al-Khidr's cheek. "Viboors?" Al-Khidr asked surprised.

Her face was beautiful. She had a dainty nose and eyebrows, and her lips were red and slightly pouty. She was wearing a white off-the-shoulder dress. "Akhom's currency," Alora laughed. "Oh dirhams," Al-Khidr uttered mechanically.

Hahaha, Alora laughed.

"What is it?" she asked.

"A coin," Al-Khidr said.

She laughed further and giggled back at her friends. The other girls were smiling at him. They were perfect, with youthful faces and dark blue hair, which exuded sex appeal. Al-Khidr had nothing to do with them, and he watched them from a distance. "Ah... okay. Yeah, I have it." Al-Khidr acted awkwardly.

He just wanted Nefertiti to come back. He awkwardly looked into his pockets and acted like he had money in them. Then he smiled and said, "Ah, I forgot to bring enough viboors – maybe some other day." Then he saw another gorgeous girl, who was coming towards him. He was ogling her, who stood out from the rest. Her eyes were the color of lapis lazuli, and her lips were red like roses. Her hair tumbled down her back, and her allure was magnetic, drawing him over just to stare at her. She came forward and said: "Hello, I am Shiphrah!" she introduced herself with a glamorously sensual smile, offering her hand to be shaken. Her perfume was intoxicating, and it smelled like spring flowers. That Al-Khidr could identify easily. "You must be tired after all day!" she said.

*What? How does she know that I have been running around all day?* Al-Khidr thought, eyeing her suspiciously, and realized that there was something fishy. He said thank you and turned around, and to his surprise, he found six men with tattoos on their shoulders and faces smiling at him. He looked back and was shocked to see that Shiphrah was not there.

*These are the ruffians*, he thought to himself. He was about to run, but the men took out their laser guns and pointed them at him.

"One move, and you will be roasted like a bird!" one warned, in a deep and booming voice that sounded somewhat intimidating.

Suddenly, a car arrived speedily outside the mall entrance and a man stepped out carrying a laser gun and a smile of absolute evil with a blend of glory.

"Master Kontar, he is finally in our clutches." Al-Khidr wasn't afraid of being captured and only hoped sincerely that his beloved Nefertiti would be safe and would run away back to Kneph. However, his heart sank horribly as he turned his face to glance to his right, wherein he noticed Nefertiti being pushed by Shiphrah, who was carrying the gun as well.

Nefertiti looked at him with a mixture of anxiousness, curiosity, and concern, as he stood there helplessly.

In a moment of desperation to save herself and her love, Nefertiti let out a fake shriek by turning her face to the right, and when Shiphrah got distracted, she smacked her face with her elbow, which caused Shiphrah to tumble backward on the ground. In that thrilling moment, Shiphrah's fingers pressed the button on her gun, resulting in a laser shot being fired, which accidentally hit the man who had his gun pointed towards Al-Khidr. The man screamed in agonizing pain and was sent flying backward. He collided with the mall's entrance glass with a gut-wrenching smash and went flying outside the mall along with the shattered glass. Al-Khidr grabbed the golden opportunity, rolled over to the side, and seized the man's gun, which had slipped from his hand and was lying on the ground. Using the gun, he fired six consecutive laser shots at the men, which hit them flawlessly in their chests, and sent them soaring back. They landed inside a supermarket with the food racks falling all over them. "Come on, Nefertiti," yelled Al-Khidr, and they both grasped each other's hands and made a run for the other side of the mall, swerving the massive crowd skillfully. Laser shots were fired at them from behind, and Shiphrah and the other pretty girls, including Alora, were chasing them and firing at them. Al-Khidr fired back at them from ahead but missed and hit a tall mannequin inside a ladies' accessories shop, which shattered into pieces. Abruptly, Nefertiti slipped and fell with a horrible thud on the marble floor, smashing her head, which started bleeding. Al-Khidr skidded and came to a halt, but before he could offer his arm to Nefertiti, a dozen lasers came flying his way, which he avoided skillfully by bending his torso backward; however, one of the laser shots struck his gun and fried it instantly. He lifted himself while the group of girls approached them.

"Think Al-Khidr", he said to himself, and his eyes fell on an array of bowling balls that lay on a shelf on his right. Immediately, he seized one ball and ideally sent it sliding across the smooth marble floor. The ball smashed against the girls' legs, and they went flying sideways like bowling pins and crashed inside a giant toy store.

"Are you alright, girl?" he asked Nefertiti frantically while he raised her to her feet. "I am alright," she assured him, holding the side of her forehead oozing with blood. "There must be a medical room here somewhere; let's get you fixed?" "No!" she cut in, clutching her forehead tightly. "Let's get the hell out of here before we attract any more trouble," and Al-

Khidr looked at her for a moment and then nodded slowly. The shopping mall was quite large, so they approached the emergency exit door at the far end on the other side of the mall after nearly ten minutes. Nefertiti let out a sigh of relief as they reached the exit door, but the moment Al-Khidr opened it... they froze in terror... as Kontar stood there with his gun. "Going somewhere, love birds?"

***

One of Kontar's men delivered a gut-wrenching kick squarely on Al-Khidr's chest making himcollapse on the ground with a terrible moan. He began coughing as an excessive pain shot across his chest. Nefertiti shouted his name agonizingly, but Shiphrah grabbed her by the hair and smacked her face mercilessly. "Shut the hell up, you bloody bitch!" she yelled at her, and grabbing her by the foot, she slid her across the ground towards Al-Khidr, who lay silently on the marble floor.

"It was a big mistake you both made by trying to escape us, girl," Kontar claimed, gazing at them distastefully. "We are Ankhamon's highly trained soldiers, and it's nearly impossible to trick us or escape from our clutches. You pathetic lovebirds were fortunate enough to have even tried to do so." Kontar snapped his fingers, and another of his men marched forward and raised them onto their knees. Al-Khidr struggled fiercely like an animal, but the muscular soldier delivered a massive punch to his cheek, and he halted his struggle. Nefertiti struggled too.

"This bitch won't listen," said Shiphrah and slapped her again furiously.

She then made Nefertiti lie flat on the ground again and twisted her leg harshly. Nefertiti flinched terribly in pain and writhed on the floor. And when she had stopped writhing, she was made to sit on her knees again.

Nefertiti and Al-Khidr were now on their knees with their hands on the back of their heads. A massive crowd had gathered across the shopping mall, watching in extreme shock and terror; however, the people could only watch helplessly as they were afraid of the ruthless new regime. The men standing behind them was pointing their laser guns directly at them, and they were ready to fire the shots at the slightest sign from their leader–Master Kontar. "What do you want from us?" Al-Khidr growled as an excruciating pain shot across his knees.

"You are well aware of what we want, filthy human!" The man said, smacking his head with the laser gun. Al-Khidr fell on the ground from the impact, and his head began throbbing with intense pain.

"Leave him alone, you treacherous dogs!" shouted Nefertiti, who attempted to hold him but was restrained by Shiphrah, who gave her a tight slap. "Silence, filthy woman! We will not kill you until you tell us about the jump-sphere," she said furiously, staring at her like a ravenous lioness. "Check his bag!" Kontar commanded, and one of his men came forward and pulled the sack of Al-Khidr towards him.

He emptied the bag's contents instantly but found nothing except some dry fruits.

"I just want the jump-sphere. I do not want to kill you," Kontar claimed, with a tinge of sympathy coming from his deep and husky voice. "Then why the hell are they pointing the guns at us?" Nefertiti shouted.

"One wrong move and you will be dead!"

"I am asking again. Where is the sphere? If you don't tell me, you will go to heaven, or perhaps even hell," Kontar threatened, with a vicious smirk forming across his lips. Shiphrah said to Kontar: "I want this bitch. Just give her to me!"

"You can take her," Kontar said casually.

Shiphrah came forward, and she pulled Nefertiti by her hair making Nefertiti flinch in pain.

"Here's the bitch from the police," Kontar's men roared with massive laughter. "Look at her. The fox is now in the trap!" they continued poking fun at her and making funny faces while mimicking her actions. "Wait. Let her go. I will tell you where the sphere is!" Al-Khidr claimed desperately as he looked at Nefertiti with immense fear and anxiety building up in his eyes. Nefertiti looked at him in shock and rocked her head in disapproval to stop him from doing the very thing that she had been dreading the most. "No, Nefertiti. You are way more precious than anything else in this whole wide universe for me!" Al-Khidr said solemnly, with a serene expression on his face. "You can kill us both here, at this very spot, or you can make a deal with us. Allow the girl to go away, and I will tell you where the jump-sphere is." "Yeah, right! We let her go, and you will give us the sphere," said Shiphrah sarcastically.

"Trust me. Just her go, and I promise I will take you to the jump-sphere myself. And then, you can even kill me if you like," pleaded Al-Khidr with the utmost desperation.

"Now you're talking," Kontar said, the smile still brimming brightly on his face.

"I am totally in love with this deal," he added with glee, gesturing his man to move the gun away from Al-Khidr's swollen head.

"You cannot do this, Kontar; it's simply outrageous!" Shiphrah howled at Kontar like a raging tigress, her eyes burning with anger and fury.

"Pappa and Hatathor will boil with fury by this atrocious act of yours. I'm telling you, they will tear you apart." She added as she stood stunned with her arms folded against her chest. "We could interrogate this bloody damned bitch to find the location of their precious Ehsis."

"Ehsis is no longer a threat, and Master Ankhamon's interest lies purely in the jump-sphere and not in this pathetic human," Kontar asserted, pointing at Al-Khidr with his laser gun.

Shiphrah experienced a frustrating feeling of powerlessness in trying to thwart Kontar's ridiculous decision. "I'll teach him a lesson!" she said to herself.

# Chapter 12

# The New Plan

KONTAR, along with his men and Shiphrah, was led by Nefertiti and Al-Khidr to the park, wherein the statue over the pond lay the one precious object sought by Hatathor and Ankhamon – the sphere.

Al-Khidr had to bend low on the park's ground with his hands behind his back, desperately hoping that Kontar would show enough empathy and honesty in exchange for Nefertiti's freedom. However, he cursed Shiphrah inside his mind for trying to dissuade Kontar into making that fair deal. Shiphrah seemed outraged at the sound of that deal and looked as though someone had tightly slapped her on her pretty face.

"Kontar," called Al-Khidr, trying to notice his face while he lay bent on the park's stone flooring, which provided extreme discomfort on his knees. "Trust me on this; we want nothing except our lives and our freedom," he appealed to him earnestly, as the pain in his knee and the discomfort in the upper part of his body intensified briskly. "I am a man of word, Kontar, and it is no less than a great sin for me to lie, cheat or to break a promise made to anyone, be it even my enemy," he asserted with clenched teeth, as a tear of pain escaped from the corners of his eyes because of the intensifying pain that had taken over his entire body now.

"It is a simple deal: we shall hand over the sphere to you, and in return, you give Nefertiti a safe passage and a vehicle to leave," Al-Khidr said. Kontar gazed at him in silence for a few minutes, thinking deeply as a storm of deep contradictions was waging inside his head whether he should make the deal and leave them both or get the sphere and double-cross them. There was a battle of right and wrong, ethics and deception, truth and lies being waged heavily inside his conscience. After contemplating in silence for a while, he looked at Al-Khidr's painful eyes and nodded slowly in agreement. "Alright, I am ready to make the deal. Hand over the sphere to me, and I guarantee that you and Nefertiti will be left free, and you would be granted a vehicle to leave," Kontar approved firmly.

Shiphrah punched the air violently and clenched her teeth in extreme disapproval at that deal that she considered ridiculously outrageous. Cursing Kontar under her breath, she immediately retrieved her mobile and speed-dialed both Ankhamon and Hatathor, but neither were picking up the phones. "Where is Hatathor?" she was wondering under her breath again and again like an ineffective mantra. She looked at Kontar and said, "I am going to see Pappa!" And she rushed in a state of exasperation. "We will leave as soon as we hand over the sphere to you," Nefertiti said. "Yes. I have already said it several times," Kontar said, annoyed.

"Arrange a small spaceship," he ordered his man, who followed his order with a quick nod.

They waited for nearly twenty minutes, and a small black egg-shaped space vehicle landed in the park right outside the mall entrance.

The pilot, a muscular man dressed in an astronaut-like black suit with a helmet, came out and gave the control keys to Nefertiti. "Nefertiti, hand over the sphere to them," Al-Khidr said.

She nodded her head slowly and most reluctantly, then thinking no further, she dived into the pond. A few moments later, her body emerged along with the sphere from the statue of Usir and handed it over to Kontar.

As soon as Kontar's eyes came in contact with the sphere in his hand, a sort of electric current flowed across his veins and his entire body, enticing all of his five senses. He was gawking at it as though he had found an ancient treasure. His eyes widened if it appeared they would pop out of their sockets in a few seconds. He experienced an intense mixture of awe, enthusiasm, and madness. He could not believe his eyes and was rooted to the ground in utmost bewilderment.

He kept staring at the sphere like a maniac, and without diverting his sparkling eyes away from it, he pointed his finger towards Nefertiti and Al-Khidr.

"You pathetic lovers are free to go," he commanded casually; his voice seemed to have changed from a deep one to that of utmost enthusiasm. He seemed like a child whose lifelong desire to visit candy land had finally been fulfilled. Al-Khidr was finally able to get up. His legs felt the most discomforting cramps that any human could ever expect to get. The blood flow in his legs seemed to have ceased, and so Nefertiti had to help him rise to his feet. She placed his hand around her shoulder and aided him in climbing the ship.

Nefertiti and Al-Khidr climbed the spaceship as briskly as their legs could, and they went out towards the south. They could not go to Kneph, as there was a ninety-nine percent chance their spaceship was tracked. They landed inside Sutekh, utterly sad, as though the world seemed to have already ended. Nefertiti felt cold and extremely frustrated. Despair seemed to have washed over her entire body and soul like a parasite, which appeared to be eating her away rapidly, and her body was trembling endlessly. Al-Khidr could find no words to utter, the ground beneath his feet seemed to have vanished, as he stood there paralyzed like a lifeless statue. "Nefertiti," he finally muttered, standing behind her and placing his numb palm on her trembling shoulder.

"Why did you do that, Al-Khidr!" she yelled at him in a trembling voice, her blood boiling with extreme rage and inexplicable fear for the lives of her people. "What the hell did you think when you made that deal?!"

"I was just trying to save your life, my love."

"Why didn't you goddamn let me die!" she screamed, turning towards him and shaking his shoulder. "I would have happily sacrificed my life instead of handing over the sphere to those killers!"

Astonishingly, tears had appeared in her eyes. Her mind seemed to blast with regret and guilt, as intense fear seemed to bubble inside her stomach when thinking about the fate of Ehsis and her people and, above all, the future of Lyra. She slipped down and fell on her knees in ultimate defeat and hopelessness.

"You do not know what you have done, Al-Khidr... What danger you have placed upon Ehsis and my people! The jump-sphere possesses the plants that drastically cure that damned disease! And now, because of you, we have lost the cure!... You made a deal to save two lives by placing the lives of millions at stake," she sobbed profusely, as a fountain of tears burst out of her pretty eyes and sprinkled on her reddish, puffy cheeks. Al-Khidr slowly placed his hands on her shoulders and lifted her.

"Look at me," he said, lifting her chin and looking into her teary eyes. "It was not one ordinary life that I saved, Nefertiti... it was the life of the woman who matters more to me than the entire universe. What would I do of this world without you, my love? I have no regrets; I would sacrifice a thousand spheres like that and put at risk the lives of millions to save you again if I had to." he paused, placing his lips on her forehead and planting a tender kiss on it. He wiped away her tears with his sleeves and continued: "It was you who said that we will prevail. You lifted my spirit, and now you have broken down. No, we will get back to the sphere. If God can give me the plants and send me back to Lyra, then he will return the sphere to us!! "It's not the end yet, Nefertiti. We can still prevail; the truth can still survive, just like you said before. You made me gather hope again, and now you are losing all of it?

His words touched Nefertiti profoundly, who slowly nodded her head and regained her inner strength and willpower to defeat the rebels and overthrow Hatathor and Ankhamon. Al-Khidr pulled her into a heart-warming embrace. And that rewarding hug seemed to suck away all the fear, guilt, and regret from Nefertiti's body, as well as lightening her heavy heart that appeared to have increased its beating because of that sphere incident. Al-Khidr and Nefertiti broke apart, and she took out a device and contacted personnel from the Kneph and asked them to pick them up.

***

Shiphrah was sitting on the right side of the empty throne while King Ankhamon was anxiously pacing in front of the throne with his hands behind his back. There were twenty-seven brethren council members who were also there.

The atmosphere was somber and unpredictable. Ankhamon's mind was blasting with racing thoughts.

*What is taking those idiots so long? Why haven't they sent any updates? Are they even alive? Or have they been killed by that human?* These thoughts didn't allow him to relax even for a second and had been tormenting him since the time Hatathor and his men left in search of the human.

"Master Ankhamon, Kontar has arrived!" one of his men exclaimed with extreme enthusiasm.

"Bring him in!" he growled impatiently.

Kontar entered the Tekhenu with the jump-sphere in his hands. He was delighted and highly enthusiastic to announce the news of getting the sphere. He was confident that today he would be rewarded handsomely or perhaps even granted the key to a treasure.

*Maybe the great King Ankhamnon would give me the Olfiva Estate – the considerable property in Akhom*, he thought as he walked past the corridors with great pomp and pride.

Kontar entered the throne room, filled with incense, and Ankhamon was right in front of him on the throne.

Kontar knelt and lifted both of his hands, which held the precious sphere that Ankhamon so badly wanted. He was sure that Ankhamon would be happy.

"Stand up, boy!" Ankhamaon commanded sharply. He stepped down and walked towards Kontar.

Kontar stood up and looked at Ankhamon, and what came next was totally unexpected.

The room started spinning in front of his eyes as the king gave him a slap.

Kontar fell on the floor, and the sphere rolled over the red carpet.

Completely stunned by his master's action, he quickly assembled himself and picked up the sphere.

"Master, what did I do wrong?" he asked softly.

"Ukha (Idiot), Hati (timid)" said Shiphrah in Lyrian as she appeared from side.

"You let the human go?" Ankhamon demanded, utterly shocked at his soldier's stupidity and foolishness.

"Master, I thought you were interested in this sphere only," Kontar said, his eyes falling to the ground in immense shame and regret.

"Yes, I am. But we could crucify the human publicly in the obelisk square to show to the entire Lyra how we are saving the planet. This could have been a big public display – the crucifixion of a human!" Ankhamon yelled and felt a profoundly intense desire, which he resisted with extreme difficulty, to shoot Kontar with the soldier's laser gun.

"Nefertiti could have given us the location of Ehsis,"

Shiphrah said, adding fuel to the fire.

"What? You let a rebel girl go!" Ankhamon roared like a lion in Kontar's face. "You brainless moronic piece of dog scum!"

Kontar's long brown hair was blown away by the disgusting breaths of Ankhamon. He knelt immediately and begged him for mercy: "Forgive me, Lord. My heart momentarily drifted from what was right, and I became merciful!" Ankhamon spat in his face and pushed him to the ground with a forceful kick.

"You are relieved from your duties, and you now are forbidden to talk to anyone about the sphere of the human. Get lost from here – asshole!"

Kontar was devastated by his king's words. Suddenly, Shiphrah came forward, snatched the sphere from his hands, and grinned mischievously at his misery.

"Abaqer (Dog) scum!" she breathed in his ear. "Why are you weeping like a baby? You should be glad that the king only insulted you and kicked you out of here.

Knowing my father, he could have had you slaughtered for your obnoxiously ridiculous actions. Get the hell out of here before I make him change his mind!"

Kontar looked at everyone, his eyes puffy with a gush of tears forming across his eyes, and with a last glance at the place, he left the Tekhenu. Shiphrah handed over the sphere to her father and walked out.

"Stop Shiphrah!" Ankhamon said and looked at every soul who was present in the room.

"I do not want anyone of you to tell Hatathor about the sphere! This is not merely an order but a deadly warning! If anyone amongst you utters a single word to Hatathor about this object being in my hands, I will have you slaughtered and fed to the birds!" he threatened ominously, and the soldiers hung their heads in shame and didn't utter a single word.

Shiphrah looked confused at this announcement, but she waved it aside quickly and left the throne room.

# Chapter 13

# The Assassination

MOTHER Ahmose entered the throne room. She was looking straight at king Ankhamon. She bowed in respect and said: “My king, I need a moment of privacy with you.”

“Granted,” said Ankhamon, and the courtiers and brethren left the throne room. “I want to remind the King about the favor he owes me.”

“Say Ahmose, what is it that you want. You have everything now. Prestige, influence and wealth.”

“Yes, Master, I am thankful for your bounty on me.”

"So now what?"

"Master, you remember when Lyra was going in the cycle 546789, I saved your life. You were wounded and chased by Shamati beasts in the Tehuti Mountains. You entered my cave –my dwelling. I have protected you from beasts because your life energy was low. But I transferred my life energies into you, and that aged me. I gave you life to save you, as you have saved me earlier from the bounty hunters of planet Akkasia. They wanted to burn me, but I escaped and reached Lyra." "Yes, Ahmose, I am thankful to you!"

"Master, I want to remind you of the promise you made me that any time in life, I can ask you to pay me for that good deed of saving your life; you will not say no to it."

"Yes, Ahmose!"

"Master, I want the hand of your daughter for my son, Desher. I want to see Desher and Princess Shiphrah getting married on this auspicious day." "Ahmose, you took the words out of my mouth. I was thinking of asking you and Desher about it. But now, since you have placed the proposal, I am glad that you are thinking the same way. Consider it done."

"But master, Princess Shiphrah, I heard she inclines towards major general Hatathor."

"Ah. No, Ahmose. I'll not let it happen," said Ankhamon."Shiphrah is a bit childish sometimes. But I am sure she will be intelligent as maturity comes," he continued.

"Thank you, Master. I am pleased today!" Said

mother Ahmose and went out of the throne room with a smile. Ahmose switched on a transmitter and said: "Minkava, it's time!"

***

Hatathor was sitting in the same place, with his face covered by his hands. The hands were wrinkled, and as he removed the hands lo-and-behold! He was a wizened man, wrinkled and leathery from years of harsh weather, hard struggle, and deceptions on Lyra. The folds of his face were deep grooves worn into the skin like that of the Tehuti Mountains. His eye-sockets were sunken deep into his head. Lyra was rotating fast, and all the people on Lyra were aging quickly. Even the children turned into older men and women. The old were crumpled and turned into dust.

Hatathor woke up. He was covered in a cold sweat.

"What was that?"

He tried to understand what the dream meant, but could not find any answer. He had this feeling that he had been stranded somewhere in his dream – hauled by his vision. He should have never gone away from where he was born and raised –Lyra.

*I have two crucial missions that I need to accomplish, without which I can neither live peacefully nor die in peace. And I can do almost anything to complete those missions, even if I had to put my life at stake. My foremost mission is to find and kill Ehsis, as she is the person who always assisted murderous Hathor. Seeking revenge for my father's death is the first and most important mission of my life.* Hatathor thought firmly, cursing himself for wasting so much time on the bloody human when his primary target was Ehsis and her people. And only when I have accomplished the dreadful murder of Ehsis and her people, I can move on to the vermin Al-Khidr! I'll find and stop him, as I despise him the most for being a human and for arriving on my beloved home planet Lyra.

Hatathor had suddenly realized that he had been spending a primarily significant amount of time in searching for Al-Khidr, while he had much more pressing matters on his mind than the darned human; matters such as Ehsis. Most of his focus and the majority of his efforts should be placed in trying to locate her whereabouts. "That bloody witch of a woman, Ehsis!" he exclaimed, gritting his teeth and cracking his knuckles out of irresistible rage that had suddenly boiled up inside him. *That old scum sent me off to Keb to get rid of me. My revenge is not over yet. She killed my father. I will never let her escape to another planet; she will pay for what she did to my father and me. I will kill her personally and bury her deep in the Lyra. But for now, I guess I must see what Kontar is doing*, he thought, and began rushing into his spaceship.

He tried to contact Kontar but he didn't reply. Then Hatathor decided to go to General Desher's office.

Hatathor's ship landed in front of General Desher's office. While he was walking towards general's office when suddenly Hatathor had a feeling that he was being watched, but when he turned there wasn't anyone behind him.

"Ah, I must be having illusions," Hatathor said and continued on his way.

Oblivious to him was that Minkava was already inside his ship, and she placed the pyramidion device right under the control panel. She smiled while she sneakily went out of the spaceship. Meanwhile, Hatathor entered general Desher office and commanded the present council members to leave immediately. "Did you find the human?" Desher demanded loudly.

"I thought your loyal soldiers, as well as your head of internal security, Kontar, are looking for the human as well. I guess they gave up quickly." "Did you find the human or not?" Desher asked again. "No," Hatathor said blandly.

"Kontar is useless, as well as you, major!" Desher exclaimed.

"What!" Hatathor was blown away by his words. "I expected you would capture the human today!" Desher taunted him.

"Where were you when Kontar and others left you?" Desher continued to inquire.

"I I" Hatathor stammered; he was not sure what to say.

"Were you a major general, my dear friend?" Desher asked sarcastically.

"General!" Hatathor couldn't take any more.

Desher didn't let him finish his sentence, and he

roared: "You gave your task to Kontar, while you should have searched the human and the sphere by yourself," he instigated him.

"Yes, I'll find that piece of disgusting human scum!" Hatathor shouted.

Meanwhile, an officer entered the General's office.

"General!"

"Yes, Berisi?" Desher asked.

"General, the human, has been tracked in Sutekh," Berisi informed.

General Desher looked at Hatathor and said: "Go, capture that dirty animal. Hatathor, remember only you can save Lyra. Fulfill your unfinished task, brother," the cunning general continued.

"Very well then. I will catch that bloody human infestation." Hatathor proclaimed and left the office.

Desher moved towards the window to see Hatathor leaving in his spaceship. Desher let out a cold and incessant laugh as Hatathor's spaceship became smaller and smaller as he flew away. "Goodbye, Savior."

Suddenly Desher's phone started ringing. "General, we had captured the human but Kontar released him," one of the general's spy informed him. "What! So stupid of him!"

Desher quickly rushed to his spaceship, while ordering on phone. "Send me the signature of the spaceship carrying human," he shouted.

***

With his full determination to find and catch Al-

Khidr, Hatathor increased the spaceship speed. After a while, when he was descending, he noticed that the controls were not working. He tried to decrease the speed, but to his surprise, nothing happened. He pressed the speed reduction button several times, but the touch-pad was not responding. The ground was approaching fast, the speed was high, and the impact was imminent.

Hatathor tried to eject his seat, but it was also not working.

"This ship is a suicide trap," he shouted, banging his fist against the spaceship's wall.

He looked for the emergency parachute, but it was not there.

"Damn!"

Using his bident, Hatathor broke the spaceship's front screen. The aerodynamic buffeting impulses were deforming his face as he came out,clinging to the ship, looking for the right moment to jump.

The spaceship was 80 Supris above the ground. It struck an abandoned building and its lower portion caught fire as its tail started burning like a meteor. In that moment of desperation, Hatathor's eyes fell on an open field, and he jumped. Eventually, the spaceship collided with the ground and created a massive hole. A fiery mushroom cloud was formed as the ship erupted into intense flames. Hatathor had jumped in extreme horror, and the mighty warrior began plummeting towards the ground. He ordered his sleeve weapon to create an energy shield, and just before a possible fatal collision with the ground, a hemispherical energy shield formed around him. Hatathor received a tremendous impact that was harsh enough to make him unconscious.

When Hatathor opened his eyes, he couldn't move. He felt as if he was paralyzed. He attempted to lift his head slightly and discovered that his vision was blurred and he couldn't make out where he was. He wasn't even sure whether he was alive, and he felt as though his soul had already left his body. A few seconds later, his head fell back to the ground. He realized that he still needed some more time to completely recover from the impact he experienced because of the fall. After being in this state for an hour, Hatathor was finally able to turn his head and look around. Although the energy shield had saved him, it had created an enormous crater into the ground. Hatathor could only notice the walls of sand and mud around him as he lay in a deep hole.

The entire pit looked like an enormous crater. An intense smell of smoke had spread everywhere, as outside of crater somewhere nearby, the ship wreck was burning. Hatathor was limping and thinking about how to come out of the crater.

He took a few steps up the slope of the crater, but the ground crumbled under his feet and he fell back into the hole.

His body landed on a colossal mound that comprised dozens of Lyrian skeletons of men, women and children. Hatathor's heart began pounding terrifically inside his chest, as though a large boulder had been banging it continuously. He freaked out like a little girl and started screaming terribly. His screams were coming out from the depths of the pit and echoed across the Sutekh.

He was helplessly lying inside a massive grave.

*How come there are tons and tons of decaying bodies here?* He thought, in a moment of utterly pitiful desperation. It was baffling to see the most courageous warrior in the whole Lyra, whose incredibly muscular physique was sufficient to make his opponents pee in their pants, was writhing and screaming like a little girl. Am I in Sutekh? All these skeletons are of the people who had died by the Mutmut contagion?

Hatathor's mind started spinning uncontrollably, and before he had the chance to control his balance, he tripped and fell. In a gigantic state of panic and utmost chaos, he flailed his arms around like a manic, but wherever he touched, there was either a bone or a skull.

He began experiencing an intensely unbearable feeling of suffocation. He was completely trapped in Sutekh amongst endless bones and innumerable skulls inside an enormous grave. His body was shaking tremendously and he was sweating profusely from head to toe. He felt he would die of a heart attack if he stayed inside that grave any longer. He simply couldn't believe what he saw! A tremendous amount of anxiety and fear dwelled within, which was more than enough to traumatize him for a very long time.

The dust and ash hadn't settled yet when a small quantity of black ash fell on his hands and face. The scent coming from the ash was eerily similar to the smell of Lyrian corpses.

Instantly, he rubbed the black ash between his fingers.

"It is neither dust nor ash," he muttered quickly, like a mentally challenged person.

Hatathor's face was as pale as a sheet, as though the blood in his veins had dried. Some black powder had been falling on him. The world seemed to slip through his fingers like sand. His legs felt thoroughly numb and heavy, as though they hadn't moved in ages, while his eyes were dehydrated and had widened in terror. He felt highly feverish as his body temperature rose. Hatathor's body slowly began swinging uncontrollably, and with a final movement, he collapsed inside the pit amongst the bones and skulls and fell unconscious.

# Chapter 14

# The End to a Curse

THE Vega was rising across the gorgeous horizon and bringing with it a new day, a new possibility, and new hope for Nefertiti and Al-Khidr. Its glowing light emerged gradually from behind the dense clouds of all shapes and sizes. The yellowish glow of the rising Vega passed through the glass of the spaceship and illuminated the faces of Al-Khidr and Nefertiti, who closed their eyes and basked in its glory. Both had been flying the spacecraft for several hours. The intense emotions of worry, hope, a bit of despair, a little of guilt, and the past scenarios kept wavering inside their minds and deprived them of a good night's sleep. No matter how much they tried to empty their minds, other disturbing thoughts entered their minds. But now, when the mighty Vega wrapped its warm and dazzling light around their bodies, it touched their minds deeply and lightened their heavy hearts with its blossoming light. They felt as though the light had nourished their souls and freed their minds of all the negative thoughts and emotions. As a result, all their tiredness and sleeplessness had vanished like a wisp of smoke in thin air.

Al-Khidr and Nefertiti were communicating via writing on paper as they considered the possibility of Kontar bugging the spaceship and listening to their conversations. "We cannot go to Kneph directly," she scribbled quickly on a piece of parchment that they had got from the spaceship.

Al-Khidr nodded his head as he understood the possibility of them being followed by Kontar and his men. Al-Khidr was looking at Nefertiti with tons of affection. He grabbed her arm while she was scribbling another note for him to read and pulled her onto his lap. Nefertiti looked mildly surprised at this spontaneous gesture of romance and gave him a flirtatious look of annoyance. She attempted to resist him, but he held her waist tightly. They kept staring at each other for a few minutes, and then he brought Nefertiti's face towards him, and their lips encountered. Then, moving their lips apart, he took her in his arms and whispered into her ears, "I love thee truly, Nefertiti. You are my whole wide world and my everything. And I want you to know that in this war between good and evil, and life and death, if I ever get separated from you, or fall into the arms of death, then know that you will always be in my heart, and have always been the greatest joy of my life." His words struck Nefertiti's heart like an arrow, as her eyes filled with tears. The thought of separation from this human meant nothing but an excruciatingly painful life and, finally death to her.

Al-Khidr then moved aside and reached her right ear and whispered again slowly: "But if we survive this battle and get destined by the almighty lord's command to stay together, then this servant takes a solemn vow that as long as there is life within me, I will be with you in health and sickness, protect you, and let no harm of any degree fall on you. That harm would have to walk over my dead body before it reaches you. And then," he paused, moving a little down to kiss the side of her right cheek. "Only death can do us apart."

Those words had the most profound effect on Nefertiti, and her heart gushed with even more love and affection for him. She felt like the luckiest woman in the Lyra for having found this man from another planet, whose worth was immeasurable and could never even be matched by a billion diamonds present in the entire Universe. Can a world like that exist? Can we ever get out of his piled-up mess and attain that ever-lasting freedom that we so desperately desire? She thought deeply, her heart bursting with desperate hope and her eyes sparkling with a clear-cut image of the fantasy world she had just envisioned. Suddenly, her fantasy world burst like a tiny bubble, extinguishing all her hopes, and she was harshly thrown back to the present reality as her racing thoughts made her imagine the evils they needed to battle and defeat before they could even try to build a world like that.

The images of the viciously ruthless monsters Hatathor and King Ankhamon flew across her eyes, and all the positive energy she had experienced a few seconds back extinguished like the flame of a melted candle.

"Nefertiti, look!" Al-Khidr shouted suddenly, moving her slowly yet hurriedly away from his lap and moving his head forward to look at the emerging view that lay ahead. They were approaching the Kurrakom Mountains, and the usual sight of huge rocks and mountainous peaks appeared slowly, making Al-Khidr's heart race with utmost joy, bliss, as well as a mixture of relief and enthusiasm.

"I am so glad that we have finally reached this place," sighed Al-Khidr, gawking at the heavily rocky area that surrounded their spaceship. "I need some fresh air to stretch out my lungs, and this stupid spaceship has nearly made me feel suffocated."

"Umm Al-Khidr" Began Nefertiti gave him a nervous smile and using the digital tablet she scribble something lengthy. She handed the tablet to him, which read: The Kurrakom Mountains AREN'T precisely a place where you can get fresh air and stretch out your lungs.

"Hmm?"

"You will find out," she replied and gave him another nervous smile.

But before they could land the ship on the mountainside, they heard a thunderous boom from behind.

"What the hell is that?" exclaimed Al-Khidr.

Nefertiti immediately looked through the spaceship's digital periscope and froze in terror and shock as she noticed another spaceship was tailing them and was sending laser blasts to subdue them.

Before she could utter a word to Al-Khidr, a guttural voice boomed in the cockpit. "Nefertiti and the human. I, Anukson, commander of the southern squadron, order you to land your spaceship. Princess Shiphrah did not allow you to leave. Land on the mountain's peak and surrender yourself to us. Otherwise, I will crash your spaceship, and you will die a horrible death. You have two minutes to comply!"

Al-Khidr was stunned and the bubble of fury blew inside his head instantly. "A mis n tkahbacht (you son of bitch), those treacherous pieces of scums!" he yelled in his mother tongue, banging his fist against the dashboard. "I should have realized that they would do this treachery and have us followed!" Nefertiti moved towards the digital periscope and took control of the ship immediately.

"What are you doing!?" he demanded harshly, fearing that she might comply with Shiphrah's soldier and land the spaceship on the mountain peak. "Trying to thwart the plan of these rascals, what else?"

"Let's thrash this imbecile commander!" he declared, as adrenaline rushed through his blood and he got ready for a battle. Nefertiti turned the spaceship sideways and raced it as fast as she could.

"Damn it!" Anukson exclaimed through gritted teeth as his ship rushed away.

"Follow them!" shouted Anukson, and one of his men turned their spaceship in that direction and chased them. Since Anukson's spaceship was faster and more advanced, it approached Al-Khidr's within seconds.

Nefertiti began circling the spaceship out of desperation, making Al-Khidr's head spin horribly giving him extreme nausea. "Let's not do that again," he said slowly in a pale tone.

"I am sorry, honey," she apologized serenely and sped up the spaceship. "Their spaceship is way faster than ours; we need to do something," said Nefertiti, but before she could complete her sentence, another thunderous boom came echoing like a shockwave. "That's it now!" Nefertiti uttered frustrated, gripping the spaceship's joystick tighter than before and ready to do something unexpectedly dramatic. "Let's give these freaks a taste of their own medicine."

And before their opponent could send another shockwave, she pulled the spaceship's joystick up and flew it upward. Turning it around from above, she fired a massive barrage of laser shots towards them. Anukson's spaceship wobbled by the hits. Anukson banged his fist against a green button on the dashboard, and a magnetic shield enveloped Nefertiti and Al-Khidr's spaceship. Anukson fired, and laser shots but they missed Al-Khidr's ship.

Nefertiti had got the aim, but Anukson hit made her seat belt break. Nefertiti and Al-Khidr's spaceship got damaged, and it began falling on the Kurrokam Mountain at an angle of sixty degrees.

"Al-Khidr!" screamed Nefertiti as they were falling into the clutches of death when suddenly Nefertiti exclaimed to Al-Khidr: "Press the button; kill the goddamned bastards!" she yelled from the top of her voice. In a blink of an eye, Al-Khidr pressed the button. The laser shots he launched hit Anukson's spaceship, and there was a thunderous boom as the spaceship blasted into smithereens, leaving no sign of Shiphrah's men.

They landed their spaceship safely on one peak of the Kurrakom Mountain. "These Mountains had a considerable amount of tectonic activity on this side of the planet," informed Nefertiti to Al-Khidr.

Al-Khidr looked around. The area was full of black rocks formed after the lava cooled down. The air was heavy with the strong scent of a mixture of melted rock and sulfur. The stench was unbearable, and they could quickly feel its reek in their breaths, making them cough excessively despite covering their mouths with their hands. "Now I know what you were talking about!" exclaimed Al-Khidr, with a rough and painful cough that nearly burst his lungs. "Oh, I can't take it anymore. Can't we go somewhere else?"

"Not yet; we have to stay here for a while till we alert someone from the Kneph about the sphere's status," she coughed harshly, and her eyes began watering. "Do something, Nefertiti," he pleaded, unable to inhale any more of the fumes. An idea flashed into Nefertiti's head at that point, and she tore a substantially large piece of her clothing and tore it further into two. She handed one bit to him and wrapped the other tightly around her nose and mouth. That piece of Lyra's clothing was enough to filter through the air. They breathed a sigh of relief.

They noticed a distant river of lava right in front of them, continuously breaking up and reforming into new shapes. The ground beneath their feet was trembling intermittently with a periodic release of intensely unpleasant gases into the atmosphere. Now that they were outside the spaceship, they assumed no one could listen to them, and so they blabbered everything that came into their heads.

Nefertiti placed her hands in her wet silky hair, removed a small hairpin, which contained a hidden transmitter. She used that tiny device to send encrypted signals to Kneph, trying to get in contact. The Kneph responded in less than a second when she uttered the shibboleth and the secret codes, sharing their exact location. They were standing on the rocks and looking at horizon that they noticed some fast-approaching spaceships that looked like flying scarabs. "Damn, Lyra forces are coming," Nefertiti said in a gloomy tone.

"Kontar deceived us?" asked Al-Khidr.

"Kontar holds the government office, but Lyra forces

are more ruthless and advanced. We need to get the hell out of here, but how" she shouted. The Kingdom forces black spaceships that looked like scarab were approaching fast, firing pulses on their way. The pulses made a wheezing sound making Nefertiti and Al-Khidr drop on the floor holding their heads.

Nefertiti was saying something, but Al-Khidr couldn't hear. The wheezing sound from their ears continued, and the spaceship's control was overridden and jammed. Nefertiti and Al-Khidr recovered from the agonizing sound, but their hearing had been slightly affected for a while. Nefertiti and Al-Khidr ran towards the control and found that the screen was blinking with a message: "Kingdom Force Override."

Nefertiti shouted: "We have lost control." The spaceship started descending vertically, and the kingdom force spaceships encircled it.

Nefertiti and Al-Khidr were both looking at each other nervously.

After a while, the door was also overridden by the Force's device, and they heard beeping and clicking sounds. "For the sake of your safety, both of you come out of the spaceship without weapons, with your hands over your head. Repeat: no weapons. This is an order from Kingdom Space Force."

Al-Khidr looked at Nefertiti and said with a gloomy face: "I'll never allow them to take you away." The Forces moved and took their positions around the spaceship. The latch at the back of the ship started opening, and they could see the Kingdom forces in black uniforms: they were seven fully armored alien men there.

Nefertiti and Al-Khidr started moving towards the latch as they had no other option left. As soon as they appeared on the latch, four soldiers moved and shouted: "On to your knees!"

Nefertiti and Al-Khidr knelt, and the soldiers cuffed them. They pulled up both of them and started pushing them towards their ships. Nefertiti was shocked. Right in front of her was General Desher. "Running away ah!"

"Desher son of a witch," Nefertiti shouted and tried to spit on his face, but a soldier pulled her back by her hair. Some spit drops fell on the face of General Desher. He rubbed his hand over his face and laughed: "Love makes people crazy, and here a Lyrian girl mad for an alien- a cursed Kebian!" Desher moved forward to slap the already forced-knelt Nefertiti. "Hold your hands!" growled Al-Khidr.

Desher said: "King and Mother will be pleased to see my hunting today."

He moved forward and pulled Al-Khidr by his hair and pushed him towards his ship. Al-Khidr turned and looked at Nefertiti.

"I am taking the alien for autopsy. Put the girl in the cage. She will be interrogated," Desher said and started moving proudly towards his spaceship while pulling handcuffed Al-Khidr with his hair.

"Let us go," Nefertiti shouted.

"Whole Akhom will watch what I will do with him," Desher said and went into his ship. The ship latched closed while Nefertiti was shouting with tearful eyes. Desher spaceship lifted vertically, and it vanished within a fraction of sight.

Nefertiti dropped to her knees.

"I am sorry" she said crying.

A soldier pulled her up and forced her to move towards one of the kingdom's spaceships. Suddenly, three soldiers fell to the ground, shot dead by a laser. Immediately, the rest of the soldiers were alerted.

"Take cover," one soldier shouted.

Nefertiti knelt and in a swift move, she kicked the only soldier near her putting him to the ground. She kicked his laser gun and the gun went into the rocks. Then she ran and got the chance to hide behind one of the parked spaceships.

The other soldiers took their positions and started firing in the direction they thought the laser shots came from. One by one, the soldiers were dropping dead. When everyone was dead, Nefertiti came out with a gloomy face.

"Hey guys, we were so damn worried about you! Where are you now?" Semed exclaimed, moving towards her.

"Why are you so late?" she shouted.

"Hey, calm down. We had reached Kurrakom Mountains, but we were not sure who sent the coordinates, so we slowed down the speed," Rostau explained in a hurry. "You did damn right!" Nefertiti shouted back while crying.

Rostau moved and hugged her.

"General Desher took him!"

"Who?" Semed asked. "Where is Al-Khidr?" Semed asked further.

"General Desher that rascal, what did he do?"

"He took Al-Khidr."

***

Kahotep came out of the Tekhenu into the dense night, which was supposed to be a special one, as Master Ankhamon had declared the night as the night of endless joy, great pomp, and world-class celebration. The brethren were drinking heavily.

Kahotep felt like he got too much to do, so the first thing he did was look out for Kontar. It had only been a few hours since he was made the Head of Security, and so he needed some tips and suggestions from Kontar on how to manage the unpredictably cruel wrath of Master Ankhamon.

He searched for him far and wide but with no luck. Kahotep was slowly losing hope, and a gloomy feeling of helplessness developed inside him. Where in Lyra did he disappear? Did he leave the place or something? Or... did he commit suicide? These fearful thoughts kept troubling him as he walked with his head bent low. He was just about to enter the Tekhenu when Lady Luck smiled upon him gracefully, and there he noticed Kontar sitting alone outside the Tekhenu in a low corner. He was heavily drunk and in a pathetically depressed state.

Kontar was in a state of complete devastation and his mind was racing with the most suicidal thoughts as he grabbed his large bottle of beer and gulped it down in one sip as if it were water.

Master Ankhamon is a monster and a venomously unpredictable snake in the shape of a human, Kontar thought bitterly, along with a mixture of disappointment and jealousy for appointing Kahotep as the Head of Security and making Kahotep's new and higher position way more responsible and challenging than the previous one. He was unhappy with the promotion and felt like murdering Kahotep and his ex-master, Ankhamon. He is a ruthless and an utterly merciless old fart! Kontar thought again as he imagined grabbing his master by the neck and strangling him to death.

Kahotep approached him with a calm mind and a mixture of happiness and relief. But before he could request any advice or suggestion from the ex-soldier of King Ankhamon, he received only a series of hatred and misunderstandings.

"So full of glee you must've been, eh, Kahotep," Kontar said. "After all, you became the Head of Security, King Ankhamon's favorite! Have you come here to gloat and mock me about my misfortune?"

"Listen, Kontar," began Kahotep, placing his hands on his shoulder and trying to comfort him, but he moved his arm away. "I am not very glad about becoming the head of security either, man. That rank has been forced on me by Master Ankhamon."

"You bloody liar! You piece of shit!" he swore at him relentlessly, pushing him aside. "You are one lucky bastard. I did so much for that king, I could have even given up my life for that ungrateful vermin, and I got that damned sphere for him as well, to shove it down his throat! But no! He kicked me out because of one goddamn mistake. And look at the irony, you scoundrel, I got kicked out because of showing mercy to an unarmed man and a woman!" he exclaimed bitterly and flung the bottle of beer towards Kahotep, who had to swerve aside to avoid it. It fell with a clash on the ground and shattered into a million pieces. "Are you bloody out of your mind, you ass?" Kahotep yelled at him, utterly shocked at his behavior. "I guess Ankhamon was right in throwing you out, and you are a brainless piece of shit who has no sense at all!"

Kontar rushed towards Kahotep and grabbed his collar. "You dare not speak to me like that, you son of a bitch! You are not worthy of being called a soldier or protector."

Kahotep freed himself from the grip and pushed Kontar back with substantial force, making him stumble back onto the ground. The exceedingly drunk Kontar got back to his feet. Immense fury and resentment were rising within Kahotep at the words that had come out of Kontar's drunken mouth. Despite knowing about his heavily intoxicated state, he felt an extreme surge of fury and hate towards him. He somehow resisted an erupting urge to throw Kontar on the ground and give him a merciless thrashing. He kept his brimming anger under control and stayed calm. The man is heavily drunk and can't seem to think straight, he told himself as Kontar went about with his rants and abuses.

"You sick bastard," Kontar swore as he swayed uncontrollably. "The Brethren have lost their morality completely; they are nothing but a worthlessly ruthless pile of bat droppings now. The brethren were the people who had left Misraim City because of the government's plan to place the innocent, diseased people into isolation." he paused, swearing harshly and uncontrollably in his pathetic drunken state. Kontar's eyes were puffy and filled with intense dark circles like he hadn't slept for various nights, and his mouth smelt pungently of the cheap beer that he had excessively consumed.

He wiped his bitter mouth with the back of his sleeves and continued: "The people in Sutekh were the ones who had died of the deadly disease while the shameless and guiltless brethren vermin migrated to the north, giving no damn about those poor people who were dying. The brethren possessed a strong conscience and empathy for people's lives and cared about the pain of others, and possessed a strong moral ground. Still, the bullshit government was pragmatic, as it possessed no cure for that bloody disease. But now, the brethren have lost their courageous leader, who was the symbol of truth and justice and valor. While this piece of a shit king by the name of Ankhamon," he made a dirty face and spat on the ground in utmost disgust as he said his name, "is not interested in saving the lives of people! That cowardly ass did all that to escape from Lyra. If I had sniffed even a tinge of awareness about his despicable intentions behind obtaining the sphere, I would have never handed it over to him. He is not worthy of being called a king. He is just an ungrateful and power-crazy moron who continuously feasted on the resources of this great planet. When the Lyra needs him, he to abscond this planet and leave its inhabitants to die," Kontar lamented depressingly and clapped his hands out of mockery.

Kahotep listened to the unending rant of his ex-senior officer patiently and hung his head down in shame. The words coming out of Kontar's drunken mouth smelled of nothing but the truth. He was right about the brethren losing their empathy and morality, as well as King Ankhamon, who was turning out to be a brutally ruthless tyrant who cared about nothing but himself.

"Kontar," he began creeping towards him and not daring to put his arm around him anymore. "I feel you brother, I completely understand your situation and admire your exceptional courage, loyalty, and bravery. But I am not here to mock you or taunt you. I came here purely for the sake of asking your advice on how to bear this bloody vicious king that I so, unfortunately, being forced to serve and bear my allegiance to."

Kontar looked at him amused in his drunken state,

as though he was a person who had escaped from a mental asylum. He then laughed uncontrollably and swayed back and forth.

"You think there is any miraculous tip or advice that I can give you which will ultimately make it easier for you to stand in the same room with that bastard who calls himself king!?" Kontar spat on the ground. "There is no way that will allow you to bear that scoundrel's bullshit except for standing like a statue expressionlessly and do EXACTLY what he orders," he claimed while pretending to be a statue to make Kahotep understand.

Kahotep looked at him serenely, and he couldn't do much to help or be of any guidance in his drunken state. Feeling quite bad for the ex-soldier, he gave him a smile of sympathy and uttered nothing further, and he left the drunken man to continue dwelling on his sad state.

# Chapter 15

# The Shocking News

GENERAL Desher's spaceship landed in front of Tekhenu. He came out and went straight into the throne room. He was moving Al-Khidr by pulling his hair as he proudly walked into the building.

The royal guards were surprised to see him.

Al-Khidr's hands were handcuffed behind his back. Desher entered the throne room abruptly. All eyes went towards the door, and as soon as he entered in full force, he threw Al-Khidr on the floor.

"Bloody alien is here!" he shouted.

King Ankhamon and all his courtiers were surprised.

"I captured him before anyone else!" proudly claimed Desher.

Ankhamon jolted out of his throne. He was standing and clapping as saliva and blood were dripping from Al-Khidr face on the royal carpet.

Al-Khidr stood up and looked at Ankhamon and the rest of all his courtiers, including General Desher and mother Ahmose. He addressed Ankhamon: "Oh King, I am a human from planet Earth. I came to your planet accidentally without my will. I saw your people struggling with the disease, so I wanted to help you find the cure for Mutmut back on my planet. You know your planet does not have the plants that contain the right elements needed for a cure. The only reason your people are here on this diseased-ridden planet is the fuel, Amris. I came back just to fulfill the promise I gave to Queen Hathor. Being King, do justice and let me go as I bring no harm to you."

"Silence, human!" shouted Ankhamon.

There was utter silence in the hall. Ankhamon continued: "It was your planet that has created havoc in our lives. Our society fractionalized, and we lost thousands of our loved ones and relatives. It was we who suffered and left our cities and decided to live in the mountains. It was our former queen's utter stupidity that she had conceived this threat-posed plan, and she wished that you be sent back to Earth. Luckily, she is no more here on Lyra. The Great Lyra did its catharsis and punished those who had adulterated its soil with the blood of innocents. It spilled over only because of you – alien. Because of you, the mutiny erupted here, and many more had died. How do you believe that I being King here would go against the wishes of my people? Nay, alien, nay. Suffer for what you have caused here," Ankhamon said in a stern tone. "I am your friend, Lyrians, not an enemy," Al-Khidr repeated.

"You said you will bring the cure. Where is the cure, alien?" Ankhamon growled. "You came back with the sphere!" Ankhamon showed the jump-sphere to Al-Khidr. Al-Khidr shivered to see that Ankhamon has the sphere – the very same sphere which had the leaves of Boraqis inside it.

If I tell them now that Earth-based plant leaves are inside, they would open the sphere and destroy them. Better not say anything, Al-Khidr decided and kept quiet. "You arrived empty-handed in a broken pyramid and created more garbage for us to clean," General Desher said in a sarcastic tone.

"You came here because of the quality of life. Your planet has nothing. Even its climate is so fragile – a little high radiation from the nearest star could melt all the ice you have on your planet, and your kind will be inundated," a courtier of Ankhamon added, and the rest of Lyrians started laughing.

"And yet we survived and prevailed not only in population but also we have cures of all kinds," Al-Khidr taunted back.

Suddenly, Mother Ahmose started laughing incessantly. Everyone turned their gaze to her, including Al-Khidr.

She raised her hand and pointed towards the human with her index finger, then she said in an electric voice, her spirits supposedly using her as a medium: "Curse on Lyra can be removed by killing this Kebian – Do this publicly."

All eyes moved from Ahmose to Al-Khidr.

"In the name of eternal Lord, I curse you, witch! You will die an agonizing death," Al-Khidr said.

Desher wanted to punch the human, but the voice of Ankhamon stopped him.

"Shut up, alien. No more words from your cursed tongue! – take him away!" shouted Ankhamon.

***

Ankhamon had the jump-sphere in his hands and was playing with it. He was sitting on his throne in Tekhenu, and was looking at the sphere with a sort of vicious glint in his eyes.

At last, the object that I desired so desperately is finally in my clutches. I just cannot believe my eyes that the jump-sphere is finally mine! No one can stop me now! He thought, with a purely wicked smile on his face, which was glowing in a terrifying triumph.

I am sick and tired of being the king of a pathetic species of dying aliens. I am so damn desperate to visit my beloved mother's planet, Mervia which is twenty light-years away and this jump-sphere is the key to me traveling back home. He thought as an evil glint shone across his eyes.

There was no one in the room, Kahotep entered and announced: "Master Ankhamon, a spaceship has just crashed into Sutekh, and it has burst into flames. I have stopped all surveillance and rescue attempts and informed everyone that no one was on board, as you advised."

"Well done, Kahotep. You are quite a good listener, and Kontar has to learn a lot from you," Ankhamon said with pleasure, a wicked smirk forming across his face as he jolted out of his throne.

"Master, I am only doing as you told me," Kahotep said to Ankhamon.

Today, Ankhamon was experiencing a considerable feeling of inner peace and joy, which was far greater than any happiness he had ever felt before, including the one when he had become the king. Hathor was dead, and Ehsis had probably ended up in some distant galaxy by now.

"I can glorify the heroism of Hatathor in every speech. How he died to save us," he said to himself with a crude sense of sarcasm and burst into laughter. He was profoundly pondering on the contents of his speech while merrily listening to Lyrian music and dancing gracefully with immense jubilation. Ankhamon looked at Kahotep with mild astonishment and asked: "Why are you not dancing, Kahotep?"

Kahotep smiled awkwardly while staring at the ground with humility.

"Dance Kahotep, Dance! I am on top of the Lyra today!" Ankhamon announced, swaying delightfully from side to side.

Kahotep was a bald and bulky man with huge muscles and a towering height of nearly seven feet. He was junior to Kontar in both age and rank; however, he had been promoted to Head of Security just a few hours earlier.

"You know Kahotep," Ankhamon began, continuing to sway his body gracefully across the floor. "My mum came from a planet Mervia. She gave birth to me here, and I became obsessed with this planet and its people. And since my childhood, I have had only one ambitious dream of becoming the king of Lyra and reaching the heights of power and control," he paused, increasing the speed of his dance moves. He then continued, "And I succeeded. I became the almighty great king of Lyra and I now possess everything I had ever desired, be it power, the valuable treasures of this planet, or control of every species that lives here. But now, I am fed up with it, Kahotep. With the jumpsphere I would like to travel across the Universe. Lyra seems more like a burdening responsibility than pleasure now," his voice turned slightly grumpy, although he continued to dance.

"Since we do not have a team that is competent or clever enough to, leave alone eradicate, but at least to control the spread of the brutal disease, it is simply not in my hands to handle this deteriorating situation any longer. So, even in my worst nightmare, I do not wish to be the king of a species that is, unfortunately, on the verge of extinction. And since there is no cure for the disease yet, I will do exactly what my dear, annoying friend Hatathor did. First, I will simply seal every city of this doomed planet and let the pathetic people of this dead planet gradually meet their painfully gruesome deaths, and then use this precious jump-sphere of mine to move away to my lovely mother's rich planet, Mervia," he began laughing like a maniac, while still swaying stupidly across the room.

Kahotep gritted his teeth, while resisting a nearly uncontrollable urge to punch Ankhamon. Immense rage and hatred were boiling within Kahotep with every despicably poisonous word that his Master uttered.

"Kahotep!" Ankhamon called so loudly that Kahotep's eardrums nearly burst as he slightly flinched.

"Yes, Master!" Kahotep chanted mechanically, shaking his head subtly and coming out of his violent imagination.

"Do something for me," Ankhamon said while being in the middle of his irritatingly disgraceful dance.

"Sure, Master. Your wish is my command. Please tell me what is to be done," Kahotep recited coldly, with a reluctant mechanical bow.

"Some scientists who worked for Ehsis are in the dungeon. Few of them died while being tortured, but we have a few more still alive. I want you to take them tomorrow to Hept Sehetch Sheta and provide them with an ultimatum that I want the facility running in a month. They have to learn all the functionalities and get everything ready for me. I wish to travel the Universe," he commanded haughtily in a musical tone.

"Sure, my Lord," Kahotep said sheepishly.

"But be warned, my dear Kahotep, it has to be kept highly confidential. If I hear anything about it from someone else, I will have your bloody tongue-tied to the flag over this building, peel your tough skin off, and use it as a carpet! And anyway, carpets of outstanding quality are quite to be found these days," Ankhamon threatened in a sarcastic tone, gazing deeply into Kahotep's light brown eyes without blinking.

"Yes, my Lord. Be assured that I will strictly follow your order and would rather kill myself than disappoint you," he stated firmly while looking at the ground. "Good, my boy. And yeah, if anyone raises an inquiry, then say that I am making the facility functional to make brethren travel anywhere they wish to go in the skies," Ankhamon said, halting his maniac dance moves and sitting down on his throne.

The Head of Security nodded in agreement, and with a final automatic bow, he left the room.

***

"Madam Secretary," called an officer, looking extremely worried and in a hurry. "We have intercepted the conversation between the brethren's top officials, and it looks like something fishy is going on at Tekhenu."

"What is it?" Ehsis demanded with a mixture of

curiosity and exasperation. “Play the conversation immediately.”

The officers began playing the conversation, and everyone, including the other officers, started listening.

“... (buzz) (Voice 1) .... Commander Kahotep has ordered that the HSS facility be made functional. Some of the equipment was damaged during the freedom struggle....

(Voice 2 replied:) Copy - where are the workers coming from? Are these the people from the Space Exploration Unit (SEU)?

(Voice 1) Around seventeen staff members are coming from SEU, and the rest are the scientists we had imprisoned. Those scientists used to work for Hathor. We will shift them tomorrow morning...... (Noise in transmission)

(Voice 2) (copy) (Noise in transmission)....

(Voice 1) Bear in mind, the task is top secret, and Master Ankhamon expects to see results within days....

(Voice 2) (co... p... y) (Noise in transmission) ....

(Voice 1) You should reach there by tomorrow at 11.12.23.28 degrees clock time.

(Voice 2) (co... p.... y) (Noise in transmission) ....

— transmission ended —

“I will not let this happen!” Ehsis affirmed loudly with firm determination.

"But madam secretary, why is Ankhamon suddenly showing so much interest in the HSS?" an officer asked earnestly.

"Ankhamon is a very cunning and secretive person, officer. He does not reveal his plans easily," Ehsis said serenely, staring into thin air in intense contemplation. "But whatever he is doing, there has to be an ulterior motive behind it," she added confidently.

"We need to dispatch a team and see closely what are they are doing on HSS," an officer said.

"Yes, we need to infiltrate the Tekhenu and stop Ankhamon in his plan," Ehsis agreed quickly.

***

Nefertiti, Rostau, and Semed entered the Cove with sad looks on their faces. They seemed anxious, and they noticed Ehsis appeared quite disturbed, too.

Their eyes narrated the sad tale of their defeat, and their shoulders had drooped with the weight of it. They were defeated.

Ehsis stood up and gazed at them emotionally; her eyes were brimming with exasperation and anxiety at the depressing look on their faces.

Nefertiti burst into tears and rushed towards Ehsis, and she hugged her.

"We have lost, Guardian Ehsis. We have been defeated!" Nefertiti wept bitterly, unable to control her overflowing emotions.

"What happened?" Ehsis inquired in a threatening tone.

"Ankhamon's men took the sphere from Al-Khidr and Nefertiti," Rostau broke it to her dejectedly while staring at the ground.

"They wanted to take Nefertiti to Tekhenu, but Al-Khidr made the deal that they take the sphere instead of her," Semed said.

Ehsis placed Nefertiti at an arm's length and looked into her eyes, and she smiled at her.

"My dear girl, you don't have to feel like a defeated person. You are way more precious than a hundred such spheres. We will get the sphere back!" she consoled her, but Nefertiti was still crying.

"What happened?" Ehsis said with a puzzled face.

"General Desher took Al-Khidr," Nefertiti informed.

"What!... Oh, no," Ehsis said and then turning towards Rostau, she said: "We must save Al-Khidr! Ankhamon will try to do something bad."

Ehsis sat in the chair holding her head, thinking deeply.

"We have intercepted a transmission. Ankhamon has ordered his man to make HSS functional. Now it all makes sense to me. Ankhamon wanted to use the jump-sphere, I believe. We need to plan a surprise attack." Ehsis asserted firmly as she continued to eye the men. "They are just not very skilled and cannot use the facility in the right manner, which will end up creating more problems. These incompetent cultists could even make the equipment malfunction," she said in a worried tone.

"We have to stop Ankhamon!" Ehsis said.

"It's not that simple," Rostau replied.

"Ankhamon's force has the most advanced and state-of-the-art technology and weapons. Besides that, their soldiers outnumber us hundred to one." "But we have to take action, Rostau! We can't watch our beautiful kingdom wither like this!" Nefertiti exclaimed, rising from her chair. "Madam Secretary, you have intercepted the brethren officials' conversations, haven't you? Then we can...," she was cut in sharply by Semed. "We still cannot attack Misraim so suddenly, Nefertiti. We need a solid plan of attack and more forces..." he interrupted Nefertiti. "Our forces are competently trained in combat, but we cannot sustain long," Semed said.

"Yes, we have been trained efficiently, but what I am saying is we need some time to plan out things," Rostau cut him in immediately and responded to his suggestion with a horrible snap.

"There is no time to plan out things! Ankhamon has the jump-sphere, and if we wait any longer to take action, he can misuse the jump-sphere!" "We do not know what they'll do with Al-Khidr. But it would not be good," Nefertiti said.

Nefertiti, Rostau, and Semed were unaware of Ankhamon's true intentions behind his desire to possess the jump-sphere. And they merely had a strong gut feeling that he was indeed up to no good.

***

Ehsis was seated in the Cove while her officers were

trying to establish a secure and encrypted communication channel. A mixture of hope and desperation was visible on her wrinkled face.

"This is our only hope to stop Ankhamon," she thought hurriedly as one of her officers attempted to form a communication link with the planet Arpat. "Madam Secretary, if you don't mind, may I ask, why are we trying to form a link with this far away planet, Arpat?" her officer inquired inquisitively.

"Iniharut is the King of the planet Arpat which is a planet in Vega system. A long time ago, Queen Hathor had helped Iniharut's father, Remi, in a time of need when I was the Secretary of State. We had a good camaraderie with them, and we had a joint defense pact that we supported each other in case our kingdoms were attacked. King Iniharut by now must have known that the queen has been murdered and another person rules the Kingdom of Akhom, but he doe not know that I was in hiding. The situation has changed now. Ankhamon has the jump-sphere, and he must be stopped. Therefore, I want Iniharut to help us in the battle against Ankhamon's army, which outnumbers ours," she explained calmly.

The mesmerized officer continued to try to create the communications link with Arpat, but failed miserably. And he slammed the panel slowly out of frustration. "Why is this goddam panel not forming a communication link?!" he exclaimed with annoyance.

"Madam Secretary," he began in a bleak voice. "The link is not getting through."

"Why? What is the issue?" she demanded exasperated.

"I am sorry, ma'am, but I do not know. Our connection is powerful. Perhaps there is some network issue on that planet."

"Damn!" she cursed loudly. Then the sad Ehsis hung her head down, covered her face with her wrinkled palms, and started slowly weeping.

The officer could find any words to console her, and he left the chamber with a disappointed expression on his face.

Our last hope has been extinguished, Ehsis' thought as a flood of tears flowed across her creased cheek that displayed her veins. "We have been defeated! All's lost!" she started wailing loudly and placed her head on the control panel while continuing to weep profusely.

Abruptly, the voice in her head shouted her name and said: Ehsis. . . get up Ehsis. . . you cannot lose your willpower and despair so pathetically. You are their leader.If you give up now, what will happen to those billions of Lyrians battling that deadly disease Mutmut? Get up now, Ehsis. . . Get up!

And gradually, she raised her head and slowly rose to her feet, and she wiped the tears off her face that seemed to sparkle on her pale face in the light. "Doesn't matter if I cannot communicate with them. I will send someone to Arpat to contact King Iniharut and bring him here directly!" Affirming that confidently, she walked out of the communication chamber—still holding on to hope.

***

Nefertiti was moving towards the cafeteria. Suddenly, a group of three heavily built men approached her from the opposite direction stopping her and glaring at her. “Well, well, well,” exclaimed the tallest one who sported a waist-length ponytail. “I heard the human traitor has given up the jump-sphere to our enemies!” The Lyrian bullies criticized Al-Khidr. Nefertiti remained calm, and she felt no need to explain anything to them. The beefy Lyrians continued to block her path and kept asking more questions about humans.

“Hey you!” shouted Rostau and Semed simultaneously, as they arrived on the scene. “What do you think you are doing?!” they demanded from the men, who were mocking and taunting.

“We cannot stand that cowardly traitor human at Kneph!” one of them exclaimed as he talked about Al-Khidr disgusted. “Watch your tongue, Gustavo!” warned Semed, pointing his finger at the heavily built man.

“You do not know about what happened over there, and under what circumstances did our friend, Al-Khidr, let go of the jump-sphere,” stated Rostau while staring at the man named Gustavo with a warning on his face.

“Oh, as if you were there to confirm that this filthy human didn’t simply betray us and present the sphere to our enemies," he jeered loudly, which rose the blood to Rostau's head.

"You say one more word against our friend here. . . "

"And what?" Gustavo demanded, flexing his muscles and getting ready for a physical fight.

"I will show you what a true Lyrian soldier does to protect the honor of his friends," Rostau finished, and Semed nodded in firm agreement.

Rostau and Semed were just getting ready to fight with the brawny soldiers when suddenly a voice sounded behind them.

"What in the Lyra is happening here!?"

Ehsis stood at the hallway entrance and glared at her people in repulsion. The guy named Gustavo immediately got alarmed and let go of his anger. Ehsis had heard the entire conversation and glared at the beefy men with disdain. She advanced towards him and demanded: "What happened? What were these guys telling you?" She asked, pretending that she had heard nothing

But before he could open his mouth to answer, Rostau and Semed burst into speech.

"Madam Secretary, these guys blocked Nefertiti's way and taunted her. Gustavo said that Al-Khidr is a traitor for handing over the jump-sphere to our enemies. We were trying to convey the truth to them," he stated with a sly smile on his nervous face.

Ehsis moved her eyes first toward the muscular Lyrian, then towards the others.

"Shame on you!" she yelled, eyeing them distastefully. "Without knowing the whole truth, you people placed such a despicable tag on a noble and brave man like Al-Khidr! Do you have any idea under what circumstances he let off the sphere? He gave it away to save your fellow Lyrian, Nefertiti, from being killed!" The muscular men hung their heads in shame and remained silent, and Ehsis continued to glare at them repulsively.

"And as for you, young man," she addressed sharply the guy with the ponytail named Gustavo, "I will deal with you later. I have much more pressing matters on my head than dealing with ridiculous rumors and issues," she proclaimed sharply and turned her head.

"Rostau!" she called, surveying him intensely. "I want you both in my office this instant!" She commanded loudly.

"Yes, Madam Secretary!" he chanted while standing in an attention position.

And with a last look of disappointment at the men, Ehsis marched out of the hallway while Rostau and Semed followed her obediently.

"Are you alright?" Ehsis asked Nefertiti anxiously.

"Yeah, I am fine," she said, feeling quite unnerved by their accusation.

She felt resentful at those men. Now the entire Kneph might think that Al-Khidr handed over the sphere to Ankhamon's men intentionally to betray us, she thought and sighed in disappointment.

Ehsis placed her comforting palm on her shoulder and consoled her silently with her tender gaze.

## CHAPTER 15. THE SHOCKING NEWS

***

Ehsis was back in the Cove along with Rostau and Semed.

"Madam Secretary, I have some good news for you!" one officer called excitedly. He had been working on forming the communications link with Arpat . . . "What is it?" she asked with mild exhilaration.

"The communications link with Arpat has been established successfully. However. . . " he paused, turning his head back towards the computer screen. The moment she heard the fantastic news, all her worries faded away, and her mouth curled into a gentle and relaxed smile that seemed to shadow her profound wrinkles. "However what?" she asked softly, in a tone of mere curiosity.

"The communication link is not very strong as the signals we can emit are weak, and it is mainly because the Kneph is quite a deep underground base."

"Hmm. . . "

Ehsis stared into space and contemplated deeply for a while. Then she jerked her head up and turned to Rostau.

"Rostau! I have an extremely crucial task for you, dear," she said calmly, as her anger seemed to have subsided the moment she heard the startling news from her office. "Yes, Madam Secretary," he chanted, standing in an attention position.

"Leave for this mission tonight!"

"Sure, madam secretary!" Rostau exclaimed firmly,

with his chest thrown open.

"But madam secretary, where do I have to go for the mission?"

Ehsis smiled earnestly, and with a casual wave of her hand, she displayed the holographic image of Lyra and expanded it to a substantial size such that area of space outside Lyra could be clearly seen.

"Rostau, you are going to go to the surface of Lyra and launch a mini satellite to establish a strong communication link with the planet Arpat," she announced. Then she turned towards her office.

"But Madam," Rostau began, looking quite doubtful at the idea. "I have an important question regarding this task." "Fire away, Rostau!" she exclaimed with exhilaration.

Rostau took a deep breath and finally asked the question.

"Um, first, if I send a satellite that flies a thousand Supris above the surface of the Lyra, won't the Brethren officials be alerted? They keep monitoring the sky constantly, don't they?"

***

Rostau marched quickly across the dense tunnel, his heartbeat racing with every step he made towards the surface. Ehsis had guided him to the exact point where he would have to launch the satellite using the quadcopter. Finally, he reached a metallic wall that appeared like a highly secured facility entrance. A computer panel was attached to the right side of the metallic wall with a small numerical keyboard. He typed the secret code that only the high-ranked officers of Ehsis knew. The moment he entered the secret code, a robotic voice called from the panel, asking for Rostau's voice identification. "Rostau," he stated after clearing his throat. The AI granted him access, and a tremendous swishing sound filled the area as the metallic wall slid aside like an elevator door. A massive boulder came into view as the metallic wall slid aside, which subsided with an ear-bursting noise. The moment the boulder lowered; a vast open space came into view.

The weather outside the Kneph was extremely windy and it was freezing, with no hope of Vega appearing soon. Ehsis had clearly instructed Rostau to walk at least two hundred Supris away from the Kneph before launching the satellite.

He moved as quickly as possible across the surface and, reaching two hundred Supris away, retrieved the quadcopter and satellite from the backpack he was carrying. Rostau pressed a series of buttons on the drone and attached the mini satellite onto its surface. Immediately, the drone that had the mini satellite soared through the air at its maximum speed.

The quadcopter had successfully launched the mini-satellite in space and was coming back to the surface as a hopeful yet nervous Rostau gazed across the cloudy sky. I hope this works, he thought desperately. The Brethren officials might have detected the drone by now.

Suddenly, the electromagnetic pulse detector in Rostau's hand started beeping constantly.

"Oh my God! The Brethren have been alerted of the drone's presence!" he said to himself anxiously, as the drone was floating back to him through the windy air. Rostau sweat with extreme fear in the chilly weather, and his body was trembling uncontrollably.

"Come on, come on, come on," he muttered like a magical chant as the drone was arriving back at him. Finally, the quadcopter was back in Rostau's hand, and he briskly placed all his electronic gadgets back inside the backpack. The moment all his devices were back in the case, the detector stopped beeping, and Rostau let out a deep sigh of relief.

"That was close!" he stated with immense relief, and hanging the backpack across his shoulder, he rushed back towards the entrance of the Kneph.

***

"Task accomplished!" announced Rostau as he rushed into the Cove with a triumphant smile on his face. Ehsis, seated worriedly with her fingers crossed, got up immediately as he entered. "You did it, Rostau!" she exclaimed with immense jubilation, along with the rest of the officers, who began applauding him cheerfully. Semed was also present in the Cove at that point gave him a tight hug and congratulated his best friend for the achievement.

"Great job, Rostau!" exclaimed Ehsis with a glowing smile across her wrinkled jaw.

"It was my pleasurable duty, Madam Secretary!" he expressed with a deep bow. "I am always ready to do anything for you and Lyra," he added sweetly with a charming smile.

Ehsis then turned towards one of her other officers and commanded softly:

"Send an encrypted distress signal to planet Arpat. I hope someone takes note of it."

The officer seated near the computer panel nodded obediently and started operating the innumerable series of buttons. A swishing sound like the fierce blowing of wind sounded across the air and the holographic image of the face of a middle-aged man wearing a golden crown on his head appeared out of thin air. Immediately, Ehsis gave a quick bow of respect, and her officers mimicked her gesture automatically.

"Greetings to the Great King Iniharut!" she chanted and smiled gracefully while her officers repeated the chant robotically. "Madam Ehsis!" nodded the King with a wide smile. "It's been a long time since we've met."

"Likewise, Great King!" she exclaimed.

"It's been so long since we've last communicated, too. Especially after Queen Hathor's death, I was completely disheartened by the tragic news," he expressed with a look of melancholy on his heavily bearded face as his hazel brown eyes surveyed everyone across the Cove. His aquiline nose and large forehead gave him a highly intimidating look.

"Yes, Great King, it was indeed a traumatic time

for the entire Lyra. Everyone was heartbroken by her death. So, how are you, Madam? And how is your ravishingly beguiling planet Lyra?" he asked with the utmost courtesy and a graceful smile on his sharp face, which displayed his sparkling white teeth. Ehsis' expression turned forlorn as she looked at the King with pain in her elderly eyes.

"Great King, Lyra has been compromised. There was a bloody rebellion led by some of our Generals who joined hands with the journalist Ankhamon," she narrated depressingly and hung her head down in gloom.

"What!" he exclaimed resentfully, and his intense look of outrage intimidated the officers tremendously. "How dare he commit such an outrageous act?! Why didn't you contact us for help back then?! We would have crushed the rebel and prevented this chaos from occurring in the first place!" Ehsis sighed gloomily and continued with her head hung down.

"Ankhamon has taken control of our lovely planet now and has become a king, or I should say, an evil dictator and ruthless tyrant who cares about nothing but himself." King Iniharut felt as though a bolt of lightning had struck him. His face turned red with immense fury and disgust. Somehow, he calmed himself and asked softly: "Madam Ehsis, where are you and your people right now?"

"We have been hiding at a secret location for the past year." King Iniharut noted that and asked politely.

"I understand. Oh, that is why we cannot discern

your exact location!" the realization hit him suddenly.

"Great King, we need your help! A dystopic man, Ankhamon, now rules our kingdom,"

"Of course, Madam Ehsis! Just let me know when I shall get my forces to Lyra. I promise we shall punish the traitor Hatathor and overthrow that vermin Ankhamon. Such acts of outrage shall be punished mercilessly!" he declared firmly.

Ehsis bowed again and continued, "The situation is getting out of hand, Great King. Ankhamon wants to use our old HSS facility, and only God knows what his viciously selfish plans are." There was a moment of silence between them, and then King Iniharut announced sharply.

"I will arrive with my forces to the Lyra as soon as possible. . . " Ehsis nodded relieved and gave a deep bow while the King returned the bow with a nod, and the holographic image vanished.

***

The Kingdom forces, mostly brethren officials, were seated lazily on their revolving chairs when they suddenly heard their motion detectors beeping. They got alerted immediately and jumped up to search for the source of the motion across the desert surface.

*What on Lyra could lurk across the surface?* they wondered. They operated their computer panels and emitted electromagnetic pulse signals to check out if any electronic gadgets were present in vicinity.

The Brethren officials were utterly perplexed as the electromagnetic pulses couldn't detect any any electronic gadget. "Holy Lord!" cried one officer who insanely operated the computer panel. "How is this possible?! The motion detectors had detected some activity in the air, and the EMP cannot detect it?"

"Calm down, man," yawned his fellow officer, who was seated nearby and looked like he was least bothered by the situation. "It must either be an error, or the device may be malfunctioning.

The other officer sent more electromagnetic pulse (EMP) waves across the air but in vain, as no electronic activity was detected. He scratched his head nervously and began pondering.

*I hope that the signal by the motion detectors was an error because if it was some foreign electronic gadget and we've missed it, King Ankhamon would have us skinned alive.*

"Guys, there is a communication satellite detected in the west of Misraim around thirty degrees in the east, at a distance of nine hundred and twenty-three point three four-point four-five Supris to be exact."

"What? Where?"

All the officers rushed towards his panel and looked at each other with apprehension.

One of them suggested: "I think we should immediately inform General Desher."

# Chapter 16

# The Bane

HATATHOR was inside the cavity. The sound of his breathing was like gravel for his ears; the sound of everything else was drowned in an infinite din.

He was looking up through the hole in the ground. The Vega lights were illuminating the nebulous inner core of the pit. He needed a jet-pack to get out of it. The crater roof was several hundred feet above him, and he feared it could collapse anytime. Fortunately, he had his transmitter with him, so he called General Desher, but it couldn't connect. Most likely

General Desher had his transmitter switched off. Then he called Kontar, but he, too, didn't pick up.

He felt like the horrible crash had sapped his energy.

*I can survive here, but the black ash is just too much,* he thought disgusted.

Lady Luck hadn't smiled on him, and his sleeve weapon's battery was dead. On top of that, the bident had been lost. To top it all, his transmitter's battery was draining quickly as well.

"I will not let this damned place be my grave!" he exclaimed firmly and looked for someone else to call. Luckily, he found Shiphrah's number, and he quickly dialed it.

She picked up on the other side and was delighted to hear Hatathor's voice.

"Hey, where have you been? I have been waiting for you," Shiphrah said in a tone of utmost exhilaration. It was one of the rare moments when Hatathor had got time for her.

"Babe, I need your help! I am trapped in a pit somewhere in Sutekh. I am sending you my location. Your father is not responding, and I called him several times," he yelled out quickly with anxiety.

Shiphrah realized that something was seriously wrong.

"Oh, are you fine, Hatathor? Where are you? I am coming to you as quickly as I can. Oh! It's getting dark!" she replied in a tone of immense anxiety. Shiphrah's transmitter beeped, and she received the location.

"Honey, do not worry, I am coming!" Shiphrah assured him.

Her mind was rushing like a bolt of lightning, filling her with anxiety and utmost apprehension at the thought of the man she loved dearly. "I will do whatever I can to help my love!" she declared firmly, ready to go.

As soon as she came out of Tekhenu, she saw a few brethren guys there. Shiphrah looked at the two sturdy guys and commanded them sharply: "You two, come with me. I need your help."

The men smiled and winked at each other, their minds brimming with fantasies as they followed her.

They sat in the spaceship, as she keyed in the coordinates of the pit.

After a while, they reached the spot of crash. The smoke was still rising from the hole which was now visible.

"You! What's your name?" Shiphrah asked one guy.

"Adjo," he replied with a smirk.

"And you?" Shiphrah asked the other.

"Anhur," he responded in a deep voice.

"I do not know how deep this pit is, but one of you will descend into it. Hatathor is stuck in there." She ordered while pointing at the deep pit. "Seka Hatathor?"

"Yes, idiot!" Shiphrah snapped irritatingly.

"Do it fast!" she yelled, gritting her teeth.

They were perplexed about the way to go inside

the pit. After pondering deeply on it, an idea flashed into Anhur's head.

"I will go inside it using the towing rope of the ship. I will connect it with my belt and descend," Anhur explained quickly, and along with Adjo, they rushed back to the ship.

The spaceship moved towards the crater and started hovering over it. Anhur buckled up, and Adjo connected the towing rope to him.

Anhur began descending into the pit. And the first thing he saw through the light of his torch was a spine-chilling scenario. There were creepy bones and skulls all around, and a dark powder was floating in the air. Anhur panicked horribly and relayed back to Shiphrah.

"Take me up. I cannot go down!" he screamed with immense trepidation. "It's a vast graveyard of Sutekh!"

Adjo heard his pleading and pulled him back up. Shiphrah looked at him with immense fury and hatred in her eyes.

*Cowardly piece of vermin!* she thought intensely as he landed back on the ground.

"You piece of cowardly shit! You are not fit to be called a Lyrian soldier!" she yelled at him mockingly, while he could only hang his head in shame. "Don't worry, Seka, I don't need any sissy to help you! I will do it myself!" saying that, Shiphrah ordered Anhur to take the pilot position, and tying the towing rope around her slim body, she started descending slowly into the pit. The eerie scenery of the pit made her blood-curdle, and her mind seemed to get numb by the suffocating dark powder that flowed across the pit.

*Oh my God! This looks like hell on Lyra,* she thought apprehensively as she descended into the pit.

Ultimately, she noticed Hatathor, who was lying amidst the mound of bones and skulls. He was sweating profusely and his body temperature was high, too. She lifted his head and tried to wake him up.

"Honey, please wake up!" she called anxiously, tapping his cheeks gently. But Hatathor was unconscious.

Shiphrah buckled him up with the belt and gestured Anuhur to pull them up. She was gazing at him with intense tenderness and worry in her eyes as they were being lifted. Soon, the lovers were finally inside the spaceship.

Shortly after they came out of the pit, the crater roof fell with an awful sound. Adjo and Anhur helped her making Hatathor sat on one seat. Anhur turned the spaceship around, and they flew back towards Tekhenu. Shiphrah sat beside the weakened body of her lover and caressed his forehead gently. There was an immense amount of love in her eyes for the mighty Lyrian warrior.

"Don't worry, honey, we will soon reach Tekhenu and you will be fine," she whispered as she planted a soft peck on his rough cheeks.

"Lord, you are great for sending us safe and sound back to Tekhenu. Thank you!" Shiphrah thanked God as they flew back to Tekhenu.

# CHAPTER 16. THE BANE

***

Hatathor was in triage. In the interim, Shiphrah went straight to Ankhamon. She entered the throne room and heard the loud music that her rejoicing father was playing. Ankhamon was dancing merrily across his room like a maniac.

Shiphrah stopped the music player device and said, "Papa, did you know what had happened?"

"What happened, dear?" he asked casually, continuing to dance despite the music being stopped.

"Hatathor's spaceship crashed over Sutekh, and he fell into a pit!"

"What! Is he fine?" he asked, pretending to be shocked of what he was hearing.

"No, Papa, he is in triage now. He landed in a massive grave in the Sutekh."

"What!" Ankhamon seemed to have been struck by a thunderbolt at the outrageous news. He gestured his daughter to come towards him, and caressing her hair slowly, he said,

"My little girl, do not go to triage. You know Sutekh has the graves of those who were killed by the horrible disease Mutmut?"

Shiphrah shook her head innocently and placed her head against her father's chest and started sobbing.

"Papa, I hope he gets well soon!"

"Oh, don't lose hope, my little girl; he will be on his feet in no time! Hatathor is a powerful man. But that guy wants to do everything without informing Desher and me," Ankhamon consoled her pretentiously while clenching his fists in frustration.

*Damn that lucky Lyrian bastard! Won't even die!* He thought desperately.

# Chapter 17

# The Rift

VILOVA, the personal servant to Shiphrah, entered the room and said to Shiphrah: "Princess, it is perhaps the happiest day of your life. Tor Ankhamon announced your marriage with General Desher," Vilova announced with utter jubilation. "What? Who told you this?" Shiphrah asked in a baffled state.

"The whole Misraim city is now engaged in preparing the most fabulous event they ever had."

Shiphrah said nothing. Her mind was frozen and she thought of why and when her father took such a crucial decision without even informing her. Vilova continued in a cheerful tone, "and you know, Princess, General Desher is the right choice, and he is the most charming man in the entire kingdom. Besides that, his mother is a spiritual person – a well-known healer. You are the luckiest, Princess."

"Shut up... just shut up and get lost," Shiphrah shouted with full force.

"Oh, I am sorry, Princess. I did not want to hurt you. I thought ...," Vilova tried to explain, but Shiphrah was not in the mood to hear more. She just pushed Vilova out of her room and then banged the door shut.

She fell on the chair and started lamenting, "What shall I do... what shall I do?"

"Damn, I cannot stand it anymore," she said to herself. "It must be some Papa's plan to engage Hatathor in some search and then marry me with that son of a witch, Desher," Shiphrah said to herself.

Shiphrah went to her father's room. Ankhamon was surprised to see her so early in the morning.

"Good morning Shiphrah," he said, while enjoying his breakfast. "How could you do this, Father?" "What?" Ankhamon asked in a surprised tone.

"How could you arrange my marriage without even informing me?" Shiphrah protested.

"Ah. Relax darling. Desher is a nice chap, and he will keep you happy," Ankhamon replied.

"I don't love him," Shiphrah said with tearful eyes.

Ankhamon stood up and approached his daughter. He wiped off her tears and then looked towards the Tehuti Mountains through the window. "Daughter, you must forget Hatathor. He is not suitable for you. Imagine the Princess of the most resourceful planet in the Vega system is marrying a major general," Ankhamon said.

"But I love him," Shiphrah protested.

"People in power have no love life, my daughter. Their marriage is a marriage for sustainable support and power," Ankhamon said. "Mother Ahmose already foretold the death of a savior," Ankhamon continued after a short break.

"That witch!" Shiphrah shouted. "She and her son are deceiving you, father. They have their ulterior motives, which I do not know yet." "Mother Ahmose proposed that for the stability of the kingdom you marry General Desher, and I liked the idea," Ankhamon said and turned around. To his shock, she wasn't present there anymore as she had run away.

"Shiphrah!" Ankhamon shouted, but there was no reply. Ankhamon felt disappointed at her sudden disappearance, and an intense apprehension bubbled in his heart that she would try to go look for Hatathor.

"Kahotep!" he shouted restlessly, and the Lord of Security rushed inside shortly.

"Yes, my king," he greeted with a bow.

"Bring Shiphrah back to me this instant! Do not allow her to go out looking for Hatathor," he ordered with a howl.

Kahotep gave a quick bow and left the chamber as swiftly as possible. Ankhamon became more and more anguished, and his blood pressure rose at the thought of Shiphrah still loving Hatathor.

Meanwhile, Shiphrah was running from one corridor to another and was about to climb the stairs to go out when she noticed a few officers carrying guns and looking hither and thither. Immediately, she skid aside and hid behind the towering golden statue of Ankhamon.

"She must not have gone far," one of them said, pointing his finger towards the ground.

"Yeah, I am pretty sure the princess must come through this corridor," the officer with the aquiline nose stated.

"But perhaps she used the other corridor."

The taller one nodded and said, "There is a possibility. Do one thing, I will guard the stairs of that corridor, and you stand in vigil over here," saying that he darted towards the other side. Shiphrah was panting as she stood behind the statue. Her heart was racing as she desperately hoped the officer would soon go away.

*Go away, go away,* she thought as a drop of sweat trickled down her forehead. The officer continued to stand there like a faithful guard dog. She was losing hope of seeing Hatathor when suddenly she noticed a steel rod that lay on a table a few inches away from her. A smile curled across her rosy lips. She tiptoed aside as cautiously as she could and grabbed the heavy rod from the table. Then slowly lurking behind the man, she grabbed his mouth with her free hand and smashed the rod against the back of his head. He fell on the ground in a pool of blood as she quickly grabbed his gun.

But before she could make another move, she heard some footsteps coming from the stairs. And the moment an officer descended the stairs, she pointed the gun at him and fired a laser beam at him, which hit in the chest making him soar backward and lay motionless on the flight of steps, dead.

Shiphrah ascended the flight of steps quickly and turned to the right where she noticed the sign at the far end of the corner, which read "Emergency exit." In her hurry she tripped on the top, fell on the ground, and hit her head against the marble floor. The gun fell out of her hands, and her head started bleeding profusely. Shiphrah's mind spun horribly and her vision blurred. Her head was aching excruciatingly, and her eyes became numb. Her ribs were burning heavily because of the impact with the ground—it was a miracle that she was still conscious. Somehow, she got to her feet and began limping across the corridor.

*I will not marry Desher! I will tell Hatathor everything about father's plan!* She thought as she limped with substantial effort. The exit seemed a mile away for Shiphrah, whose body seemed to give in to the unbearable pain that shot through her head and her muscles. She made a considerable amount of effort to go to Hatathor. Finally, she was about to get to the door when a rough hand caught her delicate wrist. Her eyes widened in horror when she heard a harsh voice.

"Not so fast, Princess," said Kahotep, who was

standing on the side along with five other officers, all carrying guns.

"Kahotep, let go of my hand!" Shiphrah commanded weakly as her forehead continued to bleed endlessly.

"I am sorry, Princess Shiphrah, but King Ankhamon ordered me to stop you."

"You fool! You don't have any idea what my father is planning!" she cried weakly, but in vain, as Kahotep turned a deaf ear to her.

"Princess, it's my duty to follow my king's command without asking questions. So please, do not make me forcefully take you back to your father's chamber. I respect you as much as I respect your father, Princess. And I do not wish to use force on you," he affirmed coldly, clutching her wrists tightly. Shiphrah struggled continuously to break free from his muscular hands, but it was in vain. She resorted to screaming and called Hatathor's name as loudly as her weak voice could allow her. But he was not there to help her.

"Hatathor!" Shiphrah continued to scream harder than ever, and eventually, Kahotep had to clamp his palm onto her mouth to shut her down.

"That's enough, Princess!" he exclaimed, grabbing her by the shoulder and taking her back to her father. "Your father is waiting for you in his chamber. He knows what's best for you."

***

Ankhamon was pacing back and forth in his chamber. Immense worry had taken over him like a burning fire.

"What's taking this darned Kahotep so long!" he said to himself. "How long can it take to find and capture a defenseless girl?"

As he pondered restlessly on the matter, his eyes fell on the jump-sphere that lay smoothly on his table. He stopped to stare at it, then moved towards it. He took it in his hands and a cunning and evil thought flashed across his mind.

The voice in his mind stopped speaking while he raised the sphere and gazed at it with a maleficent victorious glow in his eye.

Khahotep entered, bringing Shiphrah back to her father.

"What is this nonsense?" shouted Ankhamon.

"I do not want to marry Desher!" Shiphrah said.

"I heard that already. Mother Ahmose has predicted that the savior would die. I do not want you to overthink about someone who would die soon anyway," Ankhamon asserted.

"She is a witch!" Shiphrah said.

"You know little about her," Ankhamon said.

"You don't know her either," Shiphrah retorted.

"Hatathor is not even in Misraim. He has been sent on a mission," Ankhamon said.

"What mission?" Shiphrah asked.

"I cannot tell you," Ankhamon replied coldly. "Take her back to her room," he demanded and Shiphrah left the royal chambers and was taken back to her own chambers.

***

Hatathor was lying unconscious on a bed inside the triage. He was experiencing a series of blinding flashes inside his head and hallucinating dreams. Al-Khidr, the jump-sphere, the pit in Sutekh, his father's skeleton on Earth, and every other horrible incident he had ever experienced were flashing inside his head. His body was quivering heavily, as though the ground beneath him was trembling. He heard Shiphrah screaming and the shrieks tore through his dream, making his eyelids fluttered open.

Hatathor realized that he was inside the triage, and Shiphrah was seated to his side. A bandage had been wrapped around his head to tend to his wound, but it felt heavy and uncomfortable. He tried to get up, but Shiphrah stopped him.

"Take it easy, my love," she said as she caressed his forehead with extreme tenderness.

After throwing a loving look at him, she continued: "Papa said that Ahmose foretold you will die!"

"Yes. I know," Hatathor said. "Do you believe in her?"

"No. She is a witch from the planet Endor," Shiphrah said.

"Ah, so she is not from Lyra!" Hatathor asked.

"Yes. The bounty hunter chased her. Her spaceship crashed in the Tehuti Mountains and when she came out, she saw a cave and made it her dwelling there. After a few days, my father was in this area, and the beast attacked him. She did something that drove the beast away. Somehow, she healed my father's wounds. Later, the brethren women liked her as she has become famous as a healer," Shiphrah said.

"I have a feeling that she and her son are up to something," Hatathor said.

At this moment, Kahotep entered the room. Shiphrah threw a glance at Kahotep and got alarmed.

"You!" she exclaimed and panicked.

"Forgive me, Princess, I had to follow the order, but I cannot see Seka Hatathor in this state. I came here to tell you something," Khahotep said. "Now what?" Shiphrah demanded.

"Princess and Seka, I have always doubted mother Ahmose and her son for being selfish and dishonest people who cared about nothing but themselves. I eavesdropped on them while they were talking to Tor Ankhamon. General Desher and his mother orchestrated this plan to kill Seka Hatathor," Khahotep said. Shiphrah and Hatathor looked at each other.

"Yes, they planted a device in Seka's spaceship so that he would not be able to brake and finally would crash. General Desher prevented the other officers from going to Seka's help, even though he knew the spaceship crashed," Kahotep narrated slowly.

"Kahotep," said Shiphrah slowly, looking at him with immense bafflement in her eyes. "But why?"

"I do not know exactly. Maybe your father wanted to marry you with General Desher, and that is one reason," Khahotep said.

An immense rage took over Hatathor. It burned his insides like a wildfire.

*That piece of shit!* He thought, Desher was never fit to be a general.

Shiphrah looked at Hatathor with sobbing eyes.

"You may leave now," Shiphrah ordered, and Khahotep left the room.

"Shiphrah," Hatathor wanted to say something.

"No, don't talk much! You are still recovering."
"Thank you for saving my life," Hatathor said.

"No, my love. You don't understand! Papa has the jump-sphere now."

"But how did he get it? General Desher sent me towards Sutekh to search for the human," Hatathor surprised.

"Kontar took the sphere from the human and then let him go. Afterward he brought the sphere to my father," she informed him. "What?!" he shouted, as a thunderbolt seemed to have struck him at her shocking revelation.

"For your marriage, I say do what your heart says is right," Hatathor said to Shiphrah.

Shiphrah said in a low voice: "Hatathor. . . Please don't let them force me to marry someone I don't love," she said, starting sobbing quietly.

Hatathor looked at her and hugged her.

# Chapter 18

# The Rescue

It was night on Lyra. Al-Khidr was pushed and hurled through the dimly lit dungeon of Ankhamon. He had never seen this place before. To him it looked like a special place specifically made to curb the voices of the opponents, political activists, and civil society. While going through the corridors, there were many people imprisoned that by their looks the seemed to be educated people. Al-Khidr felt pity for those people, but he couldn't do much at the moment. He saw two women in one of the prison cells, and he immediately recognized them. They were the police officer Minka, and doctor Arit. Both the women looked at him with the gloomy face and said no word. Al-Khidr stopped for a moment, but the guards pushed him ahead.

"Move on, prisoner!" one guard shouted.

"This is how you treat excellent police officers?" Al-Khidr shouted back at the guards.

"Your days are numbered, human. We are just waiting for the orders to take your graveside from this dungeon. No prisoner has ever left here alive," the guards laughed ruthlessly.

The Brethren cultist pushed him into a cell that looked as if was made up of basalt stones. There were no doors. The guards moved him into the room and pressed a few buttons outside the panel. Immediately, a crisscross of tiny laser beams generated.

"This is a special security prison. If you try to move through this door, your body will be cut into pieces. So beware, you primitive human," one of the guards said, and then they left.

Al-Khidr looked inside the prison cell. Luckily, there was a jug of water to quench his thirst and a box with some food. He cupped the water, ate the food, and thanked God.

*Ah, what a fate. I'm back in a prison cell on this planet*, he thought.

***

Ehsis and Nefertiti couldn't sleep well. They were anguished for Al-Khidr and wanted the Vega to rise as soon as possible. Early in the morning, when it was still dark outside, Nefertiti's beeper buzzed. Ehsis had called her.

*That must be important*, Nefertiti thought.

She immediately rushed to the Cove and found that Ehsis, Rostau, Semed, and all officers were present.

"What happened?"

"Something urgent. We need to have a brighter team to rescue Al-Khidr. The ground surveillance found that he had been taken to the Ankhamon's dungeon. Our hackers also confirmed this as they breached into kingdom's transmission," Ehsis said.

"But how do we do it? It's the highest secured prison on the entire planet," Nefertiti said.

"We heard that Ankhamon's planning to celebrate his daughter's marriage in the obelisk square. All brethren and officials would be invited," Rostau said. "It will carry out a swift operation. Neutralizing all threats," Semed said.

"I'm ready for it," Nefertiti said.

***

The obelisk square was full of spectators. The Vega was already set and it was a starry night over Misraim city. The whole place was decorated with the most exquisite ornaments present on Lyra. The place was full of spectators of all ages, and people were sitting in a disciplined manner.

The music was playing in the background, resembling the lyre instrument from Earth. People had gathered to celebrate the event of the marriage of General Desher with Princess Shiphrah. Mother Ahmose and General Desher were already present at the obelisk square.

Female devotees of mother Ahmose were chanting the blessing mantras for the newly married couple.

The music was mixing with the mantra creating a unique atmosphere.

Suddenly, the people realized that King Ankhamon was approaching the place with his beloved daughter Princess Shiphrah.

An entourage of around twenty spaceships arrived, from which only one spaceship landed in the square. The other spaceships fulfilled the royal protocol, as required for the auspicious occasion. All eyes were looking at the black royal spaceship that landed. The latch opened, and the King appeared along with Princess Shiphrah.

She was wearing the bride's green dress, which comprised layer of cloths decorated with golden thread and colorful bead-work. Princess was wearing the crown on her head. They walked along the aisle and moved towards general Desher, who was dressed in full military attire.

Ankhamon reached the stage and went to the podium to address the people:

"Blessings of Eternal God on us all, we are here today for the marriage of my daughter with the most suitable suitor, General Desher. Being a father, I have seen many troubles in my life. My wife and sons died when Shiphrah was young. Then you all know that we had to move to the Tehuti Mountains because of the dystopian rule of Queen Hathor. And now, finally, we have the most peaceful life on Lyra. Shiphrah and Desher, you both have to prove worthy of praise by becoming a role model for our society. Mother Ahmose, I am thankful to you for proposing this matrimony."

Then Ankhamon moved towards Shiphrah. He took her hand, and they both moved towards General Desher.

"I Ankhamon, King of Akhom, give my daughter's hand in marriage to the commander-in-chief of the Kingdom forces, General Desher," Ankhamon announced.

Shiphrah looked at his father with sobbing eyes, but Ankhamon was mesmerized by the feeling that he was strengthening his rule over the kingdom. Now no military general would have dared to confront him.

General Desher smiled and bowed to the King and the Princess. He knelt and kissed bride's hand.

"It is an honor that the King of Akhom has given me. I promise and vow that I will take care of Princess Shiphrah," Desher said and looked into Shiphrah's eyes. Shiphrah, on the contrary, was looking towards the sky as if she was waiting for God to intervene and help her somehow.

"Mother Ahmose, please start the prayers which will bind them together. Begin giving your blessings to the new couple," Ankhamon said.

Ahmose was about to open her mouth when suddenly a sonic boom took everyone by surprise. Another spaceship appeared in the sky and landed on the ground. Everyone looked at the spaceship as the man who came out of it was none other but major General Hatathor.

Ahmose and Desher looked at each other.

***

Nefertiti, Semed, and Rostau were suited in protective, military-grade laser-proof suits. They were equipped with heat-sensing cameras while watching every move of the prison guards, who changed their positions regularly. Ehsis had allowed only the three of them to execute the operation. The guards were half-drunk, as today was a celebration day. The entire kingdom was celebrating the marriage of general Desher with the Princess.

"We should have a day off,! It's a public holiday today, but we have to work," one guard said with a disappointed voice.

"Yeah, I was thinking the same. But this is our job," another one replied.

"Master Ankhamon took the right decision. General Desher is the best man for the Princess," one guard said.

"You know, I wanted to marry her," one drunken soldier said, and all laughed.

"Princess Shiphrah, damn, she is one seductive girl," another guard added.

"But I heard Hatathor wanted to her too. Poor guy."

"Yeah, sad!"

Most of the guards were gathered at one entrance to the dungeon. While the dungeon guards talked, drank, and laughed, Nefertiti and her team noticed a door that was unguarded. They sneaked carefully avoiding the guards, and entered the dungeon.

"We have to move fast. However, the foremost mission is to release Al-Khidr," Nefertiti said.

"Understood!" Semed and Rostau said.

"This should work today," Rostau said and showed a small device.

As they ran through the corridor the prisoners were looking at them surprised as they hadn't seen anyone else apart from the guards walking freely through the dungeon. Nefertiti passed by the cell where her former colleagues Minka and Dr. Arit were. They had shabby clothes and worn-out faces. Minka recognized Nefertiti and before she could say a word, Nefertiti placed a finger on her lips to signal her that she should remain quiet. Minka and Arit's faces were now brimming with hope and joy. Finally, they were able to see a turn of events.

"I thought you two have died in the mutiny," Nefertiti said to them with sobbing eyes.

"Please save us!" Arit said.

"Al-Khidr is also here," Minka informed.

"We saw him yesterday passing by. Probably he's in the last cell in this corridor," Arit suggested.

"I'll be right back," Nefertiti said in a low voice, and she and the guys ran towards the end of the corridor.

Al-Khidr was sitting in the cell with his head down over his knees.

"Come on, it's time to go," Nefertiti said while Semed looked towards the entrance in case any guard came and saw them and alerted the others. Rostau placed the device on the keypad and it stuck like a magnet to iron. The keypad panel came to life and the device started working. Different numerals began appearing on the device's screen, and soon, the laser lights at the cell entrance were gone.

"It worked!" Rostau exclaimed in a low voice.

"Great, let's try this out with the other cells," Nefertiti said.

They removed the laser barrier from all the prison cells within minutes, and the prisoners filled up the corridor. "Nefertiti, General Lukmas and General Kityr are also somewhere here," Arit informed.

Rostau and Semed looked at each other.

"Guys, I'll try to clear the way out; meanwhile, you search and rescue both Generals Lukmas and Kityr," Nefertiti said. Rostau, Semed, and Al-Khidr ran, looking for Lukmas.

"Just collect whatever you have which can be used as a weapon," Nefertiti advised prisoners.

Most prisoners picked up utensils and began moving slowly towards the entrance.

Nefertiti gave her daggers to Minka and Arit. As former police officers, both ladies were well-trained in using blades. Though they were feeling weak today, their spirits were rejuvenated by the release from the cell and they were ready to reclaim their freedom.

After a search of a few more minutes, Rostau discovered two sealed off capsules installed in a prison cell. Rostau placed his device on one of the capsules, revealing a living life form inside. He repeated it on the other capsule and, to their horror, it also had a life form inside. Semed pressed the button, and capsules opened making Lukmas and Kityr fell on the ground like larvae from a cocoon. They were too weak to walk, so Rostau, Al-Khidr, and Semed carried them until they reached to other prisoners, who were now freed.

"We will take kingdom's ships to escape now," Semed said.

***

Hatathor moved towards the stage, and he climbed it, going to the podium: "The Princess does not want to marry General Desher!" he announced to the entire kingdom, as the event was transmitted live across the planet.

"Rascal, who invited you here?" Desher moved forward while gritting his teeth.

"No one!" Hatathor replied. "I came here as Princess requested that," he continued and looked at Shiphrah, who dashed towards Hatathor.

"Shiphrah!" shouted Ankhamon.

"Yes, Papa. I had asked Hatathor to come here," she said.

"I love no one other than him," she said looking into Hatathor's eyes.

"Foolish girl," Ahmose said and her face turned in disgust.

"I will not let you live any longer, Hatathor," Desher said and took out his laser gun. "Step aside, Shiphrah. I don't want to hurt you. You are not aware of how incompetent he is!" "Hatathor, I will not let this go like this," Ankhamon growled.

Hatathor looked at Shiphrah, and with a subtle movement, he required her to step aside so that he could teach Desher a lesson.

Shiphrah moved aside, and Hatathor activated his sleeve device. The hemispherical protective energy shield surrounded him. Lyrians had never witnessed such a device, so they were all awestruck. Desher fired laser shots, but they could not penetrate Hatathor's sleeve's protective shield.

People noticed that Desher could not bring any harm to Hatathor and they started shouting, supporting Hatathor: "Seka, Seka, Seka!"

Shiphrah was pleased to see the public support, and she also started calling "Seka ..."

Ahmose came to Ankhamon and said: "My Lord, shall I intervene to stop him?"

Ankhamon nodded for he didn't like the ruckus that Hatathor had provoked.

"Evaporate him," shouted Ahmose, and Desher fired, but Hatathor jumped aside and took cover.

Desher was ferociously moving forward firing continuously. He was trying to aim at Hatathor. In this struggle Desher slipped and fell from the stage to the ground below.

"I curse you, Hatathor! You will die soon!" Ahmose said as Desher was hand was bleeding. Apparently, his arm was wounded.

Ankhamon moved forward to see Desher and knelt at the edge of the stage. Many guards encircled Ankhamon, while his eyes were filled with blood as he watched Shiphrah enter a spaceship while holding the hand of Hatathor. To protect the princess, the guards stopped firing at them.

Hatathor spaceship flew and went towards the south. Ankhamon was burring in rage. Hatathor has crossed all lines. But he had more anger towards Shiphrah, who had left him, his very father and king of the kingdom and ran away along Hatathor.

"Disgusting, capture them alive!" he shouted and went towards his spaceship, heading back to Tekhenu.

Many spacecrafts flew over the guests, who were all watching in aghast. The kingdom forces received the message that Hatathor was on the run.

Meanwhile, the chaos in security setup, gave Nefertiti's team and prisoners a chance to escape so they took it and ran to take cover. The guards looked at the sky as a black spaceship passed over them at supersonic speed.

Nefertiti and her team fired laser shots at them, taking them by surprise and killing all the guards.

Then, they quickly reached a spaceship, which was

big enough to accommodate everyone. They all climbed and the spacecraft soared into the sky. Within a few minutes, it was camouflaged between the other spaceships that were looking for Hatathor's whereabouts.

# Chapter 19

# The Desert

SHIPHRAH was with Hatathor in his spaceship. She finally felt like she had become Queen – queen of none other but Hatathor, whom she had given her heart even before they truly knew each other. However, she was also worried, as the most powerful General of the kingdom, General Desher would not spare Hatathor.

*Papa will never forgive me,* she thought and then calmed herself down, as it was her destiny.

“Ahmose is a witch. She will do whatever she can to capture us,” Shiphrah said to Hatathor.

Hatathor remained silent. He was constantly looking into the control panels to see any approaching threat.

"Where are we heading, my love?" asked Shiphrah.

"Sutekh, it is probably the safest place to hide for a while. Are you okay with this, darling?" Hatathor asked Shiphrah.

"Whatever you think is good for me," Shiphrah said.

"We will leave this vessel and then move around in a hover," Hatathor said.

"I have no worries as now I can live with the best bodyguard on Lyra," Shiphrah said, and kissed him.

***

Nefertiti, Rostau, Semed, and Al-Khidr landed as Vega was about to rise. Unfortunately, the ship was short on fuel. Also, Lukmas and Kityr were shivering as their old bodies were going through a shock. Sometimes Kityr haphazardly moved his hands, so they tied him to one of the spaceship seats. They were awake but too afraid, as their memories were not coordinated and they were incoherent statements about the rebellion, Queen Hathor and the rebel generals. Their hibernation had been abruptly cut off, and they needed a complete body checkup as soon as possible.

"They will be fine after few hours," said Nefertiti.

It was nighttime, and the howling winds were blowing in this area of the planet. They were on the dry sandy floor, sitting close to each other. For the moment, only Rostau and Semed were using their light torches to establish communication with Kneph.

The protruding mountains were looking at the newly arrived guests.

"Igniting fire is out of the question," Nefertiti informed the rest as this obviously would have increased their chances of being seen and captured. "By now, they must have figured out that prisoners had escaped. If we fly longer, then they might track us on the radars," Rostau said.

Rostau and Semed were trying to establish a secure communication channel with Kneph while the others were engaged in discussion.

"Ankhamon has a priestess among his courtiers. I saw her," Al-Khidr said.

"Yes. She is from the planet Endor. She is a fugitive, and her spaceship crashed somewhere on Lyra, but she somehow survived, and then she hid in Tehuti. Somehow Ahmose met Ankhamon, and he gave her safe heaven and allowed her to live among brethren. She mingled with brethren women and became famous as a healer. When the galactic office for prisoner exchange informed us about a fugitive, we searched for her. We were looking for her, as Endor requested us to capture her. We missed her signature in Tehuti, and she was able to hide among the brethren," Nefertiti informed.

"But we never thought that she would become so influential," Minka said.

"Yes. Now she is called Mother," Arit confirmed.

"She is trying to copy the genuine Mother – our Queen Hathor," Minka added.

"I am glad that we rescued General Kityr and Lukmas. Ehsis will be glad to know that," Nefertiti said.

Rostau and Semed were finally able to set up a safe communication channel with the base in Kneph to which they sent their location coordinates. After an hour's wait, several hovers arrived at their place.

# Chapter 20

# The Return

GENERAL Desher was wounded and he was in much pain. The doctors put a device over his wound and they started healing it. After some time, the wound was healed. Ahmose was extremely stressed. She looked a lot older than before.

Desher was resting, recovering after the healing was done, when Ankhamon ordered he was shifted to intensive care facilities.

"Find that filthy Hatathor and save Princess Shiphrah from his clutches," Ankhamon shouted at the brethren.

*Shiphrah... Shiphrah, you are such a nonsense girl,* he thought while gritting his teeth, but he couldn't do anything to change her. Since her mom died, the girl became so stubborn, and I hadn't given her too much attention. Now she wants to mold me to her whims.

"She has to follow me," said Ankhamon to himself.

***

Hatathor and Shiphrah were in the Sutekh exclusion zone. Shiphrah was delighted that she was finally able to breathe freely. "If Desher is dead, we have to be careful," Shiphrah said.

Shiphrah saw Hatathor was sweating profusely, and she asked:

"My love, what happened? Why are you sweating so much?" "I don't know," Hatathor said.

Shiphrah took a device out and tuned it for temperature check and found that Hatathor's body temperature was too high than normal. "Oh my God, what shall I do? You need help, and I cannot let you suffer, my love," she said to Hatathor, who was falling asleep, with his entire body was shivering. "Think Shiphrah, think!" she said to herself.

Sutekh was a deserted place with no one around. She ran on empty roads, looking for help, but there was no one to her in agonizing moments. *I have no other option left,* she thought, and she started dragging Hatathor back to the spaceship.

She soared the ship up, heading towards Tekhenu.

Within minutes, her spaceship was detected by the space surveillance, and shortly after that it got escorted and requested to land. “Princess Shiphrah here. I’m going to see my father,” she said.

“Princess, with due respect, you must leave this vessel,” the officer announced.

They were nervous as they feared maybe Hatathor was on board and could do something severe again.

“Princess, we will now execute the orders of the King,” the officer announced and closed the transmission.

Suddenly the spaceship’s controls stopped responding, and the spacecraft plummeted towards the ground. Hatathor fell from his seat, where he was lying unconscious. “Damn you all,” Shiphrah said, and she was frantically looking at the control panels where Kingdom Override’ was blinking. Shiphrah lost all hope, and she was unconscious, too.

Shiphrah’s spaceship plummeted, but when it was around 50 Supris above ground, its control was in remote hands, and the spacecraft landed vertically on the ground. Kingdom forces forced opened the latch and entered inside. Hatathor and Shiphrah both were unconscious.

***

Al-Khidr and the rest of the Lyrian prisoners, who were saved from the dungeon, reached the Kneph. Dr. Kityr and General Lukmas were sent to the intensive care units, where a team of doctors started scanning their bodies to look for potential issues related to the sudden hibernation disruption.

"I am so proud of you all," Ehsis praised the rescue team.

"It's God's help; finally, I have hope that we will get the cure back, just as we found Dr. Kityr. The only thing remaining now is to get the jump-sphere back," Ehsis said and paused, "but there is a problem. Ankhamon wants to use the jump-sphere he has. If he charges the jump-sphere now, the Earth's plant leaves will be destroyed. We must stop him before this happens," Ehsis said.

"But does Ankhamon know what he is doing? I mean, who is he planning to send using the jump-sphere, and where?" Rostau asked curiously. At Rostau's question, Ehsis went to her station entered some data and pressed a button. A holographic image of the various stars in the galaxy appeared. "I will explain it to you," she said as they all looked at Ehsis, paying attention to her explanations.

"All the planes of the stars are moving at different levels in space," she began, as she waved her bony, wrinkled hand and medium-sized holographic images of the stars appeared aligned. "Now, as you move downwards to another plane of stars, there will always be an increase in time," she continued by drawing another alignment of stars a few centimeters away from the first line of stars with another wave of her hand.

Her impressively knowledgeable explanation spellbound Nefertiti, Al-Khidr, Rostau, and Semed. They didn't move an eyelash as they continued to stare at the appearing images . Al-Khidr's eyes' pupils were widening in awe with every word Ehsis was saying. He was listening with genuine interest and curiosity. *This is so incredibly amazing*, he thought, without moving his eyes away from the holographic images. The knowledge that Ehsis possesses is indeed unmatched. *Damn! I can learn so much from her about the mysteries of the universe.* He wondered in utter fascination.

"One cannot go back to the same point in time, where the tunnel through the stars had started in the beginning. There will always be a large dissipation of energy in the universe, and one cannot always go to the same time in the future because of destructive interference in space. Thus the same trajectory cannot be followed," she paused, taking a sip of water from her glass.

She drank some water, cleared her throat, and continued: "The time cycles between the stars' planes are different. So, Keb is at a level where the life cycles are relatively short. Here on Lyra, our life cycles are, by comparison, longer.

"I apologize for interrupting you, madam secretary," expressed Rostau and Semed simultaneously. "But wouldn't Ankhamon already know this from the scientists?" Ehsis looked at him, and a sad smile spread across her wrinkled jaws.

"That's where the problem lies, Rostau and Semed. There are only a few scientists today who know this secret, as those who developed the jump-sphere and constructed the HSS have all died," she said. Nefertiti gave her a tender look, and her eyes were a little teary and glimmered with sadness. "I am aware of all this because I worked with them and learned how to make the facility work. The charging sequence of Maft-Shespt is a delicate process, and any disruptions may alter the time and space trajectory," Ehsis said.

She saw Al-Khidr wanted to say something. "Yes, Mr. Al-Khidr, do you want to add something here?" she asked.

Al-Khidr stood up and started gazing into everyone's eyes. "When I went to Keb, I was supposed to go back in my timeline. But the slight disturbances in charging of the jump-sphere made me land ten centuries ahead in time," Al-Khidr mentioned.

"Yes. Ankhamon does not know of this. He still has the many other Galactic Space Exploration scientists in some other place, and he wants to use them for his activities."

"When Ankhamon will hand over the sphere to the scientists to charge it, that will be our moment. We'll send a team to get the sphere out of their clutches," Ehsis said.

***

"Hatathor!" This was the first word that Shiphrah uttered.

She was too weak, and with blurry eyes she saw servants and nurses around her. She slowly turned her head and found herself in a room that looked like a triage. "Save Hatathor," she said with a weak voice, but nurses requested her to remain quiet.

"He is fine!" a nurse said. Shiphrah went back into unconsciousness. After several hours, she came to her senses and she immediately sat up on the bed. This time there was no one around, and she went out of the room to search for Hatathor.

As Shiphrah went out to discover the place, she found that the corridor was empty. She began looking for Hatathor. She was weak, but her love for Hatathor gave her enough strength to go search. She soon realized that she was in some laboratory. There were many rooms where some dead alien bodies that were preserved in transparent jars. She went close to one of them and started inspecting it. Suddenly, the alien opened its eyes and moved agitatedly.

Shiphrah yelped and moved back, hitting someone that was behind her. She turned and there was a man dressed like a doctor looking at her. "Princess, stop," he said, but Shiphrah was too scared so she ran out.

She continued running until she reached the end of the corridor where she exited only to find herself in a large facility. Some staff noticed her and tried to stop her, but she continued running until she reached another triage room. Shiphrah continued running as she was looking for door to exit and the facility staff were following her closely. One staff member managed to reach her and he grabbed her. Suddenly, they heard a terrible crash. Immediately, the officers turned to see the source of the noise and saw that the triage door had been broken, and out came the mighty Lyrian warrior. . . Hatathor.

Shiphrah's blurred eyes widened in utmost bliss, and she stopped struggling as the staff person slackened his grip on her.

"Shiphrah!" Hatathor called, embracing her warmly.

"Are you alright? Your head's bleeding so badly," Shiphrah asked.

"But how did this happen?" Hatathor demanded worriedly.

"How are you feeling? You had a high fever," she exclaimed weakly.

"Where are we?" he roared furiously as he flexed his muscles and glared at facility staff.

One staff officer came forward and said: "Stop Mr. Hatathor, I am Dr. Kodika. This is Kingdom Virology Lab. You and Princess are brought here for the quarantine purposes. We advise you to stay in this lab and let Princess Shiphrah go. We have conducted some tests on your mysterious illness and test results are awaited." "What happened?" Princess Shiphrah intervened.

"My Princess, I am afraid I cannot say conclusively as test results are awaited. I request that you and Mr. Hatathor let us work and conduct tests on both of you. This might take a few more hours," Dr. Kodika said.

"I am fine. I am not in the mood to stay here. We have to go. Where is my sleeve device?" roared Hatathor. "I order you to return the Seka device," Princess ordered.

"But Princess . . . ," Dr. Kodika was unable to complete his sentence.

"Do it immediately; we are short of time," Shiphrah ordered further.

Dr. Kodika looked at his staff and with a head nod he ordered his staff to bring the sleeve device.

Within minutes, one staff member returned the sleeve device.

Dr. Kodika said: "I am afraid that you cannot go, as this facility is surrounded by kingdom forces."

There were many doctors, scientists, and soldiers who had surrounded him.

"Mr. Hatathor, please stop, you had a high fever!" another doctor said in a worrisome tone.

"I don't have it now," Hatathor replied. "Mr. Hatathor, you could be infected with some virus, and we want to investigate to see what was wrong. Now we are waiting for the results. We cannot let you go with the Princess, so don't go out, please," the soldier said.

"Try to stop me," Hatathor said.

Three soldiers had already entered the virology lab and one of them aimed at Hatathor, but their commander shouted: "Stop, you might hurt the Princess." Other soldiers communicated through the transmitter to other soldiers outside, "Hatathor is awake. He is heading out of the building. Be careful, Princess Shiphrah must not be hurt," he shouted.

***

Desher opened his eyes. He sat up on his bed and found that mother Ahmose was anxiously pacing the room. She was murmuring and looked nervous. "Mother," Desher said, and Ahmose turned to him. She immediately dashed towards him.

"Are you okay, son?" she asked in a broken voice.

"Yes, I am fine now," Desher said.

"Hatathor took Shiphrah with him. Curse him," Ahmose said.

"I knew from the very beginning that he would create a problem, but I was not expecting that he would go to that extreme," Desher said.

"But it is good. You can now shoot Hatathor anytime, and you don't need to give explanations," Ahmose said.

"Shiphrah will be your wife until Ankhamon is alive. So bear her a few more days. We will kill her once Ankhamon is dead," Ahmose said.

"I have to check what the forces are doing," Desher replied.

"Let Ankhamon handle it at the moment. You need to recover completely," Ahmose said.

Desher picked up his device, and was able to access the system to see all the details of the undergoing military operations.

"They surrounded them, and Hatathor made Shiphrah his shield. Filthy coward," Desher shouted. "I have to go. They need me," Desher said and went towards his spaceship.

"Go towards Kingdom's Virology Labs," Desher

ordered the military pilots.

***

When Hatathor came out of the place, he noticed the site was full of soldiers. He realized he could not deal with all of them at once, so he turned on the hemispherical shield around him and Shiphrah.

The soldiers were not shooting. Instead, they were only watching, as they had been commanded from the superiors.

Hatathor walked towards his spaceship but another spacecraft appeared as if out of nowhere and landed right in his path. General Desher came out of it and shouted. "You made the girl your shield, coward!" he shouted.

"I am not a coward!" Hatathor shouted back.

"Fight me with your bare hands," Desher said, hinting at Hatathor's sleeve weapon.

"Okay. I will not activate it," Hatathor said, and both lurked towards each other.

Everyone was watching the fight.

"Come on, son of a witch," Hatathor growled.

Desher kicked Hatathor making him fall to the ground. Hatathor quickly stood up and punched Desher. Blood started coming out of Desher's mouth, as he fell to the ground.

Hatathor moved forward to punch him again, but Desher took some sand and threw it in Hatathor's face. Hatathor sneezed, and with blurry eyes, he tried to figure out where Desher was. Meanwhile, Desher sneakily moved behind him and pulled Hatathor's cape, bringing him down again. Then he jumped and sat on Hatathor's face and started punching him. Desher took out a dagger which he had hidden in his clothes, and he tried to slash Hatathor's face. Hatathor held the blade in front of his face , between his palms. Despite the effort, Hatathor didn't back down. Suddenly something hard hit Desher's head, and he fell to the ground, knocked out. Hatathor saw Shiphrah right in front of him.

"Let's get away from here," she said and climbed into Desher's spaceship.

"Get out man or die," Shiphrah growled. The ship's pilot ran out of the ship in confused state.

The soldiers outside ran towards the ship, firing his laser beam guns, but the spacecraft had already taken off. They again managed to escape. "I am going to talk to father now," Shiphrah said in a determined tone.

***

The ship landed at Tekhenu, and Shiphrah asked Hatathor to stay in the spaceship while she asked her father to take back his order, he had given to Desher to come after her. As soon as she came out of the spacecraft, the guards posted at Tekhenu moved forward. Hatathor remained inside the ship to avoid further problems. "Stop Princess," they ran towards her.

"No need to stop me. I want to see my father," she said further.

Shiphrah ignored the guards, and she went straight to the throne room.

"Father!" she entered the throne room, calling her father.

Ankhamon was on his throne deep in thought. Seeing her, he just moved his face to one side and said: "Why did you come back?"

"What do you mean Papa," Shiphrah said. "Why are you behaving like this?" she asked grudgingly, with tears in her gorgeous eyes.

Hearing this, Ankhamon stood up from the throne and shouted back:

"Am I? Am I behaving oddly? Or is it you who ran off right in front of me with a stranger?"

"He is no stranger, Papa," Shiphrah said. "He is Seka, the savior, the warrior!" "Is this how nations treat their heroes?" she reminded him.

"He is cursed. I already got the news. He is sick and weak – my child. Besides that, now he is a fugitive who attacked a higher ranking general. He will be court-martialed and sent to jail," Ankhamon gave his judgments.

"I see, you are not listening to me. You are still in the clutches of that old witch and her son!" Shiphrah shouted. "Shut up!" Ankhamon said.

"You and Hatathor had created chaos in Akhom. You know he fell into a pit in Sutekh, which could be inflicted with the Mutmut virus. If this is the case, then Mutmut will reappear, child."

Ankhamon turned to his daughter and said with

tearful eyes: "I have the jump-sphere now. Come with me; it's time that we move to some other place. This kingdom has been doomed, when the curse of the planet Keb has taken over the Lyra!"

"Father, what are you talking about? You must be joking," Shiphrah said in complete bewilderment.

"No. I am serious...." Ankhamon asserted and paused. "This is a bitter truth; Lyra has been slowly dying," he added gloomily. "The damned disease will spread again across this planet and will kill our males. I am afraid that more people would die soon, and this planet would get desolate and will become an easy target for attackers due to the Amris it contains in it," Ankhamon stated in despair.

"That means...whatever Hathor and Ehsis were doing was right?" Shiphrah seemed perplexed and couldn't come to terms with the truth.

"Don't even say their names...Hathor and Ehsis – because of their mistake, your brothers contracted the disease and died. The place that you traveled to today had their bones buried in it as well!" Ankhamon growled furiously, his eyes still burning with the fire of the pain of losing his sons.

"You are running away, father, leaving your subjects behind? You are a leader! How could you do this?" Shiphrah reminded him earnestly.

"A leader is a leader only while his followers are alive. Once they are dead, he is not a leader anymore," he shouted at Shiphrah.

"I will not run away like this," Shiphrah affirmed,

with tears sparkling in her eyes again. "Use your common sense, girl! Akhom is a fool's paradise," Ankhamon yelled again with gritted teeth. "This planet has become a curse now!" he expressed, and a tear trickled down his otherwise cold eyes.

"Father," Shiphrah stepped back, shocked.

"I am not listening to anything Shiphrah, you are coming with me, and it's my final decision. I will not leave my daughter here on this dying planet!" Ankhamon stated firmly and turned towards her, but she was not there anymore.

Ankhamon rang the alarm. Tekhenu started howling like wounded Anubis. Shiphrah came out of the building, and the brethren stopped her.

"Princess, you cannot leave Tekhenu. King Ankhamon doesn't allow this," they said in a stern tone.

Suddenly Hatathor appeared behind the guards, and he smashed their heads, rendering them unconscious.

Shiphrah ran towards Hatathor and said: "Are you sick? You had fever?"

"Yes. But I don't have it anymore!" Hatathor said.

"Papa is saying that you probably contracted the Mutmut," Shiphrah said.

"What the..." he uttered in surprise.

"Ankhamon was a hacker once. I don't know where he got this data from?" Hatathor said with a sarcastic tone.

"Darling, I am just saying that you might need medical help...." Shiphrah said, but Hatathor stopped her by raising his hand with tearful eyes. "I am not sick," he shouted and he ran towards the spaceship taking off.

Shiphrah looked at the ship soaring in the sky with tearful eyes. She turned around and went into Tekhenu.

***

"Mother Ahmose, General Desher is back, but he has been wounded again," a servant announced.

Ahmose ran to look for her son, who had entered the villa on mount Tass with the help of another soldier. There was a bandage around Desher's head. "What happened? Who did this to you?" she inquired.

"Shiphrah!"

"I don't believe it," she said and looked at the bandaged area nervously.

"Mother, I cannot marry a girl who hurts me like this. Ah... my head," Desher said with pain.

"You are dead, bitch!" Ahmose said.

"Puah," shouted Ahmose.

"Contact my devotees and tell them to inform me where Shiphrah was last seen," Ahmose ordered.

Ahmose opened a drawer and took out a tiny box. She opened it, looked at the contents and closed the lid. She put the box into her pocket. "Mother, she was last seen at Tekhenu," Puah informed.

"I am coming for you, girl," Ahmose said and went towards her spaceship. Puah was unsure what mother was planning, but she walked her to the spaceship. The moment the spacecraft lifted off in Lyra's sky, Puah ran inside to see Desher, who had fallen into a deep sleep. Ahmose's ship landed near Tekhenu. She came out and moved slowly towards Tekhenu. As usual, the guards were vigilant and were surprised to see her at this hour of the night.

"I want to see King Ankhamon," she said in a stern tone.

"But mother it's..." a guard wanted to say something, but another one stopped him, and said to Ahmose: "Sure, mother, you may proceed to Tekhenu."

Ahmose looked at both before going inside to see Shiphrah for the last time.

As soon as she entered the Tekhenu, she started walking towards the throne room, and then by looking into the security cameras and staff, she smiled and said: "Oh, I need to go to the restroom. Where is it?"

A guard directed her towards the restrooms, and she went into another corridor. She now started her search for Shiphrah. She went towards the royal quarters and found it was a heavily guarded place. She went close to the guards and took the box out from her pocket, and while keeping her hand low, she went to the guards and said: "The hidden will be revealed to you."

The guards were surprised seeing her there and before they could say anything, she opened the tiny box she was clenching in her hand. The sand started pouring over the carpet, creating a heap of sand. The guards looked at it in total surprise and felt like the sand was never-ending. The guards started feeling dizzy and sat on the floor, looking at the beauty of the sand coming out of the suspended tiny box.

Ahmose moved forward to enter the royal quarter while her hallucinations were keeping the guards busy. After walking a little, she found the room she was looking for and knocked on the door. A servant girl came out, and Ahmose asked:

"Where is the Princess?"

"She is inside..." before the servant was able to say anything else, Ahmose pulled the servant by her clothes and went inside the room, locking it. "Shiphrah!"

"Ahmose... mother!" Shiphrah was surprised to see her.

"Darling, I was so worried about you," Ahmose said.

Shiphrah stood up, and Ahmose hugged her.

"I was...," Shiphrah wanted to say something, but Ahmose put her palm on her face.

"Don't say anything. I know everything. Oh, Princess Shiphrah, you are so kind. I didn't know that you were in love with Hatathor. King has not informed me about it earlier," Ahmose said. "I am sorry, Princess, if I have hurt your feelings and emotions," Ahmose knelt in front of the Princess.

"Mother Ahmose, no need for this. I understand that everything you are doing is to help Desher. He should have asked my view on the marriage proposal," Shiphrah said while looking at the Tehuti Mountains.

“Desher has to serve the Akhom. He has to obey whatever you command, Princess,” Ahmose said and went back out of the room.

Shiphrah felt relief. Finally, Desher was out of her way. She was still worried about Hatathor.

“Where are you?” she said while the transmitter was trying to connect, but Hatathor was not picking up on the other end. Ahmose was back in the corridor where the guards were playing with the sand. She walked over to the sand and clutched the box in her hand. The sand stopped pouring, and guards were looking at each other nervously. There was no sand, and mother Ahmose roared the ship vertically up, heading back to mount Tass.

“I have to maintain the status-quo,” said Ahmose to herself.

# Chapter 21

# The Deception

A spaceship landed near the HSS facility, and men and women in dilapidated clothes were pushed out of it. Their faces had signs of weariness, and they were looking afraid.

Around sixty brethren at the facility were watching the men and women being pushed towards the HSS facility. Men and women in dilapidated clothes were looking at the mountains, thinking that help might come from there to rescue them. These men and women were the scientists and engineers who had been arrested during the freedom wars when Master Ankhamon, with the help of the former military structure, took over the kingdom of Akhom.

Scientists were unaware of the men waiting for their arrival at the facility. He was the most powerful man on the planet Lyra – Tor Ankhamon. Ankhamon sat on his throne at Tekhenu with his head bowed down staring at the sphere in his hands. He had mixed feelings of victory and loss. His eyes were teary as he was not expecting his very daughter, Shiphrah, to disappoint him like this.

"You are dead for me – Shiphrah, like your brothers!" he uttered.

A man entered and said: "Master, the scientists are assembled at HSS. We are ready for you to do your live speech."

Ankhamon smiled at the news.

*Ankhamon, what are you waiting for?* Ankhamon thought.

He was ready to deliver his speech; the Brethren supporters, scientists, and engineers were all ready to listen to him. His live speech was being broadcasted to the scientists at HSS.

"Talented citizens of the kingdom of Akhom, it is a moment of great happiness for us. The excellent facility of HSS will be started once again. This facility is a symbol of pride for us, as no other planet has created such a place. Unfortunately, our people misused it in the past, and some have used it only for personal gains. The old regime of Hathor had locked it away for too long, and then Ehsis used it to send the wretched human to bring more diseases from the cursed planet Keb. Thanks to the almighty God, we stopped it at the right moment. Those were the two foolish women."

He paused and continued: "Didn't she realize this planet would be ruined if anything deadly arrived on the Lyra from Earth?! But no! She had to send our people to that accursed planet on a stupid mission!" he mocked sarcastically.

"We suffered because of the acts of our great queen. We watched hopelessly people die a gruesome death.Beloved Scientists, we have kept you in the secret chambers just for your safety. Technology is dangerous; not everyone should have access to it. We feared that your skill would be misused. I hope we all share the same thoughts and opinions that the jump-spheres should be accessible to guardians of freedom – the brethren of awaken consciousness. We can start space tourism using them, and to begin this endeavor, I would like to try out the pleasure of exploration. Ever since I had become your Tor–the King, I received invitations from heads of states of far-reaching planets. As our hearts are connected, you all know that I do not want to leave my people too long, and I want to stay among my people, more than any other king or queen.

This time we'll send our people across the galaxies in all kinds of ventures, explorations, military attacks, or spying. We give our enemies a surprise, and this is only possible with your helping hands in making HSS functional again. I want to announce hefty rewards if you finish this as soon as possible. May God make it easy for all of us. Long live Akhom!

Fearing extreme torture and death, the scientists and engineers had no other option but to do what the regime demanded.

***

Ankhamon was happy that soon he would leave Lyra to visit another far-off planet. *I will go to planet Mervia*, he thought as he closed his eyes and envisioned the moment he would land there. A booming voice brought him back to reality.

"Going somewhere, your highness?" a voice echoed with bitterness in a sarcastic tone.

Ankhamon opened his eyes and saw Hatathor standing at the entrance with his chest thrown open.

A lightning bolt struck Ankhamon at the sight of him.

"Ah! Hatathor, how are you now? I hope you are well," he asked as he sweated. "I was so worried when I heard your spaceship had crashed." "Yeah, I bet you were, Ankhamon," Hatathor retorted, staring into the king's nervous eyes. "After all, you left no stone unturned to ensure that I left this world." "I – I don't get what you are talking about, Hatathor," he lied.

"Stop betraying me, Ankhamon. I always knew that you were nothing more than an untrustworthy piece of dog shit," Hatathor spat on the floor. "I had the feeling that you were not fit to be the king, but what surprised me the most was the fact that you would betray your planet!" Shiphrah might have told him about my plans to leave the Lyra, Ankhamon realized.

Ankhamon began laughing and said: "What planet are you talking about, idiot! This pathetic piece of chunk which is on the brink of doom!" he uttered bitterly, stamping on the floor with utmost rage. "Lyra had already got destroyed when the very first case of the damned Mutmut disease showed up. I knew it since then that this accursed planet will never recover again, and I had to leave it as soon as possible!"

"Why the hell didn't you leave this planet then, you bastard?!" Hatathor swore with a growl. Ankhamon's words seemed to prick every nerve in his body. "Why did you decide to stay and become the king of this dying planet? Why Ankhamon, why?"

"Because, you nave piece of dung, I couldn't go out until your dear queen Hathor allowed me to leave. She pushed me against the wall. Restrained my movement in the mountains, and when I became the king, I felt Lyra could be a beautiful place again. But now I realized that my daughter hates me, and you opened up the pit of death in Sutekh. The spores will spread again soon, and people will start dying because of the disease. You, my dear friend, you the Lyrian savior, have become the very cause of the spread of the accursed disease!"

Hatathor clapped expressionlessly, while his eyes

continued to stare at him with immense fury.

"Hats off to you, Ankhamon. You proved you are not only a bloody traitor to your friend and your planet but also you are the worst father a daughter can ever have! Abandoning your daughter here and leaving her to die along with this planet," he said. "I tried to convince her to come with me, but if she chooses you over me, and there's nothing I can about it," he asserted with a frown. "By the way, Hatathor. You are right about everything that you have just said till now. I am a traitor and I am the worst father. But you are wrong about one thing..." he paused as he moved behind his desk. "I am not trying to get out of here, my friend. I AM getting out of here." "I will not let it happen," Hatathor growled.

"It's too bad, my friend, that you have to die here. It would have been much better that you had gotten blasted along with your spaceship, but you were lucky then. But luck won't always be by your side," said Ankhamon.

Ankhamon slammed a button that was beneath his desk, and the security alarms across the Tekhenu started ringing. And before Hatathor could make a move, a dozen Brethren officials marched into the room armed with laser guns. A maleficent smile curled across Ankhamon's lips. "Arrest him!" Ankhamon shouted. "He is a deceiver; He does not believe in values which he publicly portray. Ask him, why he wanted to leave Lyra!" Hatathor shouted back.

Brethren were confused. Their king and supposed

savior were fighting with each other.

They were anxious and perplexed at the sudden turn of events. Also, they had no clue what was going on.

"Goodbye, old friend!" Ankhamon bid farewell with a vicious smile on his face.

Hatathor pointing at Ankhamon, said: "Your great king here is planning to leave this planet using the jump-sphere."

The Brethren glanced at each other in shock and started whispering amongst themselves.

"Do not listen to him!" shouted Ankhamon, showing no signs of nervousness. "General Hatathor here is trying to defame me! He has always been jealous of me since the time I became King of Lyra!"

"That is a serious accusation! I have never wanted the throne!" Hatathor retorted back, trying his best to maintain his calm and not lose his temper. The Brethren looked at their Master.

"My loyal friends, why would I be here till now if I wanted to secretly abdicate the throne,abandon the planet and move to another planet and leave you guys to die from Mutmut in the first place? Wouldn't I be already gone long ago? Think about it, please, before doubting me!" he pleaded, putting up his most innocent face. The Brethren's whispering became louder, and one officer shouted at the rest of the Brethren.

"Master is right! General Hatathor is trying to defame him to get the throne!"

Some brethren raised their guns and pointed them

at Hatathor, who didn't flinch.

"Tell us how death feels like, Hatathor!" one of the Brethren said.

He was about to press the trigger, when a voice called from behind them.

"You tell me!" exclaimed Sambi, and the brethren man holding gun turned to see; Sambi threw a dagger into the rival man's chest and killed him. Before the officers had the time to point their guns at Sambi, Hatathor slid down and kicked one of them and, grabbing his laser gun, fired shots at three other officers, killing them on the spot. Sambi made a front flip through the air and delivered a tremendous kick to one officer's head, who went soaring backward and collapsed against a painting on the wall.

"I got your back, Hatathor!" claimed Sambi, and Hatathor nodded with a half-smile. Meanwhile, a few more lasers were shot at Hatathor, who slid across the marble floor on his knees with his torso bent to the back in order to avoid them. Upon reaching the officers firing at him, he moved his torso back up and delivered a powerful punch at the Brethren officer's stomach, which knocked the wind out of him. Then, he retrieved a dagger from his pocket and thrust it deep into the man's abdomen. There was a scream of unbearable pain, and a considerable amount of blood flowed out of the officer's abdomen as he fell on the ground and died a cold-blooded death. The rest of the Brethren cult cornered Sambi and Hatathor.

"Back-to-back!" Hatathor commanded, and they

both stood with their backs against each other to combat Ankhamon's men.

"On the count of three," said Kahotep, and once the countdown ended, they pounced over the brethren cult-like vultures with their daggers.

While Hatathor and Kahotep were battling them, one soldier sneaked from behind Hatathor after grabbing one of the two spears that lay in a golden statue's hand. Then, tiptoeing towards Hatathor, he was about to thrust the spear into his back when Kahotep sprinted towards him as fast as his legs could take him. The Brethren soldier threw the spear, but before it could reach the mighty Lyrian's back, it pierced Kahotep's chest and went right through his lung. Hatathor turned around and his eyes widened in extreme shock as he saw the Lord of Security being stabbed to save his life. Kahotep spat a mouthful of blood and collapsed onto the ground. Hatathor let out a roar of fury, and, shoving the dagger inside the eye of the officer he was fighting with, he grabbed another spear from the statue's hand and threw it at the man who had stabbed Kahotep. The spear pierced right through the Brethren officer's skull, killing him instantly. After slaughtering the man, he bent down at Kahotep, who continued to spit mouthfuls of blood.

"Kahotep," he said, holding his head and staring into his deep eyes. "Why did you do that?"

"I... didn't do it for you... I did it for the Lyra..." He managed to say as his mouth continued to fill with blood. "You are... our planet's... only hope, Hatathor.... Save it from getting destroyed." And with those words, the Lord of Security breathed his last breath. Kahotep lay there on the floor with his soulless eyes wide open. Hatathor closed Kahotep's eyes and rose to his feet.

"I promise you, Kahotep. I will save our planet from getting destroyed! No matter what it takes!"

***

Ankhamon clutched the jump-sphere and moved across a dark narrow hallway with a tiny torch in his hand, which emitted an emerald green light. *Damn you, Hatathor, I wish you had been killed on Keb by the humans. Such a thorn in my flesh! It's an immense relief to have gotten rid of him! I can't believe I am getting the hell out of this sickening planet! I will live a carefree life now! And with the help of this jump-sphere, I will travel wherever the hell I want to!* Ankhamon thought enthusiastically with a broad smile glistening across his face. Then his expression turned repulsive at the thought of his daughter. Shiphrah, I have to take you with me, even if you hate me for the rest of my life! I will not let Hatathor marry you!

The tunnel seemed to be very lengthy and very dusty. At the end of it, a small computer panel with retinal detection lay on the right side of the metallic door. A scanner activated, and a robotic voice asked for a voice and fingerprint scan along with a face scan. Ankhamon placed his chin on the frame and looked into the hole. He cleared his throat and called out, King Ankhamon.' The voice matched and a second later the computerized image of a palm appeared on the computer panel. Ankhamon placed his right palm on the scanner, matching his fingerprints. Two tiny rays of red light appeared, shot out of the computer screen, and scanned Ankhamon's eyeballs, matching the bio-information.

"Access granted to Tor Ankhamon!" called the Artificial Intelligence, and the metallic door slid aside noisily like an old elevator's door. Right in front of Ankhamon's eyes was one of his black spaceships. The day was fiercely windy and chilly as a gush of wind slammed across Ankhamon's face. His eyes gleamed with victory as he gazed at the spaceship.

However, before he could take another step towards the spaceship, a towering figure appeared right in front of him and blocked his path. "Not so fast, great King Ankhamon!" Kontar said, standing with his arms folded and his chest thrown open.

"Oh, what are you doing here? I am in a hurry, Kontar. We will talk later, so get out of my way!" Ankhamon snapped irritatingly. "I am not your bloody servant anymore, Ankhamon!" Kontar growled at him like a furious tiger. "I am a responsible inhabitant of this planet who has come to stop a selfish traitor like you from escaping. I feel disgusted! Deep down, I always knew that you were neither fit to be a king nor a responsible citizen. But little did I know you would be a traitor and such a horrible father!"

"Oh, cut the shit, Kontar! I have already had this bullshit lecture from that Hatathor! So shut your mouth!" he shouted as he held the sphere tighter than ever. "How in the Lyra did you even know that I was going to be here?"

Kontar looked at him disgusted and replied: "Kahotep informed me about it. He knew that a cowardly traitor like you would use the HSS to escape." "Whatever it may be, I have no time to waste. Move out of my way, or else-"

"Or else what?" Kontar demanded dangerously.

Ankhamon looked down to the ground, pretending to be nervous, and suddenly jerked his head upwards.

"Or else this!" he responded by firing a laser shot at Kontar using a small laser handgun. The beam hit Kontar in the shoulder, and he tumbled backward and fell to the ground while writhing horribly in pain. Kontar's agonizing screams filled the air. He got onto his feet again as he held his shoulder while flinching horribly. Ankhamon continued to point the gun at him.

"Kontar, I told you, move out of my way. I have no intention of killing you, but if you force me, I will have no other choice but to do so," he warned serenely. "Ankhamon–you are out of your mind. You are supposed to be the leader of the Brethren movement. Do not shame yourself in the eyes of the public by secretly escaping. Resign and then go!" Kontar said, looking the King straight in the eye.

Ankhamon sighed sarcastically as he glanced below.

"You have left me no choice but to kill you, Kontar.

You have been a loyal servant and faithful officer," he said and was about to press the trigger again when there was a harsh growl of Ankhamon!'

Ankhamon turned around to see the noise source and noticed Hatathor and Shiphrah rushing through the exit door. He realized he had forgotten to give the command to close it. Kontar used the distraction to his advantage and, moving towards Ankhamon, he yanked the laser shotgun out of his hand and threw it away angrily. Then, he caught Ankhamon by the collar and flung him away. Ankhamon landed on the ground with a thud, and the jump-sphere slipped out of his hands and went away rolling towards the spaceship.

"Papa!" cried Shiphrah and placed her hands on her forehead. Kontar rushed to grab the sphere, but before he could pick it up, a dozen other Brethren officers arrived onto the scene and pointed their guns at Kontar, Shiphrah, and Hatathor.

"Put your hands up in the air!" they commanded. All three of them refused to do so and stood there with extreme rage in his eyes. Ankhamon laughed as he wiped the blood off his slashed lip and rose to his feet.

"Well done, my boy!" he praised them. "You guys arrived just in the nick of time." He hastened towards the sphere, and, pushing Kontar aside, he picked it up and looked at his daughter. "Shiphrah - my darling child – come with me!" Ankhamon pleaded.

He stood on the latch of the spaceship.

"Papa, please don't do it! I beg you!" pleaded Shiphrah with tears in her eyes. "Lyra is our home; we must stay here and protect it!" "Oh, shut up, you silly girl, come with me! Try to understand the consequences of your choice, my dear daughter. Mutmut may spread again. I don't want to lose you!" saying that, he gestured to his officers to bring his daughter on the spaceship.

The guards moved forward, but Hatathor instantly turned on the protective shield around himself and Shiphrah, while Kontar rolled onto the ground and hid behind a large rock. The lasers kept deflecting off Hatathor's shield and kept landing on the ground as he and Shiphrah advanced towards the Brethren cult. The royal guards kept firing endlessly but all in vain, as Hatathor's protective shield was too powerful to be penetrated. Ultimately, their guns were out of energy, so they had to throw them aside. Kontar grabbed one of the officer's arm and struck his face with his elbow, sending him backward, on the ground. One soldier tried to get hold of Shiphrah, but his arm was caught by Hatathor, who crushed it mercilessly and flung him effortlessly onto the side. Three of the officers sprinted towards Hatathor and attacked him, but Kontar dived on top of them, bringing them to the ground.

"General Hatathor! I will take care of these bastards! You stop Ankhamon from escaping," he said as he landed a few punches and kicks at the brethren men. Hatathor nodded at him and gesturing to Shiphrah to go back inside the Tekhenu; he marched calmly towards Ankhamon. King Ankhamon was limping towards the spaceship as his foot was injured. He was holding the sphere tighter than ever and struggled to move as fast as his feet could take him. An officer bolted towards Hatathor from behind, attacking him. Still, before he could even touch him, the mighty Lyrian smacked his nose with his elbow without even looking at him. Meanwhile, Kontar took out a metallic rod and shouted: "Come on, you scoundrels! Is that all you traitors got?" he yelled and gestured the rest of them to advance.

In the interim, Hatathor rushed towards Ankhamon, twenty meters away from the spaceship. However, Ankhamon noticed Hatathor was approaching fast and would get to him before reaching the spacecraft. Thus, he moved aside, picked up his laser shotgun from the ground, and pointed it at Hatathor. "Don't you dare come any closer, Seka!" he warned, limping backward while pointing the shotgun at Hatathor and sweating profusely with fear. "I swear I'll kill you."

But Hatathor continued to advance boldly. Ankhamon fired a series of laser shots at him, but in vain, as Hatathor had activated his protective shield, and the shots were deflected. Ankhamon kept firing desperately and yelled from the top of his voice.

"Die, you ruddy bastard, die!" However, Hatathor continued to come closer and closer.

"I'll give you one chance, Ankhamon. Give me the sphere, and I shall let you live,"

"Not in a million years!" the King shouted, while continuing to fire at the shielded man. "I will not die on this planet!"

"This is my final warning, Ankhamon. Be grateful to your daughter, Ankhamon, because of whom you are getting this opportunity to live. Otherwise, I wouldn't have thought twice before murdering a double-crossing piece of rat scum like you!"

"Just get away from me! I am warning you to get lost and leave me alone!" Ankhamon shouted like a panicking child as he felt threatened by Hatathor's advancement. His shotgun ran out of energy, and in a state of desperation, he threw it at Hatathor, who swerved to avoid getting hit.

By this time, an eternal rage had taken over Hatathor, who picked up a bident. The blood in Ankhamon's veins froze at the sight of the sharp weapon, and he turned as pale as a sheet.

"This is your final warning. Hand over the sphere to me, and save your life. I promise I'll let you get out of here in your spaceship."

Ankhamon refused to let go of the sphere and held it close to his chest despite the warnings.

"Let the Princess go," a loud call forced Hatathor to turn and look at his back.

He turned to see that General Desher was there.

"You cannot force your will on us, Hatathor!" shouted Desher. "How dare you come to the palace and create such havoc!" he continued.

"Son of a witch! It's good that you came here to

see for yourself, whom you are serving," said Hatathor.

"Your king is fleeing you. He is secretly escaping from here," Hatathor shouted.

"Liar!" Desher retorted.

"Don't listen to him, Desher. Kill this bastard!" Ankhamon ordered Desher.

Desher took out a device from his pocket, which looked like a pyramidon, and threw it at Hatathor.

As soon as the device reached Hatathorits sparks made the Hatathor's energy shield dysfunctional.

"Stop this!" Shiphrah shouted. "Hatathor is telling the truth. Papa is leaving Lyra!" she said this and looked at her father.

Ankhamon shouted back: "Shut up, girl!" Shiphrah moved forward to confront her father. She was trying to snatch the jump-sphere from him. The jump-sphere fell on the ground and rolled under the ship in the struggle. Ankhamon ran and leaned to grab the sphere, which was slightly out of his reach. For a while, Shiphrah managed to stop her father.

Meanwhile, Desher jumped and reached for Hatathor. They both started fighting with the bidents.

Meanwhile, Ankhamon finally reached the sphere, and as he stood up and ran towards the spaceship; he stood on the latch and looked back.

Hatathor started feeling weak again, and Desher noticed this and took advantage, making him fall to the ground. As Desher was about to pierce Hatathor's belly with his weapon, Shiphrah ran towards both of them to stop them. Hatathor's fury broke out, and with a tremendous growl, he aimed the spear-like rod at the stubborn Desher, determined to kill him. General Desher suddenly moved his bident to pierce Hatathor... when Shiphrah rushed in between them and received the full blow. Shiphrah screamed and fell to the ground.

There was an excruciating silence of agony... as the razor-sharp weapon pierced through her chest...

Desher froze in terror. His body became numb at the sight of what he had done.

"Shiphrah! Shiphrah!" Hatathor called in shock.

Ankhamon, still on the ship's latch shouted in tears: "Shiphrah!" Desher stood up and ran off from the scene. A gush of blood filled Shiphrah's mouth as she conveyed her last few words to Hatathor.

"Seka....I have always loved you... I will always be there in your heart," she muttered, placing her weak hands on his chest, and with a last gesture, she passed away and remained lifeless in her lover's arms.

Hatathor looked up into the sky and let out a thunderous bawl of rage and agony . Seeing his girl's dead body made him realize the pain that Al-Khidr would have felt when he had accidentally killed Estelle, back on Keb.

Hattahor rose in furry and his eyes rested on Ankhamon: "It is all your mistake!!" he shouted.

"You left your daughter and you wanted to ran away like a coward! You don't deserve to be called a father, let alone a king!" Hatathor moved towards the King, who was looking in shock at his daughter's dead body. Hatathor raised his arm to punch him when Ankhamon received another shock as he noticed Hatathor's hand.

Hatathor's tattered shirt's sleeve was revealing his left arm, which looked like a dried-up twig. Ankhamon shrieked like a maniac and he pushed Hattahor out of ship with a kick in his belly. In this attempted , Ankhamon lost his balance and fell on the latch. The jump sphere dropped from his hands and it rolled out of the ship latch and finally rested between the legs of Hatathor, who was now lying on the ground.

"Aaaaaaaa", Ankhamon growled and he quickly pressed the button to close the latch, and ran into the ship's cockpit. "Move Bovar at hypersonic speeds and go far from here!" Pilot Bovar looked at him.

"Hurry, you idiot!" Ankhamon growled as he looked through the window to see any signs of Hatathor.

The pilot engaged the controls, and Ankhamon's spaceship lifted vertically into the sky.

Seeing Hatathor's hand the chaos and horror took the soldiers. They were clearly panicked and started screaming in immense fear. "He's got the curse," an officer said, and they all sprinted away, yelling like mad. In the meantime, Kontar, who was badly wounded by the soldiers, lay writhing in pain on the ground, praying:

"O, God! Help Lyra!"

Kontar was wounded and he was looking helpless at Hatathor.

Hatathor picked up the sphere and looked at the

people who had left him. He realized that he is now cursed. The Mutmut took him; his people abandoned him.

***

General Desher ran like a mad man across the passage inside the Tekhenu. His mind was bursting with the guilt of killing Shiphrah. A volcano of guilt seemed to erupt inside of him as he sprinted across the place. Upon reaching back into Ankhamon's chamber, he tripped and went rolling across the ground. Panting heavily, he managed to retrieve the phone out of his pocket and called his mother, Ahmose.

Ahmose picked up instantly and blabbered anxiously: "My boy where are you? Are you okay? Did you capture that darned Hatathor?

"Mother... I killed... her," he managed to say, as he gasped for breath.

"What? Killed whom? What happened, son? Tell me clearly."

"Mother... I killed... Shiphrah!" he finally articulated through the extensively heavy breaths that he was taking. The news struck Ahmose like a storm as her jaw dropped and eyes widened in shock.

"What! How? How in the universe did this happen?

"I... I was battling Hatathor... and I threw the spear at his... but Shiphrah... Shiphrah came in the middle and it struck her instead." Desher began to sweat profusely as he narrated the incident to his mother.

After listening to the entire story, Ahmose's voice turned surprisingly calm. "Ah, my dear boy, listen to me. You did not kill Shiphrah, it's not your fault-"

"No mother! I am the cause of her death! We can no longer stay in the kingdom! I will be hunted down and punished!"

Ahmose made various attempts to console him and calm him down but it was in vain. Finally, she raised her voice and said sharply: "Now you listen to me Desher! You did not kill Shiphrah! That was just an accident which happened when you were trying to kill Hatathor! Plus, that stupid girl Shiphrah decided her own fate by getting in the middle. You had no intention to harm her in any way! Do you understand!?"

Desher slid down along the wall and rested with head down. He was panting and panicking and was slowly returning to his senses. "Now listen to me carefully, Desher," Ahmose said in a very serious tone. "Tell me, where are you?"

"I am at the . . . " Before he could say anything else to his mother, he heard heavy footsteps from outside Ankhamon's chamber. The Brethren soldiers were approaching. Instantly, he cut the call and rushed outside the chamber.

Desher began to move across the palace. His leg was wounded and he knew that he couldn't make it in time to his ship. He started looking for a place to hide as Hatathor could have attacked him at any time. He headed to the top floor, desperately looking for a room to hide only to find out, to his dispair, that all the rooms were locked.

***

"Your father left you darling."

Hatathor lay Shiphrah's dead body on his lap. His eyes were bloodshot, and the pain in his weak twig-shaped arm was agonizing. His mind was a ticking time bomb that could have burst in any moment.

"Shiphrah... my lovely Shiphrah," he lamented.

He was surrounded by an unimaginable physical and emotional pain. He had lost the only person who loved him and cared for him. His heart seemed to have been snatched out of his body at Shiphrah's death.

"I never expressed my love for you. I had involved myself so much into hatred, bitterness, and revenge that I had forgotten to care for the only one left to love me. I am sorry, Shiphrah! Please forgive me!" he wept bitterly, and his tears trickled across his rough cheek and fell on his dead lady love's eyelids. He caressed her forehead gently, surveying her soulless body with the utmost affection that his heart could muster.

"Desher!" he shouted in rage. And his agonizing voice echoed across the horizon. Unfortunately, there was no one there to console him or to share his pain. "I will get you, Desher!" roared Hatathor while Mutmut was taking over every cell in his body. "No matter which corner of the universe you hide in... I will find you!"

"You will pay for your sins, Desher! No matter which hell hole you hide in, I will find you! And I will give you a merciless death that even your soul would shiver!" Saying that, he gave Shiphrah a last glance and dashed towards Tekhenu. He ran through the secret entrance in Tekhenu through which they had arrived. He wanted to search Desher as fast as he could. Blood was rising to his head.

*I must get to that bastard before his spaceship goes out of sight*, he thought intensely while he pushed himself to continue running. He reached the throne room and then darted outside as quickly as his legs allowed him.

"Where are you, Desher!" he roared with a mixture of agony and desperate fury.

Suddenly he saw someone's silhouette on a side corridor and rushed to see who it was. The moment he entered the corridor, his eyes widened in rage and his blood began to boil, as the man who had killed the love of his life stood right in front of him.

Desher seemed to have been hit by a thunderbolt as he was facing the last man in Lyra that he would have wished to meet at that point. "Desher!" roared Hatathor and lurked on him like a ravenous lion. Desher fired with his laser gun but Hatathor turned on his protective shield and continued walking, panicking the young General. He reached him and as soon as shield touched Desher's gun, the gun melted and Desher threw it away to avoid getting hurt. Hatathor switched off his shield. He ran and punched Desher in his face.

Hatathor and Desher fell over the exquisite art pieces used to decorate the palace. Hatathor caught

Desher's collar and punched his face. Desher tried to get up but Hatathor grabbed him by the hair making him scream in pain, and slid him across the marble flooring. Desher's head hit one of the doors and he cried in agony. Desher managed to stood up and he punched ferociously Hatathor, making his face bleeding.

"I am not afraid of any disease. I am not even a Lyrian. You people are the worst in galaxy," Desher shouted vehemently.

Hatathor switched on his sleeve and created a shockwave, which threw away Desher and his head smashed on the wall making him moaning in pain.

Hatathor ran and kicked Desher stomach several times. Then he placed his foot on Desher's neck, he started crushing it.

"This is for you, Shiphrah!" called Hatathor.

"No, Hatathor no, please forgive me! I beg you!" pleaded Desher through his mouth full of blood. But he couldn't attain General Hatathor's mercy as the Lyrian continued the pressure until Desher's neck was broken, rendering him motionless on the ground.

Hatathor began to pant heavily as he stared at the lifeless body of General Desher.

"Shiphrah, my love, I have avenged your death!" he exclaimed, trying to maintain his balance.

Suddenly, he heard a vibration and realized that it was Desher's transmitter. He shoved his hand inside the dead general's pocket and grabbed the phone. It was Desher's mother who was calling.

Hatathor answered the call and Ahmose spoke in a highly anxious tone.

"Desher where are you?! Why did you cut my call then? Are you in trouble?" Ahmose ranted and Hatathor listened silently with an evil smile on his sickened face. "Your dear son Desher is dead," he declared calmly.

"What!? What nonsense is this?" she began shouting and cursing angrily.

"I, General Hatathor, murdered your son and took revenge for the death of my dearest Shiphrah, you witch!"

"You are lying! You filthy scumbag! You are lying!" she screamed, and Hatathor began to laugh coldly.

"Well, witch, I won't deprive a mother of her right to bury her son. Desher's body is lying here in Ankhamon's palace. Come get him," saying that he cut the call and crushed the transmitter into pieces.

Ahmose let out a horrendous scream of agony and fell onto her knees on the ground. She began to wail loudly and began pulling her hair insanely. Slowly, she managed to gain control of herself.

"Hatathor, you have killed my son! Now, this entire planet will bear its consequences along with you . . ."

# Chapter 22

# The Revenge

ANKHAMON was in his spaceship's cockpit. The Lyrian space force noticed that the royal vessel was airborne. Ten military spaceships got airborne within a few minutes, chasing the royal vessel.

"We are being followed, my king!" the pilot shouted in exasperation.

The space force on the ground contacted the royal vessel.

"Is King Tor Ankhamon on board? Or is this a drill? Answer quickly. Otherwise, we will be forced to make you land!"

"I do not want anyone to follow me!" Ankhamon shouted irritated. "Contact the space force and give me the microphone," he ordered.

Bovar established contact with the ground control room.

"King Tor Ankhamon has ordered that this vessel should not be followed!"

"We have received none such order from Tekhenu!" the ground officer claimed.

"Useless cursed people!" Ankhamon muttered, gritting his teeth.

"Activate Shtat-Sqeb quickly!" Ankhamon yelled frustratingly.

Bovar turned off the communication with the ground space security office and activated the cloaking technology.

Immediately, Ankhamon's vessel became invisible and its signature completely vanished from the radars.

***

An inexplicable sadness took over Hatathor, which seemed to infest every inch of his insides. He lost his love and now his body is dying. "I am cursed only because I went to planet Keb", he said to himself.

"I'll destroy the Keb."

He was sweating profusely, and as he put his hands on his face to wipe it off, he felt the dry skin of one of his hands. He looked at it, and the hand looked like a dried twig, though his fingers were still movable. He pulled up the sleeve of his shirt and found that the hand had dried up to his elbow. "I have got that accursed Mutmut from the Sutekh! Soon I would die!"

He started crying agonizingly.

"Everyone, get away from me and run away as fast as possible!"

He continued crying and then said to himself. "I will destroy the Earth and every human presence on it!"

He retrieved a long glove from inside the dashboard of his spaceship and slide it on his infected arm. Then, he changed the course of the ship, heading towards the HSS.

***

Hatathor jumped out of his spaceship and went towards the HSS facility. As he entered the facility, he noticed the scientists were still working on the ancient Lyrian technology, trying to make it functional again.

"General Hatathor!" one scientist uttered as he saw him entering the Hall of Stars. The rest of the scientists took a glance at him and then returned to their work. The scientists murmured amongst themselves, but Hatathor raised his hand and they all got silent immediately.

"Everyone! I want to know how close we are to creating Tepta Ankh?"

"We are still working on it, general," one scientist informed him. "We will be mostly done by next week..."

"Shut your bloody mouth!" Hatathor growled.

Another scientist spoke up: "Tepta Ankh–the wormhole will open up as soon as we are able to configure the orrery for the sphere trajectory. We are still working on it, and Secretary Ehsis knows it better..."

"Ehsis! I don't want to hear her name ever again here, you understand?" Hatathor shouted grudgingly.

The scientist got frightened with Hatathor's outburst because he did not want to make him angry.

"I cannot wait longer; I came here just to inform you I am coming back with Qeqt-Qemau (The deadliest weapon)!"

"Qeqt-Qemau!"

"Yes, I will destroy that cursed planet Earth," he said with an intense growl. "I don't have much time! I don't care what you all do, but I want the HSS ready by the end of today! If anyone of you doesn't speed up the work, I will have you beheaded in front of the entire Lyra!" Hatathor threatened and marched out of the HSS facility, leaving the scientists shaking with intense fear.

***

King Iniharut was seated on his throne inside a battleship while his soldiers were in the front seats.

"My king!" called one of the soldiers with an extreme concern on his face.

"What is it?" the king inquired calmly.

"Some hostile Lyrian spaceships appear to be heading towards us! Shall we attack?"

“No. Let’s talk to them first,” he affirmed and they halted at the entrance of the Lyrian atmosphere.

Shortly, the fleet of Lyrian spaceships faced the Arpatian battleships.

“Who are you, intruders? And why are you approaching the kingdom of Akhom?” demanded the commander of one of the Lyrian spaceships.

“I am King Iniharut of the planet Arpat, and we do not pose any threats. Our fuel is diminishing, and we need Amris to return to our planet.” Iniharut cooked up a story as his deep voice boomed.

“We cannot allow you to enter the kingdom without the approval of our king. We received no prior order to allow your landing. You better get away from our planet, or we will have to open fire against you and your troops!” the Lyrian threatened firmly.

“Forces of Lyra, understand us; we are merely seeking help from you... “ Iniharut started explaining, but he was rudely interrupted by the Lyrian commander. “I will say this once more, get the hell out of our planet, or we will destroy all your ships!”

Iniharut waved his hand, and his officers cut off the communication.

“We turn to contingency plan. Establish contact with Secretary Ehsis.”

***

Hatathor reached the Gerh-en-eha, the battle control station of the kingdom of Akhom. The soldiers stationed at the facility entrance saluted him quickly upon arrival.The battle station had been closed for a while, but the weapon system was routinely checked to ensure that it was functional in case the kingdom needed protection.

Gerh-en-eha was located close to the military headquarters amd it had cosmic guns and laser cannons which were bigger and stronger than the ordinary ones. The cosmic guns were able to generate powerful laser beams to blast a meteor into pieces. Apart from that, there were also many biological weapons, like missiles that had glass tubes attached to them that comprised nanomites – a nano-particle-based weapon which, if unleashed, could devour the toughest metal in the entire universe. Hatathor went straight to the core of the inner sanctums of Gerh-en-eha. He knew the building well as he had been the head of weapon systems before going to Earth. He went to the weapons room and looked at the many spheres that were attached to metallic clamps and girdles.

Hatathor looked closely at one of the spheres. As he approached the sphere, the sphere's color turned dark green from black, and it started glowing. He noted the number visible on the sphere's surface and went to the control panel. As soon as he placed his hand over the scanner, the voice issued: "Welcome, Mj. General Hatathor! Activate unclasping sequence for weapon number 1002001. Authorization requested. Enter Sheta Terf (password)," the voice demanded the shibboleth to unclasp the weapon.

Hatathor entered the password and voice issued.

"Qeqt-Qemau dislodged." The sphere fell on the floor with a loud thud.

Hatathor moved closer to the sphere. There was a handle on one of the sides which he rotated and quickly pulled towards him making a device come out of the sphere. As soon as he activated the device, a beam was fired and engulfed the spherical bomb. Hatathor started moving back towards his spaceship as the beam held Qeqt-Qemau like a balloon above him.

He placed the weapon inside his spaceship.

Finally! I will destroy the Earth and take revenge for the death of my father, and the countless fellow Lyrians who have died because of the Mutmut! Hatathor thought firmly as a maleficent smirk spread across his lips.

But as soon as he was airborne, the entire Misraim started shaking with sirens.

Is someone attacking the Lyra?

***

Ankhamon's spaceship was still moving across the Lyrian atmosphere when the pilot informed him that a large fleet of spaceships was entering Lyra from the outer space. "What?" he demanded anxiously, looking out of the window immediately, although they weren't in a position where they could have seen anything relevant. "Who the hell are those intruders that you speak of?"

"I have no idea, my king. But they do not seem to be from any nearby planet."

Suddenly, a fleet of massive battleships got into their visuals, and Ankhamon recognized them. Instantly his jaw dropped and his eyes widened in intense fear at the sight of the ships.

"Damn! It just cannot be!" he exclaimed, jumping out of his seat like a monkey.

"I don't believe my eyes! King Iniharut of Arpat arriving in Lyra after such a long time!"

King Ankhamon remained silent in shock for a few moments and then gave a furious command.

"Officer, I want this spaceship to be landed this instant!" "But, my king-"

"Just do as I say!" he bawled irritatingly, his eyes brimming with intense fear and dismay. "Land it anywhere; I don't bloody care, but let's get the hell down as fast as possible!"

"Okay, my king, as you wish!" saying that, the pilot changed the course immediately, heading to the ground.

A huge cave was nearby, and the pilot directed the spaceship towards it as quickly as possible. Ankhamon took an enormous sigh of relief as they entered the cave and jumped back into his seat.

***

Semed, Nefertiti, and Al-Khidr were hiding in the rocks outside the HSS. Al-Khidr noticed Hatathor had come out of HSS, and some soldiers were still around. They slid down through the rocks and landed on the sand. Their mouth and head were covered, camouflaging them and they managed to sneak into the HSS through a broken glass window. Nefertiti entered a hall first that looked like the docking station. Semed and Al-Khidr followed her.

As soon as Al-Khidr entered it, he recalled that this was the Hall that he had seen first when he had entered Lyra for the very first time.

"This hall is abandoned, but it is connected to the Hall of Stars," Al-Khidr informed Semed.

"Look over there," he pointed hurriedly to a small space in the corner. "That passage leads to the abyss, and I guess the Hall of Stars is directly above us," he continued.

"You are right," Semed agreed with a firm nod.

"There must be a way to go up," Nefertiti asserted as she surveyed the top contemplatively. "Be careful; Ankhamon's people are stationed all over the place," she advised firmly.

Everyone gazed intensely into each other's eyes as they readied their laser guns for engagement.

***

Hatathor turned his spaceship's direction and landed near Gerh-en-eha; the security alarms across the facility were ringing heavily with the warnings Red Alert.' Hatathor entered the facility and zoomed into the battle station–the Hall of Death. The officers clutched their laser guns and moved towards a computer panel that lay right in the corner of the room.

One of the officers operated the buttons on the computer panel, and the gigantic screen switched on displaying a massive battleship entering Lyra's atmosphere. The battleship was unlike any other they had ever seen before and was much bigger than the spaceships Lyra had. It appeared to be a massive dome with three scissor-like flaps attached on either side.

"We have got intruders!" one of them exclaimed.

"What!" Hatathor yelled and rushed towards the computer screen.

What the hell is happening? Who are these bloody intruders?

"They are from planet Arpat," one officer said as he slammed the button on the computer panel to zoom in and have a closer look. *Why have they come without permission?* Hatathor wondered desperately. Could they be helping the human?, whispered the voice in his head. However, he shook his head to get rid of the negative thoughts.

*Don't be ridiculous, Hatathor! How could anyone dare to attack Lyra?*, he thought again. Hatathor commanded the soldiers.

"I don't care how formidable those foreign battleships look! I want them destroyed right now!"

"But we are waiting for General Desher's order. . ."

"I won't let any more foreign scum invade my planet! So destroy them before they even have the chance to escape!"

The officers glanced at each other and nodded firmly a Yes, sir' and gave an order for the Lyrian spaceships to be deployed.

***

Hatathor was watching the entire confrontation on the screen. He banged his fist against the display panel.

"What the hell are these brainless soldiers doing?! Why are they wasting time arguing with these foreign maggots! I better have a word with them!"

Saying that, he pressed a tiny button on his communicator earpiece and spoke to the commander of the spaceship who had engaged the Arpatian ship.

"What the hell do you think you are doing, idiot! Blast those vermin into pieces!"

"But general..."

"I don't want to hear anything! Just destroy their battleships and get your asses down as soon as possible!" he yelled.

"Okay, general," he muttered.

The moment the call disconnected, the commander ordered.

"Open fire!"

A large laser gun emerged out of the Lyrian spaceship towards King Iniharut's battleship. And a massive laser beam was fired at the battleship; however, to the Lyrian soldiers' horror, the laser beam deflected off the battleship and went towards one of the Lyrian's spaceship, blasting it into pieces. King Iniharut's battleship was enveloped by an immense hemispherical protective shield.

King Iniharut sighed disappointed and ordered calmly: "Destroy their spaceships."

The moment the words came out of his mouth, the first officer pressed a large red button, and a sophisticated cannon appeared out of the battleship's hull. A giant blast of fire went zooming through the cannon, and within a fraction of a second, the spaceship was blasted into smithereens with a blood-curdling noise that sent shivers down the Lyrian soldiers.

"Let's enter the planet," said Iniharut, and the enormous fleet of Arpatian battleships made their way into the Lyrian atmosphere. Hatathor looked utterly stunned at the shocking sight.

*How is this possible!* he thought, staring at their enormous vessels making their way into Lyra. Have they come to put a stop to my plans? How the hell do they know about my plans?

For the first time, an inexplicably intense fear rushed across the mighty Lyrain's spine at the sight of an enemy. Never had he been so anxious when an enemy was approaching.

"I must act fast and send the quantum weapon to Earth before anyone stops me!" he said quickly and began moving towards the center of the Hall of Death. However, sudden dizziness took over before he could make another move. He stopped in his tracks for a few moments and shook his head slowly, but before he could move any further, a sudden rush of intense pressure rose across his throat, and he puked horribly on the metallic floor. His entire face pricked as though tons of tiny red ants were moving inside it. He looked at the floor, and a lightning bolt struck him. . . there was a small pool of blood on the ground. Slowly, he wiped his mouth with the back of his sleeve, and it got stained with blood. He froze in horror, as he couldn't believe his eyes. . . Mutmut was drastically taking over his body.

***

"How far are we from the Kneph?" King Iniharut demanded.

"It is 34,456 Supris away, my king. If we breach the defense line, we will reach there within seventeen minutes. . ."

Before the officer could finish his sentence, his eyes widened in shock as he noticed in display panel nearly fifty Lyrian spaceships were approaching them. "What happened, officer?" Iniharut inquired coolly.

"My king, more fleets of Lyrian ships have arrived!"

"These people never learn. Alright, show them what we got," Iniharut ordered, maintaining his unshakeable calmness.

The officer nodded and turned the battleship around while the fleet of spaceships was consistently firing beams at them. The Arpatians shot a fireball at them, which a few ships avoided by swerving or rotating aside. But one spaceship wasn't very lucky, and it blasted into tiny pieces when it got hit by the ball of fire. The Lyrian spaceships zoomed at tremendous speeds across the enormous Arpatian vessel. They fired laser shots continuously from each side, but in vain as the protective shield deflected them.

"Be very careful, officer. Remember, we are here to save this planet, not destroy it."

"Understood, sir."

Meanwhile, one of the officers on the Lyrian spaceships that moved across the right, asked the pilot to fly the spacecraft over the vessel. Once the spacecraft was over the Arpatian vessel, he looked down over the battleship that moved slowly and opened the spaceship's deck, intending to jump onto the battleship to enter it. "On the count of three," he said to himself nervously. "One... two... three... " and then he made the jump. However, his efforts were futile as the protective shield surrounding the vessel blasted him into wisps of smoke.

"No!" cried one of his comrades from the spaceship. "That's it now! I can't take it anymore! There is only one weapon that can destroy this foreign filth!" saying that, he moved over to the dashboard and retrieved a peculiar gun which had a glass tube attached to it that contained a greenish fluid: nanomites. "Don't do that, Remmao! If you miss, the missile will either hit a building or, even worse, the ground, and the nanomites will eat up everything, causing mass destruction!"

"Jorge! You always forget one thing!" he asserted, turning towards him with the nanomite-filled missile gun directed towards the battleship: "I never miss my shot." He pulled the trigger and the lethal missile went flying below. Unfortunately, Remmao's fear came true, and right at that moment the colossal vessel rushed forward making the missile collided with a building under construction instead. The green fluid enveloped the entire building, and the nanomites feasted on the metal and turned it into wisps of greenish smoke within seconds.

Jorge's eyes widened in fear, and he moved backward in shock.

"You dumbass! I told you this would happen!" Remmao shouted agitatedly. "If you ever use that darned weapon again, I will skin you alive!" Remmao stopped shouting and looked ahead with death staring intensely into his eyes.

The officers yelled as the spaceship smashed into a massive building ahead, and they all perished instantly.

The other spaceships continued the chase and attacked the Arpatian ship at the same time in the interim.

"My king, they are too many! If they continue firing like that, the laser beams will eventually break through our protective force field!"

A soldier that sat on King Iniharut's right side suggested releasing demolishing waves to destroy the Lyrian spaceships, but the king put down the idea.

"No! The frequencies will also demolish the buildings and kill the people of this city along with the spaceships! So, it's too risky to use them." "My king, what shall we do then?"

Iniharut paused for a few seconds as he stared into the air in intense contemplation. "Officer, use the cloaking technology!"

"But, my king, it has not been perfected yet, and we might lose cloaking effectiveness after a short while," he informed quickly.

"That is not a problem, officer," he said with a bright smile. "In those few moments, we will turn these annoying Lyrian spaceships into wisps of smoke. So, do it!" The Arpatian officer raised his eyebrows, thoroughly impressed by his king's brilliant idea. He opened a glass flap below the dashboard without wasting a second and slammed a fist-sized red button. The entire battleship vanished within a fraction of a second and went completely out of sight. Without a visible target, the Lyrian spaceships had to stop firing.

"What the hell just happened? Where did that battleship disappear?" a soldier from one of the spaceships exclaimed. "Did it get destroyed?"

"No! I don't think so. If our laser beams had damaged it, surely there would have been a blast!" cried a driving soldier.

As the Lyrians continued to debate on the battleship's disappearance. King Iniharut gave the last command: "Officer! Get rid of these annoying rebels! We save only the forces supporting Secretary Ehsis."

Instantaneously, he targeted all the Lyrian spaceships simultaneously and informed his king: "Targets locked sir, deploying fireballs in three. . . two. . . one."

At the end of the countdown innumerable cannon-like guns emerged from every corner of the battleship. A series of loud blasts occurred as the fireballs raced towards their respective targets and collided. All the citizens of Misraim gathered across the city and gazed fearfully into the sky. The blasts caused them to run hither and thither out of intense fear, and the streets soon emptied.

After all the Lyrian spaceships were destroyed the Arpatian battleship was visible again.

"Good job, officers!" Iniharut praised, and they all cheered. "Now let's get to the Kneph as quickly as possible; Ehsis must be waiting for us." The battleship turned around and soared towards the Kneph.

***

Hatathor's insides were burning fiercely as he attempted to hold his balance and move forward. But to his utmost horror and shock, his legs felt thoroughly numb, as though they had no feeling left in them. He struggled to move, but he simply couldn't. Every muscle in his legs seemed to have paralyzed. He shouted frustrated: "Must move... quickly!" he uttered. "There is no time to waste! Move Hatathor, move!" he said to himself. Abruptly, all the muscles in his legs gave in, causing him to fall onto the ground pathetically.

"Place the Qeqt-Qemau weapon in the cannon," Hatathor ordered.

The soldiers glanced at each other.

"Do this fast or I'll kill you," he growled.

Within a few minutes, the weapon was ready to launch.

"General Hatathor, King Iniharut, has decimated the Lyrian forces. Soon they will attack Misraim," they informed him with extreme worry on their faces. "He has used cloaking technology, and we are unable to track him."

"Hunt him down!"

The officers frantically started scanning the sky and engaged the satellites as well in the search for the Arpatian ship. "Iniharut's ship was spotted in the east, near the crater of Sovidos."

"The crater of Sovidos," Hatathor uttered with extreme bewilderment.

"Zoom in all the spy satellites over there and get me all the visuals!"

The officers entered the data, and all spy satellite probes started moving towards the crater of Sovidos.

Hatathor jumped out of his seat.

"We have intercepted their communication," one Lyrian officer said.

"They are communicating with someone deep in the crater, almost 2500 Supris below the surface!"

Another officer with a baffled face looked at generals in the hall of death.

"I want to listen to what they are up to!" growled Hatathor.

The nervous officer put the communication on the speaker: [Buzz. . . noise. . . ] "King Iniharut here." . . . "We have arrived at the coordinates. Contact quickly secretary Ehsis."

The voice of King Iniharut sounded, and Hatathor was furious.

"[buzz...] King Iniharut, Ehsis here, we have detected your spaceship; I am coming up to greet you."

"Ehsis!" "All this time, she was in Lyra!" another general shouted in surprise.

"So it is she who has invited Arpat forces for her support."

"Damn, cursed bitch!"

"Throw Qeqt-Qemau on his spaceship," Hatathor shouted with disgust.

"Ehsis!" he exclaimed, punching the air. "All this time, you were in Lyra, right under our nose! But finally, I have found you, you bloody old hag! Now, before I destroy the Earth, I should melt your existence, along with every Lyrian who has ever supported you! I will kill you, Ehsis. Your death is inevitable!" he yelled. "General, launching to that range will take a few minutes."

"Do it!" growled Hatathor impatiently, unable to contain his rage over finally having the opportunity to crush the rebels.

The officers pressed the touch screen, and the launching sequence was initiated taking Hatathor closer to avenging his beloved father's death.

# Chapter 23

# The Fall

AL-KHIDR, Nefertiti, and Semed sneaked through the tiny passage at the corner of the abandoned hall. The passage was narrow with poor lighting, but they were able to go through it. It was an air-conditioning duct in which they were moving, and they took many turns and climbed many times until they could see a corridor.

"Shush!" Nefertiti waved her hand and asked them to be quiet. Semed tried to say something, but Al-Khidr gestured him to remain silent with a finger on his lips. They noticed two soldiers walking from the other end of the corridor, conversing deeply amongst themselves. They waited until the soldiers passed away. As soon as the corridor was clear, Al-Khidr pushed the cover and jumped out of the duct. Nefertiti and Semed followed him.

After they had passed, he peeped at the hallway from the side, and when he was assured that the hallway was cleared, he gestured to the other two to follow him. As cautiously as possible, they moved towards the Hall of Stars.

But before they could get any closer to the entrance, there was a shout from behind them that alarmed them greatly: "Hey, you!" roared one brethren officials. "What the hell are you three doing here?"

Three Brethren officials moved towards them while directing their laser guns at them. Semed tried to open his mouth to speak, but they shut him down with a shout. "Place your weapons on the ground and put your hands up in the air!" the brethren ordered crudely.

Al-Khidr looked at Semed and Nefertiti and gestured them to follow the order. The three of them had bent down and were about to leave their laser guns on the ground when Al-Khidr retrieved two daggers from his boots and quickly threw them instantly at them. The Brethren officials cried out pain while Nefertiti raised her laser gun and gunned them down, killing them. Semed looked at them foolishly and felt stupid for not thinking of such an excellent tactic. "Let's move!" Al-Khidr said and they continued on their way. A computer panel was hung on the right side of the entrance door of the Hall of Stars. Nefertiti swiped the security pass of one of the dead soliders on the touch screen, and a robotic voice asked for a fingerprint.

"Damn it! How can we enter the Hall of Stars now? Why didn't we think of this before!?" Semed lamented, punching the air. The three of them paused for a few moments in immense frustration.

Think of something, Al-Khidr, think, the tiny voice in his head called as he intensely pressured his mind. Abruptly, his eyes fell on the dead body of the brethren soldier lying on the ground, and a brilliant idea flashed in his head. He dashed towards him and dragged his body towards the computer panel. He read the soldier's name on his ID tag: Kabuto. Instantly, a palm-sized image appearing on the panel. Al-Khidr then removed the glove from the soldier's right hand, placed his palm correctly over the image, and the AI scanned his fingerprints, accepting them as correct.

"Access Granted. Welcome, Kabuto," called the AI, and the doors slid open.

"Brilliant, Al-Khidr!" Semed praised him as they rushed into the Hall of Stars. Semed was awestruck by the gigantic hall that stood in front of his eyes upon entering. His jaw dropped as he gawked like a hawk at the enormous place. As they moved further inside the great hall, he witnessed the gigantic circular ring that floated right in the center of the Hall of Stars.

There were many scientists present, and soon they

started to notice them and turned to look at them.

Al-Khidr noticed the jump-sphere, which was placed on a stand.

"Look! The sphere is there."

"This is fantastic!" expressed Semed, surveying the celestial place in awe while his arms were wrapped around his body as he shivered slightly. "I have never seen a place like this before!"

"Never mind the place; we got the jump-sphere, now let's just get the hell out of here."

The group of scientists turned around and looked at the trio in an intense mixture of shock and amazement.

"Nefertiti!" one of them exclaimed and moved towards her. He gave her a one-armed hug and expressed immense happiness at seeing her after such a prolonged period. "It's been a while, Minka," she expressed with a generous smile.

"Help us, please," another female scientist moved forward towards Nefertiti. "I saw you earlier in this hall when we had sent him to Keb," she pleaded for help. The remaining scientists also mustered around them.

A scientist named Destro hugged Semed and showed his utmost surprise at seeing them.

"How come you all are here?" he inquired.

"Never mind," exclaimed Al-Khidr, staring at him sharply. "We are here to rescue you all and take you out of here."

Al-Khidr paused suddenly as a question rose inside

his mind. He gazed at Destro with an expression of fear and confusion and asked him. "What have you guys been planning to do with the jump-sphere, by the way?" At his question, Nefertiti and Semed, too, stared at Destro curiously.

Destro glanced at the sphere and sighed.

"Hatathor can come back here at any moment. He wants to destroy Keb by sending the most destructive weapon we have." "What?!" they were shocked.

"Hatathor has been hatching the despicable plot to destroy the planet Keb. And if any of us had refused or resisted him, he would have killed all of us in an instant," he explained with a somber expression on his face as he looked down guilty. "But what weapon is that?" Semed asked sharply.

"He planned to send the Qeqt-Qemau weapon. It is a bomb which, if it falls on a planet, would obliterate it right from its core," Destro replied, and Nefertiti clamped her mouth with her palm in intense shock.

*You murderously ruthless man, Hatathor. You are not a part of this peaceful universe, and you are nothing but a disease, much worse than the Mutmut that needs to be removed as quickly as possible,* Al-Khidr thought furiously as a gigantic wave of rage and hatred grew inside his head. Destro hung his head down in utter shame.

"Where has Hatathor gone?" Nefertiti demanded sharply. "He has gone to the Hall of Death."

"Thank the almighty Lord that we reached here before Hatathor had the chance to return!" Al-Khidr exclaimed, and turning towards Destro, he commanded. "Take the jump-sphere out of the charging stand immediately before either Hatathor or the brethren forces arrive." "Sure!" he exclaimed with exhilaration and turned towards his fellow scientists. "Everyone, remove the jump-sphere from the stand now. These people are Secretary Ehsis' soldiers, and they rescue us!"

The rest of the scientists started muttering gleefully amongst themselves, and one of them removed the sphere out of the stand and passed it on to Destro. However, before Destro could hand over the sphere to Al-Khidr, ear-bursting explosions sounded from outside the hall, which caused them all to cover their ears tightly. "What in the world is going on outside!?" Nefertiti demanded as she continued to clamp her ears tightly.

"We should inform Ehsis immediately!" Al-Khidr said with gritted teeth, unable to bear the gut-wrenching noise of the bombardment. Gradually, Semed unclamped his palm, tapped his ear's communication device, and contacted Ehsis. Ehsis picked up the call instantly.

"Hello! Madam Secretary! We heard some explosions," he roared on top of his lungs, but her voice wasn't audible because of the constant bombing. "Hello, hello," he kept shouting, but the call was disconnected.

"Nefertiti, Semed! Let us rush to the Hall of Death and stop Hatathor!"

However, before they could make a move, the doors of the Hall of Stars slid aside, and a dozen Brethren officers marched inside quickly. "Put your hands in the air, people of Ehsis!" one of them ordered, aiming his gun at Al-Khidr.

The Lyrian forces aimed their guns at Al-Khidr, Nefertiti, and Semed.

"Place your guns on the ground and place your hands behind your heads!" they shouted.

The three of them did as instructed and raised their hands.

Suddenly, the alarms resounding in the entire Misraim were heard.

"What's going on?" Semed said.

"Kill these Arpatians," one soldier said.

"Wait, we are not from planet Arpat, and we are Lyrians like you," Nefertiti shouted.

"Imprison them until Seka Hatathor comes back!" their commander ordered.

***

King Iniharut's battleship had landed near the crater of Sovidos and was waiting patiently for Ehsis' response. Abruptly, one of his commanders exclaimed, "My King! We are receiving the transmission from the commander Hemiyan."

"Establish communication,"

Commander Hemiyan was relying on his battleship. He said: "Our system has detected the heat signatures of a brethren spaceship. But it is inside a cave, near us!" "What? Who could that be?! Is it Secretary Ehsis' hideout? Then how in the universe can a brethren spaceship be here?" he demanded, utterly perplexed. After a moment of intense contemplation, he commanded:

"Enter the cave and neutralize all threats."

"But my king, it could even be a trap, laid by Ankhamon himself."

"No! I don't think so! We indeed surprised the Lyrian forces. They were not expecting us. King Ankhamon, I am not sure where he is."

Commander Hemiyan and a dozen Arpatian soldiers entered the cave while the rest stayed back on the battleship to guard the area. The commander of the Arpatian army was carrying a portable heat detector and moving towards the site where the heat signatures were coming from. As they marched across the cave, the heat signatures became stronger.

"Commander!" the soldier whispered, turning the heat detector towards the right. "The Brethren ship is just a few meters away toward the right." "Excellent!" he said softly, and they immediately turned towards the right and continued to walk. The soldier was sweating profusely, not out of the cold but due to the possibility of an ambush or a trap.

Finally, as the passage came to a dead-end and right in front of them lay a giant black spaceship with words Brethren' embossed on its surface at the center. "This is the Lyrian vessel!" whispered one of the Arpatian soldiers.

"But what is it doing here? Commander Hemiyan uttered in surprise.

And before he could contemplate any further on the matter, a croaked yet lively voice sounded from behind him, and they all turned around. "I can tell you the answer to that."

Commander Hemiyan's eyes widened, and his stiff jaws let out a gleeful smile, and before turning, he uttered the words joyfully. "Secretary Ehsis!"

Hemiyan turned, and all of a sudden shots were fired. Hemiyan fell to the ground. He also fired and wounded the enemy before closing his eyes; he saw a man with a tattoo on his forehead coming towards him.

Master Ankhamon had neutralized the Arpatian forces inside the massive cave.

***

King Iniharut's ship landed and established communication with Cove, giving him the opportunity to descend into Kneph alongside his entourage. Ehsis and Rostau greeted them. He was immensely pleased to see finally Ehsis.

He moved towards her, and both gave a bow of respect to each other.

"Thank you for coming to help us, great king Iniharut!" she expressed with a weak yet lively smile.

"This is our duty madam secretary to help our firends!"

After the warm welcome, she led them all towards Kneph. As they entered Kneph, Iniharut asked her courteously,

"Madam Secretary, my army has discovered a ship in a cave nearby. Does it belong to you?" Ehsis sighed and replied carefully.

"My king, we are going through very chaotic times. We don't know much as our systems cannot detect all signatures."

"What happened here? Why you haven't contacted me earlier?"

And Ehsis narrated the entire incident to him.

When she finished her story, King Iniharut's blood boiled and he turned extremely red with intense rage.

"Why didn't you kill Ankhamon?" he asked, trying his best to maintain his calm.

Ehsis shook her head. We were outnumbered, and people were afraid, so we kept quiet.

"Ankhamon is that bloody traitor due to whom Lyra had to face such a bloody rebellion. He is the reason you were all forced into hiding!"

He let out his anger while Ehsis continued to stare at him calmly. King Iniharut heaved heavily and tried to let go of his intense anger.

"Okay, whatever happened, happened. But please don't tell me that you let him walk away?" "No, I didn't, great king," she informed him, and a substantial bubble of relief broke across his face.

"Yes, indeed, he is the reason the entire Lyra is in grave peril. But we Lyrians have our rules. We don't kill simply because we can or have the power to. Tor Ankhamon will be punished for his despicable acts. Yes, he will. But he will be placed on trial in the

Lyrian court of law once we have cleared the mess that he has made. If we kill him now without placing him on trial and giving him an appropriate punishment, what difference would be there between him and us?" she told him peacefully.

King Iniharut stood there rooted to the spot motionless and suddenly gave her a deep bow, which blew everyone's minds, including Ehsis'. "Hail Secretary Ehsis!" he exclaimed, moving himself up. "You are a true Lyrian and the perfect heir to Queen Hathor. Your just ways and fairness have immensely increased the respect I had for you."

Ehsis thanked him serenely and continued to walk towards the Cove.

"Secretary Ehsis, I think I should order my forces to attack HSS and kill Hatathor," he suggested.

However, she shook her head slowly and said: "No, great king. The HSS is a vital facility, the heart of the Lyrian technology. Before Ankhamon and Hatathor took over Lyra, HSS was where our scientists worked on scientific innovations to better our planet and its people. Destroying the HSS will take us back in time," she enlightened him, and he contemplated over the matter deeply.

"And besides, some of our most competent officers have gone there to release the scientists from the ruthless Brethren Cult," she added and began pondering about the reason it was taking them so long to come back and the horrible noise that she had heard while Semed was trying to speak with her on the call. As they approached the Cove, one of her officers, came running towards her with a terrifying expression on his face. "Madam Ehsis, madam Ehsis!" he bawled, sweating profusely from head to toe.

"What happened, officer?" she demanded anxious.

"Ankhamon forces have activated the Qeqt-Qemau weapon system in the Hall of Death, and we believe they are targeting the king Iniharut ship right above Kneph. It is a matter of seconds, and we must evacuate the Kneph right now!" "No!" she yelled. "We don't have time to move." "Everyone come inside the Cove!" she ordered with intense consternation.

Some of the Arpatian soldiers called the rest of the soldiers from their battleship, but the intense electromagnetic surges stopped any communications. "It is too late, officer," he said in a gloomy voice and shook his head while the soldiers slowly wiped the tears off their eyes, following Ehsis inside the Cove. When all the officers of Ehsis and King Iniharut had safely entered the Cove, Ehis ran to her central station and broke the seal of a button visible through the glass. "All put on the seatbelts!"

"Yes, ma'am!' the officers said.

She pressed the button, and a swishing noise sounded across the Coveas metallic walls enveloped the entire place within seconds. A crushing sound erupted from across the Cove and everyone, including the Arpatians, began to lose their balance. "Hold tight, everyone!" Ehsis called.

They were experiencing the ground beneath them

moving drastically, as though a humongous tremor was occurring. The computer screen displayed that the missile was merely a few feet away from colliding with Kneph, and everyone's heartbeats halted for a second.

The entire Cove fell under the gravity of Lyra with an enormous splash that shook the soul of every man and woman that was inside.

The missile hit King Iniharut's battleship over Kneph, but there was a soul-ripping blast that destroyed the entire area and everything that was fifty Supris within its radius, including. The cameras inside the Cove turned black, and the loud explosion was heard. The unfortunate Arpatian soldiers that stayed back inside the battleship to keep watch perished horribly, and they sacrificed their lives for their king, and their loyalty remained unmatched.

The Cove sped up as the explosive gases created pressure to push the gases in the caverns underneath the Cove. The Arpatians and the Lyrians began to scream horrendously as the Cove started to rotate as it fell. It seemed like the end was near, and they were falling into the arms of death. Almost everyone was experiencing an intense amount of terror, and their hearts seemed to be moving out of their chest as the Cove rotated and moved. The Cove accelerated in the water-filled caverns, flowing like a ball chased by the burning gases. Suddenly it jerked out of the cave, and it was a thousand Supris above a large lake. The cave was opening at the top of the mountain, and the water was falling from the cave into the lake in a waterfall.

But now, the cave was roaring like a dragon as combustible gases were coming out from it.

The Cove shooted out and landed into the lake with a massive splash.

# Chapter 24

# The Tremors

ANKHAMON was flying the Arpatian spaceship across the Lyrian horizon. The Vega was emerging gradually from behind the clouds. Ankhamon took a sigh of relief and, placing the spacecraft on autopilot, he moved his revolving seat back and relaxed. Just a few moments earlier, he managed to kill the commander of the Arpatian army. Unfortunately, his loyal pilot died in the clash.

"I do not need him anymore; after all, nobody should know where am I am heading," he said to himself.

*Finally! I am far away from the dreaded Lyrians and that damned Hatathor*, he thought as he placed his hands behind his neck. But his calm mind suddenly jolted back to anxiety. He was thinking of the place where he could hide from the mad general Hatathor. Excessive fear bubbled inside his stomach, causing him to get enveloped by goosebumps. He buried his face in his palms and contemplated deeply. Within a few seconds, an idea blasted into his head that doubled his worries. "Honkira would be the last place any Lyrian king would like to go. Curse on me. I have no other option left now," he said to himself. "Commander Hemiyan!"

"Commander Hemiyan!"

Arpatian forces were trying to establish contact.

He moved towards the communications panel and switched off the Arpatian communication channel. Also, he quickly activated the cloaking to hide his spaceship. He took out a device from his helmet and inserted it into the Arpatian ship.

"I should hack their codes and block them!" he said to himself.

Being an experienced and skilled hacker, it didn't take him much time to override the security protocols.

"I am all set to open my communication channel," he said to himself and tried to establish a communication with the ambassador of the planet Honkira, who was stationed in Lyra. Both Kingdom of Akhom and Kingdom of Qumrud of planet Honkira had fought over Amirs. The last battle happened during the time of King Ptah, and finally, both kingdoms reached an agreement, and a diplomatic relationship was established.

"Come on, come on, come on!" Ankhamon muttered desperately, struggling to establish a channel with Honkira. Nothing happened for a few seconds. Then suddenly, a husky voice boomed through the microphone, and Ankhamon nearly jumped out of his seat with joy. "I am Tor Ankhamon, the king of Lyra and I would like to speak to the ambassador of Honkira."

The husky voice paused for a second and turned into a soft voice: "The ambassador of Honkira here. Your Excellency, I am all ears to you."

"Ambassador, I would like to inform you that there is a clear and persistent danger to your life. The Mutmut disease has reappeared on our planet. I am informing all the ambassadors stationed in Lyra," Ankhamon said on a nervous tone.

"Oh, thank you, Your Excellency. My team also informed me about unrest in the capital," the ambassador spoke.

"Madam Mosaka, I advise you that you leave Lyra as soon as possible. There is a military coup going on here. Many ambassadors have been assassinated, but I can help you get out of Lyra safely. I will provide you a safe passage, and your safety is ensured as long as we are on board on the same spaceship".

"I see, I see," the Honkira ambassador said on a nervous tone. She was pretty worried now, and that was what Ankhamon wanted.

"Your Excellency, I will get back in a few moments." The communication ended, and Ankhamon was smiling.

***

The Cove emerged over the surface of the lake like a spherical submarine. The thunderous experience thoroughly shook every soul inside the gigantic floating vessel. The lights inside Cove were flickering, and most were either unconscious or sleeping after the jolting ride, and the experience had sapped their energies. Ehsis and King Iniharut were still in their seats. Their eyes were closed, and their heartbeat was high. They were waiting for the moment their heartbeat stabilized. After a while, a voice sounded in Cove:

"Madam Secretary," called one of her officers, who seemed to shake with trepidation.

"Are you okay, Guardian?" "His highness, King Iniharut. Is he fine?"

Some officers removed their seat belts and went to Ehsis and the King. Ehsis nodded; due to her age, the whole experience had been too much for her, but she had the strong nerves to recover from it. King Iniharut and the soldiers mourned the officers' deaths from their spaceship while guarding the Kneph.

Ehsis moved towards the king and consoled him serenely.

"Great King Iniharut, I am sorry for your loss. Their blood is on my hands," she expressed with her hands folded and an expression of extreme guilt on her wrinkled face. "Please, Madam Ehsis, do not consider yourself responsible for their deaths!" he exclaimed as he placed her folded hands between his palms. "My soldiers were merely martyrs who sacrificed their lives for their king. There is no higher honor than martyrdom for us Arpatians."

King Iniharut asked Ehsis:

"Where to now, madam? What shall be our next move? Kneph is gone."

"We will prevail. We salute the martyrs who died at Kneph and King Iniharut's ship," Ehsis said.

All were saddened and had tearful eyes. Suddenly, the Cove received a transmission: "Neymar here. We are in Misraim city now, and just a few moments ago, we saw a huge Qeqt-Qemau in the sky, heading east. Also, we heard that Arpat had attacked Akhom. The ground was trembling here..."

"Yes, we lost Kneph," Ehsis informed in a stern voice with tearful eyes.

"What. No, no!" Neymar was in shock.

Ehsis cut off the transmission, and she growled: "Take us to the Hall of Death, officer."

"I will capture you, Hatathor. People knew me as a huntress," she shouted.

Inhiharut was looking at Ehsis with admiration.

"Okay, madam," he obeyed firmly and swiftly slammed a series of buttons on the computer panel. Suddenly, a whizzing noise resounded from beneath their feet as two booster rockets emerged from the Cove, and it rose over the lake water. The Cove rose nearly six feet above the water and zoomed forwards at a tremendous speed. Ehsis nodded her head slowly as the Cove zoomed towards the Hall of Death.

***

Hatathor lay writhing in excruciating pain on the floor. His body had gone completely numb, and he couldn't move an inch. A greenish liquid was dripping from his mouth, and his teeth were chattering uncontrollably.

He pressed his hands against the ground in a struggling attempt to lift himself. Finally, with great difficulty, he managed to stand again. His eyes had turned inexplicably puffy and blood-red, and there were deep dark circles beneath his eyelids.

"What has happened to General Hatathor!?" some Lyrian generals asked and moved forward to help him.

"What happened?"

"Nothing. Just stressed out!" Hatathor said.

The officer looked at each other and continued monitoring the battle situation.

"Apart's battleship is annihilated. Now they will run away, but we will not let them go," Hatathor said.

***

Meanwhile, Al-Khidr, Nefertiti, and Semed were thrown into a large circular cell at the HSS. An extreme feeling of frustration mixed with rage and fear zoomed through the trio as they lay inside the cell helplessly.

After a few frustrating moments of silence, Semed lost his patience and banged his fist against the cell wall. "Damn it! I can't take this anymore! Get us out of here, you bloody bastards!" he bawled as he moved towards the cell's metallic rods and kicked it furiously. "Relax, Semed! There is no point in shouting and letting your anger out on the walls and rods!" Nefertiti exclaimed, trying to calm him down. She, too, was losing her patience, and anger was surfacing from within her.

Al-Khidr was surveying the walls of the cell intensely.

"What are you looking for, Al-Khidr?" she inquired curiously.

But before she could get the answer, Al-Khidr punched the air and jumped to his feet.

"What happened?" Semed and Nefertiti asked together. However, Al-Khidr ignored their question and moved towards the wall.

"Nefertiti, quickly give me a dagger!" he exclaimed as he moved his eyes upwards at the metallic ceiling. "But-"

"Quick!" he said, moving his hands towards her while continuing to gaze at the ceiling. Nefertiti retrieved a dagger from her shoe and handed it to him.

"Semed, come here fast!"

"What?" "Pile up your palms and lift me," he ordered gently. Semed placed one palm over the other and helped Al-Khidr to lift himself. Semed and Nefertiti glanced at each other, and Semed shrugged in confusion.

As he rose, the clever Berber man moved the dagger up and used it to unscrew four nearly camouflaged screws on the ceiling. After that, he cautiously pushed the metallic plank upwards, and the entrance to a duct opened up.

"I like the idea," Semed nearly shouted, but Nefertiti shushed him. As slowly and cautiously as they could, the trio got into the duct. It was extraordinarily squishy and sweaty inside, and they had to be very careful while they crawled through it.

After a few moments, they turned right and continued to move forwards. Suddenly, they could hear voices from below and halted for a second to listen. There was a tiny hole in the duct through which they saw a few Brethren soldiers aiming their laser guns at two scientists who were kneeling on the ground. The trio had a shock when they realized the scientists were Destro and Minka.

"Listen here, you two rascals!" Destro shouted, looking at them fearlessly in the eye. "We didn't call those three here. They just came out of nowhere and tried to get us out of here! We have nothing to do with those people! So, leave us!"

"Shut up, you traitors!" one brother soldier snapped at them. "We saw you both hugging them through the cameras. And how could they break into the Hall of Stars without inside help!"

"We don't know, officer! Please, I beg you! Spare our lives!" Minka's eyes had turned puffy as she was shedding tears.

"We don't spare traitors like you, woman! You both have to pay the hefty price of treason and letting intruders into the facility!"

The rest of the scientists stared at the two in immense terror and were rooted to the spot.

"What the hell are you people looking at? Get back to your duties, or it will be your turn next!" an officer growled at them. Scared to bits, the scientists instantly returned to their work.

The officers turned their attention back to Destro and Minka and got ready to shoot the innocent scientists. "Say goodbye to each other!"

But before the brethren soldiers could press their triggers, Al-Khidr kicked open the metallic plank of the duct, and the three of them jumped out. Before the officers had the time to look upwards, Al-Khidr delivered a solid punch to one of the soldier's heads, throwing him backward against a computer panel near the entrance. Nefertiti performed an impressive front flip in midair and gave a tremendous kick to another officer's head, making her fall backward and roll on the ground while the laser gun slipped out of his hands. Semed landed firmly behind the third soldier and used his remarkable strength to lift him in the air, and threw him on a table. Al-Khidr and some scientists moved and quickly picked up the laser guns.

"Nefertiti! Semed! Before any more of these scums

show up, let's grab the jump-sphere and get the hell out of here!" Al-Khidr yelled. They locked the soldiers into a room and managed to come out of the Hall of Stars together with the scientists. The scientists decided to run into the mountains. Suddenly the ground shook underneath their feet, and they fell on the floor.

"What was this?" Al-Khidr asked, "planet tremors?"

"No. Some sort of huge explosion caused this," Semed said.

They all looked at each other. Al-Khidr and the team took one hover and started moving towards the Hall of Death.

***

Ankhamon lay on his seat and landed the Arpatian spaceship in a valley. It had been two hours since he had spoken to the ambassador of Honkira. *What is taking the damned Honkiran Ambassador so long to speak to her king?* he wondered irritated as he smacked the dashboard out of immense frustration. *Did she even try speaking to his king? Or she merely lie to me about trying to speak to her king?* Ankhamon's suddenly turned fearful, and his heart sank at this thought.

Suddenly, the communications panel on the dashboard beeped loudly. He dashed out of his seat and slammed the button in excitement, and the voice of the Ambassador of Honkira rang across the spaceship.

"Your Excellency, Tor Ankhamon," she greeted in a pleasantly positive tone, and Ankhamon returned his greeting loudly. "Mosaka here, our great King Romvalan has advised me that I should leave Lyra. It will be an honor for me if mighty King Ankhamon would like to accompany us in our vessel." "Yes. Sure, Madam Mosaka. I am glad that you realized the gravity of the situation."

"I also like to convey his Excellency, King Romvalan, message to you, Sir. Our king has given an offer, as I understand that you might need time to return to the home planet," she paused and continued, "he offered you a home on our beloved planet Honkira." Ankhamon realized where the conversation was going.

"Thank you, madam. It is great hospitality, and I am honored to have it."

Mosaka continued: "My government laid this offer on your table in return for your pledge of allegiance to us and the promise that you will support us for the rest of your life!" "Under present circumstances, we need the help of each other," Anhamon stated.

"Yes, Your Highness," Mosaka replied.

"I accept this offer," Ankhamon said.

"Send us your coordinates, Your Excellency; I will meet you soon," Mosaka said, and the communication ended.

Ankhamon jumped with exhilaration and punched the air ecstatically. He began rejoicing like a maniac. He got out of his seat and danced merrily across the vessel. His heart was blooming like a butterfly, because for a moment all his worries, anxieties, and fears seemed to have evaporated instantly, giving his mind lightness and relaxation.

Damn! I just can't believe it! I am finally getting out of this doomed planet and its sick people! I will lead a new and much better life now in Honkira! That will be free of any sort of cursed diseases like Mutmut! he pondered mirthfully as he continued to dance with grace and passion.

Who in the universe wants to return to this doomed planet!? And besides, it's only a matter of time till it gets wiped out completely by Mutmut. Suddenly, there were electromagnetic field surges due to a weapon explosion, and the communication was out. "Why? Surges? I haven't sent the coordinates yet."

Ankhamon was banging his fist on the communication panel.

***

The Cove reached near the Hall of Death, and it descended as the booster rockets folded back into the vessel. King Iniharut, the Arpatian officers and the Lyrian soldiers moved out of the Cove when Ehsis expressed an intense desire to go with them. "But madam secretary, it's too dangerous for you to come. The Brethren officials will be there, and trust me, they will not see whom they fire against!" one officer exclaimed earnestly.

"No! I am your guardian! And I won't act like a coward and let my soldiers fight this crucial battle while I stay back!" "But madam-" he opened his mouth to argue back but was cut in by her.

"Officer, I am coming with you."

The Arpatian officers, too, tried to dissuade their king from accompanying them, but he also turned them down.

King of Arpat looked at Ehsis with a sense of intense admiration and nodded at her with a smile.

The Lyrian supporters of Ehsis, accompanied by the Arpatian force, neutralized the Lyrian guards at the entrance to the Hall of Death and moved cautiously across the place. The rest of the soldiers followed them while guarding Iniharut and Ehsis. They were finally entering the Hall of Death.

***

Nefertiti, Semed, and Al-Khidr just reached the Hall of Death. They saw the Arpatian forces around.

"We are on Ehsis side," they spoke loudly.

"Hatathor is inside, and he is planning to destroy Earth," Nefertiti informed.

"We already lost our battleship and Kneph," Apratian soldier said in a gloomy voice.

"What" Their mind froze. "What happened to Kneph?" Nefertiti shouted.

"Destroyed!" the soldier said. Nefertiti fell to her knees. Al-Khidr knelt to console her. She was crying and looking at the sky. "God, why?

Secretary Ehsis, I am sorry." She continued crying.

Semed and Al-Khidr tried to console her with tearful eyes.

"Secretary Ehsis and King Iniharut survived." The soldier came closer by now and said in a loud voice.

"Don't stay here. Take cover fast!" he ordered.

Nefertiti stood up, and she removed her tears.

"Don't lose hope, darling," Al-Khidr said. She smiled and hugged him.

# Chapter 25

# The Salvation

ANKHAMON sat on a revolving seat with his hands behind his back. He imagined all the amazing things he could do once he left the dying planet and was humming merrily. However, he was also a bit anxious. What is taking that ambassador of Qumrud so long to arrive here? It has been an hour since I sent the coordinates to them. Have they doubled-crossed me? Were they simply lying to me?

As these anxious thoughts circled his mind, he considered contacting them again to ensure he hadn't been deceived. He had barely opened his eyelids when he noticed a tiny dot across the horizon. He jumped out of his seat instantly and ran towards the dashboard to get a closer look. The spaceship was coming closer: finally someone was coming!

The humongous Qumrudan spaceship landed beside Ankhamon's vessel, and its doors slid open. A wide mechanical plank zoomed out of the spacecraft and attached itself to the Lyrian vessel. Ankhamon walked across the plank nervously and made his way into the Qumrudan vessel. As he entered, the spaceship doors closed automatically. The surrounding atmosphere turned colder, and a ravishing smell of state-of-the-art Qumrudan technology filled the air. Taking a deep refreshing breath, Ankhamon observed the ship's interior, which was much more advanced and different than the Lyrian one. Besides that, there were no pilots, and the humongous advanced vessel was being flown by artificial intelligence.

"His excellency, King Ankhamon!" a voice greeted, and Ankhamon turned to notice Madam Mosaka seated on a revolving chair at the center. "Madama Mosaka, it is an honor to finally see you."

Ankahmon was just about to move towards the ambassador of planet Qumrud when he got a tremendous shock. Seated behind the Qumrud ambassador was mother, Ahmose. Her shocking appearance caused Ankhamon to be frozen on the spot.

"What... she is doing here, Ahmose? Her son – the stupid Desher killed my daughter Shiphrah. I'll never forget it!" he shouted, pointing his finger at her.

"Well, Tor Ankhamon, we, the Kingdom of Qumrud, cannot leave our citizens on a war-ridden territory," Mosaka claimed calmly with a mechanical smile on her face. "Uh, Madam Mosaka, I. . . I don't understand what you are saying?"

"Ahmose is from planet Endor. . . " Ankhamon said further.

"Tor Ankhamon, perhaps it is now necessary that you see people around you in their true colors," Mosaka said and turned to mother Ahmose.

"Let me introduce you to Ahmose, the greatest spy in the entire Qumrud!" she said proudly. "What in the Lyra are you saying, Mosaka?! She ain't a Qumrudan!"

Ahmose was in a saddened state. She looked exhausted and she burst with furry.

"I have been Qumrudan since the day I was born, and I will remain so until the day I will die, Ankhamon. You Lyrians have butchered my son! I'll teach all of you a very bitter lesson."

The news hit Ankhamon like a bolt of lightning, which shook him from head to toe.

"Yes, it is true. We had sent Ahmose and her son Desher as spies on this doomed planet."

At the mention of Desher, Ahmose caught her breath to stop the tears forming across the corners of her eyes and to maintain a straight face. Ankhamon opened his mouth to fire a question at Mosaka when she quietly raised her arm to stop him.

"Tor Ankhamon, why and how we sent Ahmose

and her son as spies to Lyra is not important right now. The important thing right now is that our king has granted you asylum on our planet." Ankhamon's eyes turned gleeful, and he let out a beam of excitement.

"Oh madam Mosaka, how can I thank-"

Before Ankhamon could utter another word, she cut him in.

"On the condition that you, Tor Ankhamon, the king of Lyra, agree to sell the Amris mines to us."

"What? Are you out of your fricking mind?" he shouted, throwing them looks of pure disgust. "How dare you think of this? The Amris mines belong to Lyra! I will never do such an outrageous act!" Ahmose threw her head back at this statement and let out a howl of cold laughter.

"This is the hilarious thing I have heard today! You are so funny, Ankhamon!" Ahmose commented, trying to catch her breath.

"I am the King of Lyra–" "Oh, give me a break, will you!" Ahmose remarked in a severe tone. "What king and what Lyra are you talking about, you piece of scumbag! You are ready to abandon your precious' planet to save your dirty worthless skin and leave your people to die! And then you claim loyalty?"

In disgust, Ahmose spat on the floor and threw Ankhamon the dirtiest look she could muster.

"Tor Ankhamon, have you ever thought – who would like to come to a death zone like the kingdom of Akhmon?" Mosaka said.

"Death zone...I don't understand." Ankhamon

said with a puzzled face.

"Yes, your planet and this kingdom, in particular, has no worth. It is a diseased planet. But you are sitting on valuable Amris... Ah, the Amris we all want. Look, Tor Ankhamon, this planet and its people are anyway going to perish. And that's precisely the reason you are here on this ship in the first place. So, if there won't be any people on Lyra, what will you do with the Amris? Rather, you sell it to us, and we shall make good use of it."

"Ahmose - what a disappointment. I protected you when the bounty hunters were chasing you. I gave you the title of mother and gave you respect. I am sad that you repay me in such a way!" "This was all done to fool you, Ankhamon. I am neither a healer nor a mother. I am a scientist, and I did what my Government asked me to do. What I did was all science, not witchcraft. Ah, poor Lyrians – I pity them. They lost so much in science, technology and so bad luck struck them," Ahmose said. This statement profoundly affected Ankhamon, who seemed to have finally realized how things were.

He stood motionless for a few moments staring at the ground. Finally, he raised his head, and moving towards Ahmose and Mosaka; he sat in front of them. Mosaka nodded at him approvingly with her mechanical smile and waved her hand across the air. Instantly, a holographic panel screen appeared before him. The display brought King of Qumrud in front of Ankhamon.

"Tor Ankhamon, greetings from Anmehotan! I am glad to see you in one piece. This is the loveliest day for the planet of Honkira. For ages, the planet Lyra and Honkira conflicted on almost every occasion; we fought wars, killed our people, and bombed cities. But you see, we cannot live in isolation in this vast galaxy. We need to share each other's resources. This was when we were waiting for Lyrians to come to terms with us. I learned from the ambassador that you seek asylum in our kingdom. I would be glad if the honorable king helped us and gave us a little handshake to close the deal we are offering. I am sure by this time you know what our terms and conditions are!" King Anmehotan said with a mischievous smile, and the transmission ended.

Ankhamon's mouth was parched. He wanted to speak, but the words were not coming out.

Ankhamon waved his hand across the panel, and holographic text showing Sell Amris' appeared on the screen. Below the heading there was a massive amount of text with various clauses. Ankhamon was not in the mood to read it. He had already made up his mind to get away from Lyra. Without thinking any further, he placed his hand on the tablet, which scanned his fingers, generating an identity record. Ankhamon further pushed his hand, and the deal was closed. He had sold all the Amris mines to the King Anmehotan of Qumrud.

Ahmose and Mosaka gave him a wide beam while he returned their smiles with a look of utter disapproval.

"King Ankhamon, you have made a wise decision by selling the Amris mines to us!" Mosaka exclaimed and pressed the button. The data and contract with the kingdom were sent to Bayrosim, the capital of Qumrud.

"Indeed! You have earned yourself a new free life on our planet!" the ambassador remarked gratefully.

"And we give you our word that you will face no issues at all on our lovely planet, and you shall be treated equally to a born Qumrudan!"

Ankhamon muttered a thanks' and lowered his frown as he began to look outside through the massive glass as the gigantic spaceship flew out of the Lyrian atmosphere and towards the promised planet of Qumrud.

***

Hatathor's condition deteriorated with every passing second, making his body become weaker and weaker. His right arm seemed to have lost all the strength it had left and became numb.

In the interim, Al-Khidr and his team peeped through the entrance. They noticed the Brethren soldiers guarding the scientists and the officer coming towards the door. "On my count, we move in and start the onslaught," Al-Khidr instructed, and they nodded.

"Three... two... one..."

Al-Khidr kicked open the door, turned towards the Brethren officials, and running across the hall, they started firing lasers. Most of the officers, including the one heading towards the entrance, were quickly struck by the lasers shot, and they perished instantly. However, Hatathor activated his hemispherical protective shield and thus saved himself. At the same time, the other Brethrens managed to dodge the lasers and started firing in return. As Nefertiti and Semed were busy battling the Brethren officers, Al-Khidr and Hatathor's eyes met, and a tremendous rush of intense hatred and rage boiled up inside them both. They glared at each other like two ferocious lions ready to pounce on each other.

*Human, I have waited a long time for this moment. Your luck has saved you from my wrath on numerous occasions, but now you will die by my hands!* Hatathor thought furiously. Al-Khidr recalled the dreadful moment when the ruthless Lyrian had murdered Estelle. Throwing the laser gun aside, he clenched his fists tightly. *I don't need any weapon to fight you, you ruthless man!* Al-Khidr thought, and slowly, the two men began moving towards each other and increased their pace as they inched closer. "You bloody pile of earthly shit! Finally, you have come into clutches, and I swear, you will not remain alive to see the daylight tomorrow!" Hatathor growled, looking at the Berber with intense hatred in his eyes.

"Forget about me seeing tomorrow's daylight, Hatathor. I will stop your breathing at this moment!" Al-Khidr responded furiously as he clutched his fists tightly. "You and your bloody planet Earth are a curse! And that curse needs to be broken!"

"Hatathor, that curse is hanging around your neck! It's not my planet that is cursed, but you! You are cursed because of your insufferable hatred and negativity inside your head! You are so engrossed in your ego and blind thoughts that you won't try to see the truth!"

"That's enough! I will crush every bone in your body and hang it on the tallest obelisk in Lyra so that every Lyrian will curse you there and know about your dreadful fate; the human who tried to mess with our planet!" Hatathor growled and rushed towards Al-Khidr.

As the two warriors clashed, Hatathor raised his arm and smacked Al-Khidr's face hard. The Berber man was lifted off his feet, rolled onto the ground, and ended up inside a large room containing various handguns and laser weapons. Despite being infected by the Mutmut disease, Hatathor still had a considerable amount of strength left in him. He entered the room that Al-Khidr lay in and closed the door.

Al-Khidr got onto his feet and wiped the blood off his lip, which had been cut.

"Is that the best you can do, mighty Hatathor?" he asked with a tiny smile on his face.

"Oh, darned human, you have no idea about my true strength. That was just a taster!" He dashed towards him again and the fight resumed. In the meantime, as Ehsis and King Iniharut, along with their respective armies, entered the battle station inside the Hall of Death, they noticed Nefertiti and Semed fighting the Brethren soldiers.

"Praise the Lord! Nefertiti and Semed are here!" Ehsis exclaimed happily.

"Soldiers attack!" Ehsis and King Iniharut commanded simultaneously, and their armies joined the fight.

Ehsis and Iniharut's armies opened fire at the Brethrens and killed many of them instantly while injuring a few others. Nefertiti and Semed punched the air with immense joy upon seeing Ehsis and their fellow Lyrians, and their morale was intensely boosted. "But where is Al-Khidr and that bloody Hatathor?" she murmured furiously, looking around for any sign of them. Suddenly, her eyes fell onto the weapons room on the right, and through the transparent laser-proof wall, she noticed the two mighty warriors fighting hand-to-hand. Al-Khidr and Hatathor were clutching each other's fists and roaring like two furious ravenous tigers ready to tear each other apart. "Filthy human, I will murder you for everything you have done to ruin my planet and my people!" Hatathor bawled, trying to push Al-Khidr behind, but the human was quite strong himself and could effectively resist the sick alien.

"And I will make you pay for killing Estelle!" Al-Khidr roared back.

Hatathor moved and pulled Al-Khidr towards him, headbutted the human, making him stumble and fall on the ground. Flinching slightly, Al-Khidr held the side of his head and got up. His vision was somewhat blurry due to the intense force of Hatathor's blow.

Shaking his head slowly, he bawled like a devil, dashed towards Hatathor and aimed a punch at his ear. The Lyrian moved swiftly onto the side and, catching his fist, grabbed the human from his waist and lifted him high in the air. He then threw him forcefully against the wall.

Al-Khidr crashed against the wall and fell to the ground. His forehead started bleeding heavily, and a flood of excruciating pain rushed through his muscles. Meanwhile, the Brethrens had managed to wound a few of Ehsis' men. Nevertheless, her men still had the upper hand as their force was assisted by King Iniharut's highly trained army, whose one soldier was equal to three Brethren fighters. Together, they managed to subdue nearly the entire Brethren soldiers and were on the brink of victory.

Nefertiti, whom three enemy officers surrounded, managed to stun them with her acrobatic kicks and began running towards Ehsis. She had nearly reached the Secretary when a Brethren officer began firing at her continuously from ahead.

"No one can stop us now!" she roared and swerved sideways effortlessly to dodge the laser attacks. Finally, she leaped high into the air, and with a skillful front flip, she delivered a tremendous kick to the terrified soldier's face and landed on the ground near Ehsis. "Madam Ehsis!" she exclaimed with glee and Ehsis smiled at Nefertiti. They turned their eyes towards Al-Khidr again, who lay pathetically on the ground against the transparent wall.

At that point, Kontar made his way into the erupting hall and growled on top of his lungs.

"Stop this ridiculous fight!" At his intervention, the entire battle came to a sudden halt, and everyone stared at him curiously. "That so-called treacherous king Ankhamon deceived us all and now he cannot be found anywhere on Lyra. He is the root of all evils and the reason behind all this chaos on our planet! I order all the Brethrens to surrender to Secretary Ehsis's army. We have wronged her and the entire Lyra, and so we must bear the consequences!" Kontar's words profoundly affected all the Brethrens, and they immediately dropped their weapons and surrendered. Madam Ehsis looked at Kontar and nodded at him in approval.

"What! Where did that treacherous man go? Did you search every place that he could have possibly gone?" demanded King Iniharut, eyeing Kontar sharply. Kontar gave him a brief bow and said,

"Yes, Your Highness, King Iniharuut. My fellow trusted Brethren officers and I have looked into every nook and corner of the planet. Unfortunately, he is nowhere to be found. Moreover, there is no sign of that cunning witch from the planet Endor, Ahmose. We feel that they both have escaped the Lyra in some foreign spaceship that possesses some kind of untraceable technology,"

King Iniharut punched the air in a fury and gritted his teeth.

"If you are right, and that bloody pile of treacherous scum has truly escaped, then I promise you, Madam Ehsis, the Arpatians will search the entire universe and throw him at your feet! He shall not escape so easily! He will indeed bear the consequences of his atrocious actions and will be punished!" King Iniharut declared with intense rage in his otherwise calm eyes. Secretary Ehsis gestured with her wrinkled arms to calm him down. "King Iniharut, let's worry about Tor Ankhamon later. As of now, we need to stop Al-Khidr and Hatathor's fight. Both of them are heavily burning in the inextinguishable fire of revenge and will end up tearing each other apart if we don't stop them. Nefertiti and Semed, find a way to break that wall !" she commanded firmly.

So, after all the Brethrens had surrendered and were being led away by Ehsis's army, Nefertiti and Semed sprinted towards the transparent wall and tried to destroy it with their laser guns but in vain, as the wall was laser-proof. They struggled to break through the wall by utilizing various other weapons like tiny bombs and throwing chemical bottles at it, but it just wouldn't break.

"Damn this bloody wall!" Semed cursed as he aimed a kick at it in frustration. Finally, all they could do was watch Al-Khidr and Hatathor fight mercilessly. Al-Khidr slowly moved sideways, mustering all his strength to get onto his feet, but failed. At that point, he noticed a gleaming rod that lay a few inches away from him. He made a substantial effort and crawled towards it. He grabbed the rod, and mustering all the strength left in his body, he managed to get onto his feet and flung the rod like a javelin at Hatathor. The rod zoomed across the air and struck the mighty Lyrian on his leg. He let out an agonizing groan, and after swaying for a while, he collapsed on the ground. Al-Khidr then dragged Hatathor's unconscious body, he brought him outside the weapons room and placed him in the center of the hall. King Iniharut's blood began to boil at the sight of Hatathor, and he was about to command his officers to seize him when Ehsis stopped them with a quick wave of her hand.

"Nobody goes near Hatathor!" she declared in a thoroughly severe tone. "The deadly Mutmut has infected him, and now he is in an infectious state due to the virus. We should stay away from him till we have come up with an antidote to cure him!"

"Cure him?" King Iniharut demanded incredulously. "Madam Ehsis, this bloody man, along with that cowardly rat Ankhamon, is the reason behind millions of deaths across your planet as well as destroying the Cove. And have you forgotten that he is the one who killed Queen Hathor? Despite all the heinous crimes that this beastly Lyrian has committed, you still wish to save his life?"

"King Iniharut," Ehsis began calmly. "I haven't forgotten anything, and I can never forgive Seka Hatathor for his horrendous crimes. And we Lyrians show mercy even to the ones who have wronged us. But... he is still a part of this planet, an unstable and evil one, yes, but he still is. He will be placed on trial in the Lyrian Court of law and punished for his crimes legally. But, leaving him to die a horrible death like this is against everything that Lyra has ever stood for..." At her compassionate and sagacious words, King Iniharut bowed before her.

"Madam Ehsis, the respect I have for you has increased beyond anything. You are a true leader and a true Lyrian!"

Madam Ehsis smiled weakly and ordered her soldiers to stay away from the diseased Lyrian. At her command, all the soldiers stood rooted to the spot in extreme fear and didn't dare to even move.

"But we can't just leave him here!" King Iniharut exclaimed indignantly. "We have to do something and capture him somehow before he regains consciousness and creates more trouble!"

"We don't have the jump-sphere. Otherwise, we could have cured him using the earthen leaves that are concealed within it, which are the antidote to this lethal disease," she sighed with extreme disappointment. At that point, Nefertiti exclaimed, "We got the sphere, Madam Ehsis!" And she handed the jump-sphere to Ehsis. "Excellent job, my girl!" She remarked with a loving tap on her cheek. And without wasting a moment, Ehsis called Rostau, who lay fearfully in the hall's corner and the other scientists. "Rostau! I want you to open the sphere and give it immediately to Dr. Kityr. He can extract the cure from the earthen leaves!" "Yes, madam Ehsis!" Rostau affirmed and instantly rushed outside the battle station, to start looking for virologist Dr. Kityr. Within minutes, he found him and brought him back with him to the Hall of Death.

Rostau opened the sphere and handed the earthen leaves to Dr. Kityr. "Dr. Kityr, Madam Ehsis wants you to use these earthen leaves to make an antidote for the Mutmut!"

"Of course! But I need you to take me to the virology lab where the proper equipment is."

At that point, Kontar and his trusted Brethren officers marched forward.

"Here, we will accompany you to the virology labs and help you make quicker the antidote made," Kontar offered to help. Semed nodded at him approvingly, and they all left for the virology labs. In the interim, everyone, including Madam Ehsis and King Iniharut, was left confused.

"I can go close to Hatathor, but he might try to kill me," Ehsis said. "Why don't we throw a blanket or a large piece of cloth over him?" one of the Lyrian officers suggested sharply.

"No! Any man who even gets an inch close to Hatathor will get infected within a moment," Nefertiti claimed instantly.

"Let's have him airlifted with one of our spaceships!" another officer advised confidently.

"That won't work either, because there is a high chance that the Mutmut will be released across the air due to the strong winds that are blowing right now.

Besides, we will have to try to burn a hole through the heavily unbreakable metallic ceiling of this battle station, which is more or less impossible!" Semed explained wisely. Ehsis let out a sigh of contemplation, and there was a pin drop silence all over the battle station. They pondered deeply for a few minutes. Suddenly, a dazzling idea struck Ehsis. She looked at the commanding officer of the Lyrian soldiers and ordered, "Officer, quickly place the force field around Hatathor,"

The officer nodded and pressed a button on his wristband, and he unleashed a circular force field around the diseased Lyrian warrior.

***

A few hours passed when finally, Dr. Kityr marched into the battle station holding the jump-sphere in one hand and two test tubes filled with a bluish liquid in the other. "Madam Ehsis! I have extracted the cure from the earthen leaves and made a potion out of it!" Dr. Kityr declared enthusiastically as he handed over the sphere and the test tubes to her.

"Ah! Brilliant work, Dr. Kityr! I knew you could do it!" she remarked joyfully and slowly began to move towards Al-Khidr. "Great!" cheered Semed as he punched the air, and Nefertiti wiped a tear from the side of her eyes. Dr. Kityr handed one potion containing the power booster to Al-Khidr, who gulped it down immediately. The moment the bluish liquid made contact with his throat, the human experienced an exotic feeling inside him that seemed to repair and refresh every cell in his body. He felt a rush of blood inside his veins, which appeared to restore the strength in his body. Besides that, his wound seemed to heal miraculously as the skin stitched itself where it had been cut. Nefertiti and Semed rushed to hug him tightly and rejoiced at his recovery.

Dr. Kityr walked over to Hatathor, who lay on the verge of a gruesome death, as he could neither move his muscles nor move his lips to speak. Ehsis gave him a look of pity, and Dr. Kityr injected the vaccine made from earthen leaves. As the miraculous vaccine entered his body, he began to recover gradually; his weakened arms and legs regained their strength and returned to their proper shape. And finally, he was able to open his eyes and then to get to his feet and talk.

He gazed at everyone present in the hall, and finally, his eyes landed on Al-Khidr. However, his expression was far from being angry and vengeful. And instead, it was tender and grateful. Turning towards Ehsis, he hung his head in shame.

"Madam Secretary, I feel extremely guilty about all the chaos that occurred and the huge troubles that you had to go through. And despite being your and the entire Lyra's culprit, you decided to save my life." Ehsis looked at him with a mixture of anger and pity and said, "Hatathor, your father committed a murder, and he got the death sentence. You didn't know the details, as we didn't want to shame your family publicly. But you committed a grave crime. You killed our mother and my friend, Queen Hathor. Have you ever thought about the chaos that you lead us into?" Hatathor sighed, looking at her regretfully in the eye.

"I beg for forgiveness from you and every Lyrian that has ever suffered because of me. I have wronged you and the entire planet. I am not fit to be a general of the noble Lyrian army anymore."

"You have to face the punishment for the crimes you have committed," Ehsis declared and ordered her soldiers to arrest Seka Hatathor. Hatathor nodded in agreement, turned towards one of the Lyrian officers, and raised his wrists to be handcuffed. The officer pressed a button on his wristband, and a pair of semi-transparent but solid cuffs were fastened around Hatathor's wrists. Hatathor looked at everyone apologetically, including Al-Khidr, who nodded at him gently with a tiny smile, and Seka Hatathor was led away by the Lyrian officer.

***

All the citizens of Ankhom gathered in Obelisk square. Ehsis was sitting on a throne at the far end of the square with an obelisk on her right and left. The place was jamming of people.

On the stage were also the police commander Nefertiti, Al-Khidr, King Iniharut, Rostau, Semed, and some other loyal Lyrian soldiers, who were standing and waving at the crowd.

"People of Lyra!" Ehsis addressed the Lyrians while beaming gloriously. "By the Lord's grace, we have treated all the people suffering from the deadly Mutmut, and they have all recovered. So from this day onwards, all our hardships end! And I want to request all of you to join me in rebuilding the glorious Lyra we all knew and loved. The Lyra that our dearest Queen Hathor had once ruled! The Lyra that we all want to be a part of!"

Ehsis's inspiring words caused an enormous roar of triumph and hope amongst the citizens of Ankhom. They all shed tears of joy and began shouting Ehsis' name. At that moment, Nefertiti moved forward and placed a golden tiara on Ehsis' head. She took the microphone from her hand and declared, "People of Lyra! I present to you the new queen of our beloved planet, Queen Ehsis! Hail to the queen!"

"Hail to the queen!" King Iniharut chanted along with the Lyrian soldiers.

The crowd grew even wilder, and Hail Queen Ehsis' chants echoed across the entire city. People from across the planet witnessed the glorious scenario from massive holographic screens. "My beloved people, being the newly appointed queen of the Lyra, I pronounce Al-Khidr a citizen of the kingdom of Akhom, and I give him the highest honor of our kingdom. Without him we would have never been able to defeat our enemies and save our people and our planet from Mutmut!" The announcement sent a jolt of electricity across Al-Khidr's veins as he looked at Nefertiti, whose smile widened in a state of immense joy. Ehsis gestured Al-Khidr to move forward and placed the badge of highest honor on his chest. The chants of Al-Khidr' spread like wildfire throughout the entire square while he stood there with a humble smile on his face.

However, before he could move back, Ehsis gave another announcement, which nearly knocked his brains out with intense bliss and exhilaration.

"Everyone! On this glorious day! I would also like to announce the wedding of Mr. Al-Khidr and commander Nefertiti!" She gestured Nefertiti and Al-Khidr to come forward and handed two golden rings to Al-Khidr and her. Nefertiti and Al-Khidr stared into each other's eyes intensely for a few seconds; their hearts were beating louder than ever. Gently, they placed the rings in each other's fingers and continued to gaze deeply into each other's eyes, which were sparkling intensely with immense bliss. They had finally accomplished the mission they had dreamt of for so long and became man and wife. Then, moving forwards, they embraced and whispered into each other's ears, "Till death do us apart ..."

Little did they know that it was not a happy future they were looking forward to. The future was rather darker and it was soon to come...

# About the Author

Nassim Odin holds PhD degree in Aerospace Engineering and he teaches engineering. He likes to read about the pyramids and ancient civilizations.
https://www.nassimodin.com

**The Revenge of Hatathor**

**— book blurb —**

**Challenged by Destiny. Driven by Duty. Desperate to Survive.**

Al-Khidrs destiny has brought him back to the planet Lyra, which was as beautiful and majestic as it was before, but this time there was something odd about it. Apart from delivering the Lyrians the precious cure for the Mutmut disease, Al-Khidr must now find out what has happened in his absence, before its too late. Not being able to find his friends, he starts looking for clues with a racing heart. On the other hand, Hatathor is set to finally get his revenge and is hunting Al-Khidr relentlessly. Will Hatathor catch Al-Khidr? Will Al-Khidr be able to find his friends and help the Lyrians get over the terrible epidemic that has been decimating them?

The Sphere Trilogy

Following QR code will lead you to the Sphere Trilogy page at Amazon store.

Made in the USA
Columbia, SC
24 July 2025

844e9db7-74cb-40a6-9905-9e9d118eef33R02